MARSHAL

LOYALTY AND WAR 1

DEVON VESPER

MAGELIGHT PRESS

WANT TO KNOW MORE ABOUT GOD JARS?

Visit the wiki to get more information about The God Jars Saga.

There you will find interesting things like an overview and map of the continent of Peralea, a glossary of terms, the ranking list of the Aesriphos order, the full book list, and more information on each character. The information grows with every book written.

Come find out more about the intriguing and volatile world of The God Jars, and continue your immersive experience!

Head to the Wiki now!
https://devonvesper.com/wiki

For Cassie, because she's awesome. You and your wife are one. Literally. May they live on into eternity. <3

CHAPTER ONE

"No. NO! PAPA!"

It had to be Kerac. Tymor wouldn't be carrying anyone else, and Valis would know that silver stallion anywhere. Even in the darkness of night where Valis had trouble seeing anything else but moon-silvered grass and the darker darkness of the distant tree line, he could make out Tymor's coat and the distinct, elegant shape of his breed. The moon lit up the surrounding area just enough that Valis could see the glint of the horse's silver coat and the shine of armor. And the person slumped over the saddle had long, dark hair that dragged through the tall swaying grasses. Just the sight made Valis wish he could fly. Kerac *had* to be alive. He just had to.

Another horse exited the tree line with a tired whinny, and Valis cried out, "Xyna! That's Father's horse! I know her whinny anywhere!"

But Xyna bore no rider, and Valis's stomach pitted. Where was his father? Valis coughed to clear his throat and let out a cracked scream, "PAPA!"

"Valis! Don't kill your horse!"

"Something is wrong with Papa," Valis called back. "Where is Father?"

Valis's heart thundered, sending jolts of panic through his veins. It thumped faster than Rasera's hooves, even as he urged his horse to go faster, farther. And even though Valis knew his heart was in his chest, trying its damnedest to crack his ribcage, it felt like it was in his throat, strangling him as he wheezed for every gasping breath as if he ran instead of riding his horse.

"Papa, I'm coming!"

The body slumped over the horse didn't even twitch with Valis's choked cry. With every thundering beat of hooves, Valis felt his entire world tilt on its axis, and feared he would fall off. And as he raced, he frantically tried to call his friend.

Thyran! Thyran, please answer me!

Thyran took only a moment to answer and sounded harried. *Gracious. What is wrong, Child?*

I found Kerac slumped over his horse's saddle, but I don't see Darolen anywhere. I need a search party to my location. Can you see it in my mind?

No, but I can scry after you. Leave it to me. Bring him home and let me handle the rest.

Thank you!

Clouds passed over the moon, obscuring Valis's vision.

He pushed magic into his eyes until the area lit up again. As he neared Kerac's silver stallion, he urged Rasera to slow down so they wouldn't bowl the poor horse over or terrify him. Rasera didn't have his augmented vision and trusted him not to let them run into anything.

"Papa!"

He pulled Rasera to a stop next to Kerac's horse. The poor beast looked exhausted, his head hanging down. He neighed tiredly when Rasera pressed his nose to Tymor's neck.

Valis let Rasera comfort Kerac's horse while he vaulted out of the saddle and brushed Kerac's matted hair away from his face.

"Valis?" Tavros called.

"Here! Push magic into your eyes with the intent to see."

"Got it. I'm coming!"

Valis frantically searched Kerac's neck for a pulse. Tears scalded his chilled cheeks, but he ignored them. Finally, he found it. Kerac's pulse came thready and weak, but it was there. Now that he wasn't as frantic, he could hear Kerac's shallow breathing. With as much care as he could manage, he pulled Kerac off his horse's back and laid him in the grass to start removing armor.

Tavros approached, his horse letting out a snort as they stopped. He dropped out of the saddle and knelt on Kerac's other side, and without a word, he helped Valis get the armor off. Between them, they made quick work of it, and Valis got up to get Kerac's bedroll from his saddle and unrolled it, using it as a makeshift bag to carry the armor pieces in.

Once he had that tied to the silver stallion's saddle, he tied the poor beast's reins to Rasera's saddle, Xyna's reins to Tavros's saddle, and mounted up. Tavros didn't need asking. He just hauled Kerac up and helped situate him in Valis's lap, knowing what Valis needed.

"We'll get him home, love," Tavros murmured. "He's hung on this long. He won't give up now."

"I know," Valis whispered. His voice wavered, but all he could do was hope.

Feeling Kerac's soft, shallow breaths waft across his throat gave Valis something to focus on as he waited for Tavros to mount up. The moment he was in his saddle and ready to go, Valis wanted to race home, but he didn't know the extent of Kerac's injuries, nor did he feel comfortable making his fathers's horses run with as exhausted as they were. Instead, he held on to Kerac and let Tavros lead them home.

The festivities in Cadoras were still going strong as they neared, the sounds of revelry echoing into the night as they navigated their horses through the whiptail trees that bordered Cadoras Lake. It offered Valis a little peace, especially when they boarded the ferry and the feeling of *home* washed over Valis. Even Kerac seemed to relax. But that only made Valis's heart plummet and his fingers fly to Kerac's throat to search for his pulse.

The weak beats that fluttered against his fingertips made

Valis only marginally relax. It was a small comfort, just like the soft puffs of breath against his collarbone. And the moment they stepped off the ferry and onto Cadoras Island, Valis suddenly felt like he would break apart at any moment if he didn't urge Rasera into a gallop.

But the Autumn Festival was still in full swing. There were people everywhere. It wouldn't be safe—not for the city's citizens, and not for the horses.

It took too long to get through the masses of people and in front of the monastery. People were everywhere, some drunk on ale or wine, others drunk on the fun they were having. All Valis wanted to do was scream at everyone to get out of his way, but he let Tavros do the talking while he focused on Kerac and those puffs of breath on his skin that let him know his papa was still alive.

"Valis?" Aenali's voice carried over the revelers. "Valis!"

"Aenali, wait!" Jedai called.

Valis glanced over to see his group of friends rushing through the crowd. Seza, the faster of them, stopped at Rasera's side and laid a gentle hand on Kerac's back, her eyes huge. "Jedai. Get over here. Valis, pass him down to Jedai. Maph, take care of these horses, will you?"

"Of course," Maphias said as he rushed over.

Jedai reached for Kerac, and Valis carefully lowered him down. "Be careful. I don't know what injuries he has."

"No problem, man." Once Jedai had Kerac in his arms, he cradled him tenderly just like he would his baby sister. "Get down here so we can get him inside."

"What's on Kerac's horse?" Seza asked.

"Kerac's armor," Valis said as he dismounted. "I bundled it into his bedroll."

"I will get his armor," Zhasina said. "You and Tavros get him to the Master Healer."

Jedai carefully handed Kerac back over when Valis reached for him. "I'll go with you in case you need anything. That okay?"

"Yeah," Valis said. "Thanks."

By the time they made it to the healer's ward, his friends had raced to catch up with him and met him at the door. Tavros never left Valis's side, so Jedai knocked to get Firil's attention. When the Master Healer poked his head out of his office, his eyes widened, and he threw the door open, motioning Valis to head into the main sanctuary with the rows of cots. "Come in. Get him on a cot while I rouse my assistants."

Valis's friends parted to let him through. In the stark white light of the healing ward, if Kerac's breaths weren't ghosting across Valis's skin, he'd think his papa was dead. Kerac had deep purple bruises under his eyes. His face was so gaunt and pale, and he was so emaciated, that Valis wondered when he'd eaten last. How long had he been slung across that saddle?

Most of all, his thoughts went to the sinking feeling in his stomach. *Where is father?*

Darolen and Kerac were inseparable. They never went anywhere without the other. Not unless they had to split up to keep someone safe, or they had a short errand to run. This was no short errand. Darolen would never let Kerac get like this unless he was dead or captured.

Valis laid Kerac on the cot and stroked his matted hair, picking out dead twigs and bits of grass from the ends. He stroked his papa's cheek, ghosted his fingers over his forehead and down the side of his face to his chin, down to rest on his pulse point just to prove to himself that Kerac was still alive.

"Let us in," Firil said gently. The Master Healer squeezed Valis's shoulder and nudged him out of the way. "I will not ask you to leave, but your friends should return to their rooms or duties if they are not going back to the Autumn Festival."

Valis glanced over at his friends and Jedai stepped forward, drawing Valis into a tight hug. "We'll wait for you in the sitting room of your suite. Meet us there when you have news, okay?"

"Yeah," Valis whispered around the lump of emotion in his throat. "Thanks."

Jedai nodded and gave him another squeeze before ushering the rest of the group out of the room and shutting the door behind him. Only Tavros remained. He stepped up behind Valis and wrapped his arms tight about Valis's chest, resting his chin on Valis's shoulder. "He'll be okay," Tavros whispered. "He's fought hard to get here. He won't give up now that he has help. Not now that he has you so close."

All Valis could do was nod and pray that his husband was right.

And then that thought hit him. Tavros was now his *husband*. Even as fear for Kerac's life weighed him down, Tavros's love kept him from drowning in that fear. It had only been two days since their joining night, and everything was still so new and vibrant before they found Kerac in the field.

"What are you thinking about?" Tavros murmured against the shell of Valis's ear.

Valis shrugged. "I still can't believe we're finally married. Worried about Papa. Wishing I could do more than stand here like an over-emotional idiot while other people work on him."

Firil's voice, strained from working and his magical focus, filtered over, "You are doing plenty by just being here. Your presence is keeping him at peace."

Valis felt a small, brief smile tug at the corners of his mouth. It seemed foreign, as if he hadn't smiled in weeks instead of just hours. Leave it to Firil to comfort him while he worked.

"Do you think he'll make it?" Valis murmured, careful to keep his voice down so he wouldn't break the four healers' concentration.

"I believe he will, yes," Firil said, just as quietly. "He will need you when he wakes, I think."

"He can stay in our suite," Tavros said. "I won't force you to part with him, Valis. We can either bring a small bed into our room or set up a cot or something in the sitting room."

Valis leaned back into Tavros's chest, his heart swelling with pride and love until it became hard to breathe. "Thanks."

Firil glanced over with a small smile, then turned back to his work as he spoke. "I am afraid he may be remaining here for the foreseeable future. We can heal much, but he will need to be monitored for some time yet. Unfortunately, we cannot heal illnesses or weight loss with magic. He must be medicated and put on a special liquid diet to regain his lost weight and battle the infections in his system."

"I don't mind," Valis said. "I'd rather he be in capable hands."

The Master Healer merely nodded. Sometime later, Valis glanced at the clock in the room. It had been hours, and Valis hadn't moved, watching the healers work. Finally, Firil rose from his stooped position over Kerac's body and stretched his back, craning his neck from side to side with a series of pops and snaps as his spine realigned. "We have done all we can for now."

"How is he?"

The three other healers who had worked with Firil all smiled at Valis and disappeared through a door in the back of the room as Valis neared Kerac's cot. He glanced up at Firil, waiting for news.

Firil took his time stretching, and Valis waited as patiently as he could until Firil let out a sigh and started speaking. "He is critically malnourished and dehydrated, has a chest infection, stomach infection, kidney and urinary tract infections, and is severely magically fatigued. My apprentices and I healed his wounds, but the infections from them are still in his blood and tissues. All must be cared for with medications, nutritious foods, treated water, rest, and around-the-clock care."

"But he'll live?" Valis asked, his voice cracking on the last word.

The Master Healer gave him a sympathetic smile as he squeezed Valis's shoulder. "I believe he will, yes. So long as he receives the proper care, he should pull through. But, the first few days will be critical to his recovery. I must start on his treatment plan immediately."

"Can we stay a little longer?" Tavros asked.

Firil gave him a nod and motioned to the chairs along the walls. "Neither of you will hinder me. Stay as long as you like. Just be sure to take care of your own health as well. And if you need me, I will be in my office."

Valis glanced at the office door and nodded. "Thank you."

Once Firil was gone, Tavros gave Valis a hug from behind, pressed a kiss behind his right ear, and went to the side wall. He brought back two chairs and placed them beside Kerac's cot, then reached for Valis's hand and drew him over.

"Come on, love. He needs you."

Valis didn't hesitate. With that single tug, he let Tavros lead him over to the chairs and sat himself down, his hands automatically reaching for Kerac as if they had minds of their own.

"He needs a bath," Valis whispered.

"You can bathe him," Firil said from close behind Valis's chair. "I was going to have my assistants do it soon, but there is a bathing room through the door on the left if you and Tavros wish to do it yourself.

"I'll go get him a change of clothes from his suite," Tavros said. He stood, pressed a kiss to Valis's temple, and left, leaving Valis alone with Kerac and Firil.

Firil took Tavros's vacated seat and rested his clasped hands in his lap. "Once you get him bathed and on a clean cot to rest, you and Tavros should go on to bed. I will send for you both when he wakes, but it is very late, and you need your sleep if you want to stay strong for him."

All Valis could do was nod. His vocal chords wouldn't work, so he didn't try to force them. Instead, while he waited, he contented himself with petting Kerac's head to ease his own heart, to remind him that Kerac was *here* and he was *safe*.

Tavros returned sometime later, and after spending an hour getting Kerac clean and into clean clothes that looked ten times too large on him, they tucked him into a clean cot and Valis sat down to try to relax. Everything was pressing down on him, and he needed a moment to get his body to stop shaking from the adrenaline crash from finding one of his fathers half-dead.

Then, out of nowhere, Kerac sucked in a wheezed gasp.

His eyes fluttered open. He clutched at the bed sheets as if they were a lifeline.

Then he started screaming.

The sound was like nothing Valis had ever heard before—broken, pained, lost, agonized... *tortured.*

Valis tried to calm him down. He stroked along Kerac's head, whispered words near his ear, but it was like Kerac couldn't hear him, like he was lost in his own mind, seeing and hearing terrible things. He screamed so hard, only stopping to refill his lungs, that Firil rushed back into the room and placed a glowing hand on his head.

Kerac instantly went limp, and Valis turned accusing eyes onto the healer. "What did you do?"

Firil frowned down at Kerac. "I put him into a magical coma. Not stasis. That would prevent him from healing. Instead, I forced him to sleep. He must rest, and I feared he would hurt himself. We will try removing it tomorrow."

"But—"

Tavros grabbed Valis's hand and squeezed. "Listen to Firil, love. Let's go rest. We can come back in the morning and see how he's doing."

"I'm afraid," Valis whispered. "What if—"

"He will be monitored constantly," Firil assured. "Nothing will happen to him during your respite. Go rest, Valis. He will need you when he wakes."

With a deep sigh, Valis forced himself out of his chair at Tavros's insistence and gave Kerac one last look before he let Tavros lead him out of the room.

"Come on, love," Tavros said as he linked their fingers and drew him down the hall. "Let's give our friends the news, kick them out of our suite, and get some sleep. We'll send Seza out to alert Thyran that you won't be teaching anyone tomorrow."

"Yeah," Valis said on a gusted breath. "Yeah. Thanks."

He would humor his husband, but Valis doubted he would sleep at all.

CHAPTER TWO

THE NEXT DAY, Valis didn't wake until lunchtime. Tavros lay snuggled up to his back, his arm snug around his waist. Valis closed his eyes, enjoying his husband's soft, rhythmic breaths that puffed against the back of his neck. He tried to move but gave up with a soft chuckle when he realized Tavros was lying on his hair.

Just that little chuckle felt strange after the heartache of the previous night. Valis itched to go check on Kerac, but he didn't have the heart to wake Tavros to start their day. They'd both had a rough night with Valis tossing and turning for hours before his body had finally had enough and he passed out sometime after dawn.

Settling into a doze, Valis laid there for another hour before Tavros finally stirred. He grunted and squeezed

Valis's waist as he stretched out his back and legs, pressing his morning arousal into the crease of Valis's ass.

"Good morning," Tavros murmured, his sleepy voice thick and gravelly.

"You mean good afternoon?" Valis glanced over at the clock on his nightstand and stretched, too. "Lunch is halfway over for the day."

Tavros groaned, burying his face in Valis's hair and rocking his hips. "Lunch or sex? I'm leaning toward sex and more sleep."

Valis huffed a laugh, reaching behind him to swat Tavros's hip through the covers. "I want to check on Papa soon."

"So, no sex?"

The pout in Tavros's voice made Valis grin and roll over in the circle of his husband's arms. He ran his hand teasingly down Tavros's arm, tickling his fingers along his ribs, over his waist to rest his hand on his hip. "I never said that. We just have to be quick, so we can bathe and get food before we head to the healing ward."

Tavros's eyes glittered with mischief. "I can be quick…"

Sex with Tavros was rarely quick. But as Tavros lined their dicks up and grabbed them both with his callused hand, Valis's breath hitched, and he moaned. This might not take as long as he thought.

Tavros claimed Valis's mouth in a hungry, possessive kiss as his hand stroked their cocks from root to tip. Valis mewled into his husband's mouth, bucking his hips for more friction. As their tongues entwined, Valis let his hand roam, mapping out the hills and valleys of hard, defined muscles in Tavros's back, gripping his rounded, muscular ass. He pulled Tavros closer, smiling into the kiss as his husband gasped, stealing the breath from Valis's lungs.

With the way their hips alternated in thrusting up into Tavros's pumping hand, creating a delicious variance in friction, it didn't take long for both of them to fall apart, moaning and panting against each other's necks.

Valis rested his forehead against Tavros's as they fought to catch their breath. His heart stuttered when Tavros grinned, showing his slightly crooked teeth. Valis's voice wavered as he whispered, "I love you."

Tavros tilted his head for a chaste, sweet kiss. "I love you, too."

Valis looked up and combed his fingers through Tavros's shaggy black hair. Soulful cloud-gray eyes stared back at him, searching Valis's face. He leaned in for one more kiss before brushing his knuckles across Valis's cheek. "Come on. Let's get bathed and dressed so you can go see Kerac."

It no longer surprised Valis that Tavros knew what he needed just by looking at him. He followed his lover into the lavatory, and after Tavros lovingly bathed him and helped him get dry and dressed after hastily bathing himself, they stopped for a quick lunch and were in the healing ward within an hour.

Firil was already by Kerac's bed when Valis walked in, Tavros close behind. "How is he?"

Firil glanced back and smiled at them. "Better than he was last night, but still very weak and sick. I just finished medicating and feeding him."

Tavros rested a hand on the back of Valis's neck and squeezed, relieving some of the tension that started building the moment they entered the ward. "How do you feed a sleeping man?" Tavros asked.

Firil smiled and turned back to pull the covers up to Kerac's chin. "The swallow reflex works whether you are asleep or awake, but I used a tube to inject his liquid meals directly into his stomach to ensure he wouldn't aspirate it. He will be on a high-nutrition liquid diet for more than a week in my estimation, even if he wakes."

"Will you wake him today?" Valis asked.

"No," Firil said. "No, I do not believe that is wise. I would like to get more medication and food into him before I remove the sleep spell."

He stepped back and sat on a chair next to Kerac's cot and started writing in a chart that he had resting on Kerac's chest. "I must warn you, Valis. His recovery will be very slow. First, we must deal with the infections while rebuilding his tolerance to solid foods. Then we must work on his strength. He may need therapy to enable him to walk again based on how much muscle mass he has lost."

He turned his head and stared up into Valis's eyes as Valis approached and buried his fingers in Kerac's hair. "It is a miracle he made it home, Valis. He has suffered greatly. It appears he was tortured, so be wary. When he wakes, his mind may also be broken. With as sensitive as he was before he left, it may take years of therapy for him to regain any sense of normalcy." Then he shrugged and went back to writing notes in Kerac's chart. "With your care, he may pull through faster. We will have to wait and see."

"What can I do to help him?"

Firil reached out with his free hand, still writing with the other, and squeezed Valis's wrist. "Once I finish my notes, I will show you how to work his body. His muscles have atrophied for the most part. We were able to reverse most of it, but he will need his muscles worked at regular intervals to help him regain range of motion, and the strength to sit up on his own, and eventually stand and walk."

Valis inhaled a shaky breath and nodded, taking a seat in the chair Tavros brought over. He idly played with Kerac's hair while Firil finished his notes, then helped as Firil showed him the exercises to put Kerac through. When they finished, Firil squeezed his shoulder and gave him a sad smile. "You can sit with him as long as you like, but I recommend going and doing other things with your day. Visit with your friends, get your own strength training done. There is nothing else to do for him at the moment but wait until his next feeding. His next exercise session isn't scheduled until after dinner."

"We'll stay a few minutes more," Tavros said. He squeezed the back of Valis's neck, then slid his hand over his shoulder to rest over his heart. "Then I'll drag Valis out for a while. We'll be back often, though."

Nodding, Firil headed for his office, Kerac's file tucked under his arm. "Come as often as you wish. You will be bothering no one. Just don't neglect your own needs, yes?"

"Yes, sir," Valis and Tavros said.

Tavros only let Valis fuss over Kerac for half an hour, just long enough to brush out Kerac's hair and braid it so it wouldn't get knotted again while he was bedridden. After he finished, Tavros drew him out of the healing ward by his hand and paused outside the door. "Anything you want to do today other than hover over Kerac?"

Valis smiled weakly at the tease and rested his forehead on Tavros's broad shoulder while he thought. Then he drew in a deep breath through his nose. "I want to visit Aryn, see how he's doing."

"Are you sure?" Tavros asked. He took a small step back and cupped Valis's face in both of his hands, tilting up so they were eye-to-eye. "It hasn't been very long..."

Valis shivered as Tavros pressed a soft kiss to his lips and brushed their noses together. He closed his eyes and soaked in Tavros's quiet love for a moment as he searched his heart for the truth. When he found the answer, he reached up and gently squeezed Tavros's wrists and turned his face to press a kiss to one of his husband's palms. "I'm sure. He wasn't himself, Tav. I can't believe that if he was in his right mind, if he was in control of himself, he would have hurt either of us. I can't believe that. I *won't*."

After a moment of staring into his eyes, Tavros acquiesced with a small nod. "I won't give up on him, either. But I have to admit, I'm not in any hurry to see him yet."

"You don't have to go," Valis said. He closed his eyes and leaned into the comfort when Tavros kissed his forehead.

"You're not going anywhere alone today. You've been through too much since last night, barely slept, and I can't stand the thought of you being out of my sight for more than fifteen minutes." He gave Valis a small smile and pulled him into a tight hug, breathing out a sigh that tickled Valis's left ear. "Seeing Kerac in that condition hit a little too close to home."

Valis nodded. He knew exactly how Tavros felt. Their future was set, at least it was in Valis's mind. He had to find out where Darolen was, rescue him, and find the missing god jar to return it to the other nine. Tavros would be accompanying him, and he'd had nightmares all night about Tavros getting left behind, sending Valis home, half-dead on his horse while staying behind to keep fighting, dying only moments after Valis's horse thundered away. Thankfully that dream didn't feel precognitive.

Precognitive or not, it left Valis feeling cold long after he thrashed awake, long after he woke up hours later to start the day, and even now, as Valis let out a shaky breath and tried to revel in Tavros's intense warmth and love, that chill remained coiled tight about his spine.

Valis did his best to shake off that feeling and gave Tavros a small smile. "Aryn might fight harder and do better in therapy to get well if we show him he's still loved. We have to try." He leaned in and kissed the tip of Tavros's nose, making him scrunch it adorably. "And I wouldn't want you anywhere else but by my side. I don't know if I could visit him alone, anyway. It's still... *raw*."

"It is for me, too," Tavros whispered. "He and I used to be so close. I just... he's my baby brother. I should love him, just like I used to. But I don't know if I can after what he did."

Valis tugged on Tavros's hand, drawing him down the hall toward the stairs that would take them to the prison. "That's okay. If you can't, you can't. But, keep an open mind, and let him prove to you he's worth it. If he can't do that, then at least we tried."

"Yeah," Tavros murmured softly. "Yeah. I can do that."

Once they made it to the Duty Captain's office, Valis took a deep breath as they waited for Captain Girnas to finish his thoughts on whatever he was writing. When he looked up, he perked a brow. "You two look like you're about to be led to your beheading. What's going on?"

Valis laced his fingers with Tavros', squeezing his lover's hand. "We want to visit Aryn Sadovin."

The Duty Captain shook his head. "Probably not a good idea. He's been a little bastard of late, demanding to be released. Fairly certain that boy's mind is gone."

Valis's stomach dropped, but he swallowed down the nausea and nodded. "Even so, I'd like to see him, and I'll be visiting him often."

Girnas smirked at him and waved to the two seats on the

opposite side of his desk. "Have a seat. I'll send guards down to fetch him."

The two Aesriphos guarding the door to the prison nodded and called to the other side, relaying the message, and Valis and Tavros settled in to wait.

After about fifteen minutes according to the clock over the door, the two guards started unlocking the gate. "He is ready for you."

Valis and Tavros stood, their hands still linked. Valis took a steadying breath, then led Tavros through the door and followed the waiting Aesriphos to an interrogation room.

"We will wait outside," their escort said. "If you need anything, or have any trouble, let us know."

She unlocked the door, removing a large, heavy bar and swung the door open. Just as it had been with Roba, Valis's birth father, Aryn was encased in a tiny cell that was too small for him to even sit down. He leaned against the back wall with his arms crossed over his chest. He wore the prison uniform of a gray tunic and matching loose pants. His black hair was slicked back and braided, the long braid draped over his shoulder to hang down near his stomach.

As Valis and Tavros entered and took their seats, Aryn glanced over at them, his dark gray eyes dull and almost life-less. "What do you want?"

The door to the room boomed closed, making Valis wince. He waited until he and Tavros had taken their seats before replying, "I wanted to check on you and see how you're doing. Have you begun therapy, yet?"

Aryn rolled his eyes. "Why do you care?"

"Because you were once my best friend, and I want my best friend back." Valis kept his voice calm and steady, trying to fight back the tremor that wanted to come out. "If you do as you're told, do well in therapy, you might not be in here as long as you think." Valis shrugged and met Aryn's steely stare. "While I won't say what you did wasn't your fault, I will say that mental illness played a large part in your actions toward Tavros and I, and if you *try*, we can all get past it."

Aryn drew in a shaky breath and blew it out. He lowered his eyes to the floor and hugged himself as he whispered, "I thought you hated me..."

"Neither of us hate you," Tavros said. He gripped Valis's hand tight. "We want you to get better. We want you back, Aryn. I want my baby brother back. I miss you. We both do."

Twin tears dripped from Aryn's eyes. He shrugged, wiped his face with the back of his hand. "I'll try, okay?"

"That's all we can ask," Valis said gently. "That's really all you can do."

With a small nod, Aryn sagged further against the wall and wrinkled his nose, rubbing his eyes with one hand. "I feel different, too."

"I removed all the black magic from your system," Valis said. "I also locked your gold away until you're well enough to use it wisely."

Aryn's lower lip wobbled. "I—I had black magic?"

"You did," Tavros murmured. "It was terrifying as fuck,

too. At the end, even I had it, though a bit less than you had. Valis took care of that, too."

Aryn let out a shaky sigh and tossed his black braid over his shoulder, but it bounced off the wall and fell back onto his chest. "I'm sorry," he whispered. "I didn't—" He cleared the squeak from his throat and tried again, "I didn't mean for it to go that far. I was just… so… so *jealous*. I couldn't think, couldn't eat, couldn't sleep, and the more I thought about it, the worse I got. I don't even remember the last few weeks."

He shrugged again. "I'm still jealous… but…"

"I know," Valis said. "It won't go away overnight."

"No," Aryn whispered.

Then he took a deep breath and glanced over again. "You got married?"

"We did," Tavros said proudly. "Valis and I had our joining night three days ago."

"Congratulations," Aryn said, sounding half-dead. "I'm sorry I missed it."

Valis gave him a small smile. "It's okay."

He needed to change the subject, so Valis rubbed over his heart and murmured, "I have some news."

"Oh?" Aryn only looked mildly interested. "What's that?"

"Papa returned home." Valis told him about finding Kerac the night before when he and Tavros left the Autumn Festival for some time alone outside Cadoras's walls. When he finished, Aryn's eyes were filled with tears.

"Will he make it?"

"We're fairly sure he will," Valis said. "He just needs medicine, food, rest, and to rebuild his strength. Firil thinks he was tortured, so his mind may be messed up."

The boy shivered and grabbed his cell bars. "I'm so sorry. Did… did you find any sign of Darolen?"

Valis shook his head. "No. Thyran sent out search parties, but none turned up any sign of him. Scries turned up nothing, as well, so we have to wait until Firil removes the sleep spell so we can ask Papa about it. Firil is waiting until he's built up a bit of a tolerance for food because of how emaciated he is."

Aryn glanced down at himself and winced. "Yeah."

"You'll fill back out again," Tavros assured. "You went a long time without sleeping or eating right. The dark circles under your eyes started to look like you got punched in each eye twice a day. It… it was kind of awful."

"I'm sorry," Aryn whispered. "It still hurts."

"Then will you stop giving the guards a hard time?" Valis asked. "The Duty Captain said you were causing a lot of problems."

The boy shrugged. "I didn't know why I was in here until yesterday, and I didn't believe them until you came in. It all feels like a really bad dream." He took a deep breath and rested his head back against the wall. "But yeah. I'll behave."

"Good," Tavros said. "If you're good, you won't be in here for long, I think. Valis and I will talk to the priests and see what can be done if you prove you're no longer a danger to anyone."

Aryn gave his eldest brother a small, tired smile. "Thanks, Tav."

The door to the room opened, and the female guard stuck her head in. "Time's up. Are you ready to head back?"

Valis let out a soft breath. "Yes, ma'am."

He looked back at Aryn and smiled. "I'll be coming to see you as often as I can, okay?"

With a nod, Aryn wiped his eyes on the neck of his tunic. "Yeah. Thanks."

As Valis and Tavros left the interrogation room, Valis rubbed over his heart. "Think that was really him?"

Tavros squeezed his hand and brought it up to kiss the backs of Valis's fingers. "I'm pretty sure it was. Thanks for making me come today."

"You're welcome." Valis turned and pressed a kiss to Tavros's shoulder. "Thank you for coming with me."

"Always, Valis. Always."

CHAPTER THREE

AFTER DINNER with his husband and friends, Valis led the group back to the healing ward to visit Kerac. He had planned to go alone with just Tavros, but everyone wanted to go, so they filed through the halls until they made it to the side of Kerac's cot.

To Valis's surprise, Kerac blinked up at him, awake. Firil entered from a door at the back and smiled at the group. "Good, Valis. I am glad you came."

With a wave at Firil, Valis sank into the chair beside the cot and took his papa's hand. "How are you feeling?"

Kerac's lower lip wobbled, and he shook his head.

Valis leaned in close. "Was Darolen still alive when you separated?"

His adopted father's golden eyes glistened with unshed

tears. He opened his mouth to speak, but nothing came out for several moments. With each second that ticked by, Valis's stomach dropped further and further into the floor. Was Darolen dead?

All Kerac could do after a bit was nod. Relief flooded Valis. He leaned in and pressed a kiss to Kerac's forehead. "It's okay, Papa. You can tell me all about it when you're feeling better. Don't stress yourself over it."

Valis wanted to ask so many questions, but the devastation in Kerac's face made him keep his mouth shut as he stroked a hand over his papa's hair. "I missed you," Valis whispered. "I missed you so damned much."

The tears that had gathered in Kerac's eyes spilled over to the sides of his face and dripped into his ears. He sniffled, let out a whimper as he tried to raise his hands, but was too weak to get them more than a couple inches off the cot.

Valis smiled softly as he gently helped Kerac into a sitting position. Then he wrapped his arms about Kerac and held him as tight as he dared without hurting him. Kerac buried his face in Valis's hair and took long, deep breaths as if he couldn't get enough of Valis's scent.

Then he started sobbing. It started off gentle at first, then grew in intensity until his entire body shook with his pain. Throughout it all, he remained so quiet that it worried Valis. He knew how Kerac cried. He was vocal to the point where he would make sound both when exhaling *and* inhaling. What had happened to him that when he cried this hard, he made no sound except quiet gasps and wet sniffles?

"Oh, Papa." He rubbed his hands up and down Kerac's back and kissed the side of his head. Valis gently rocked him back and forth while Kerac sobbed uncontrollably and clung to Valis with every minuscule ounce of strength he still had, his bony fingers clenched in Valis's tunic, hands shaking with exertion.

It took long minutes for Kerac to calm, and the moment he did, he collapsed. Feeling Kerac go limp in his arms, Valis's heart stuttered painfully, and he held his fingers under Kerac's nostrils to make sure he was still breathing.

"Valis?"

Valis glanced over at Seza and let out a breath. "I think he just passed out from exhaustion. Will you fetch Firil?"

She nodded and strode quickly away toward the Master Healer's office. When she returned, the rest of their friends parted to let Firil through. The frown that marred his face worried Valis, but then it disappeared and Firil smoothed a gentle hand over Kerac's head.

"What happened?"

Valis took in a deep breath and held Kerac a little tighter. "He couldn't stop sobbing, and then he just went limp."

Firil relaxed and smiled. "He only exhausted himself. He needs sleep, Valis. All is well. Lay him down and let him rest. He has been through too much to get over it in a day."

No matter how much that made sense, Valis didn't want to let Kerac go. When he looked up at Firil again, the Master Healer chuckled and patted him on the back. "Hold him a while longer if you wish. It will hurt nothing. Your presence may help his mental state when he wakes next. I took the coma spell off him to gauge his reaction, and he's done remarkably well under the circumstances, so he may not need it again."

With a nod, Valis buried his face in Kerac's hair, breathing him in. Now he understood Kerac's reaction. He had been gone so long that Valis couldn't get enough of his scent, either, wanted to breathe him in forever. Then a thought occurred to him. "When can I take him back to our suite? He may be more comfortable there."

Firil thought about that for a few moments. When he finished whatever assessment he did in his mind, he shook his head. "You may be right. If it will make you feel better, you may take him now. I can feed him and help him through his physical therapy there. It will be no trouble."

"No, Valis," Seza rested a gentle hand on Valis's shoulder. "Take him to his own suite. He'll be more comfortable with his own things, in his own space. We can take turns keeping watch over him. That way he's never alone."

She gave Valis a small smile. "I know you wanted him close by, but I do think this idea is best. You and Tavros need time to yourselves so soon after your joining night, and you'd never get it sharing a suite with Kerac there."

When Valis sighed and drooped his shoulders in defeat, Seza chuckled. "Don't give me that look. You also need to not smother him, and you'd fuss so much he'd never get any rest."

"You know she's right, man," Jedai said. "No sense fighting her about it."

Valis cast a glance back at the traitor. Jedai shrugged negligently and ran his fingers through his wavy auburn hair. His blue eyes didn't seem the least bit sorry.

When he glanced over at Tavros who stood by his side, then Maphias, Aenali, and Zhasina who stood a few feet away, they all smirked at him. "She's right," Zhasina said.

Sighing, Valis acquiesced with a nod. "Fine."

"Then let's get him situated," Tavros said. "We can keep the first watch."

Seza nodded and helped pull the covers back from Kerac's legs. "Let's get him comfortable first, then we'll have a meeting in his sitting room to discuss a watch rotation."

It both did and didn't feel right to be taking Kerac out of the healing ward. As he carefully lifted his adopted father off the cot, Valis tried to remind himself that nothing would happen. Firil would still take care of Kerac. His friends would help Valis keep an eye on him between the Master Healer's visits. Kerac would be safe, and he would get better.

But with every step, it felt like he was taking Kerac into danger.

Your mind is delving into the realm of stupidity again, Roba muttered. His ghostly voice made Valis shiver but made him feel less alone. Sure, Valis was surrounded by friends, but at least Roba had permanent access into his mind and could call him out on his bullshit and self-flagellating thoughts.

Thanks, Dad.

Just remember that whether you take him or leave him, he will progress just the same. And being in familiar surroundings may help his mind heal faster even if his body takes longer.

Valis let a small smile creep onto his face. *When did you turn into a softie?*

Roba didn't deign to answer that with anything more than an indignant huff in Valis's mind.

Still, Roba's concern made Valis feel lighter, and that feeling of danger passed. Now, Valis recognized it as a small bout of anxiety, and could more easily dismiss it. And when they made it into Kerac and Darolen's suite, Valis felt a small wave of nostalgia wash over him. He hadn't spent any real time in this suite since his fathers left for their mission. It felt strange to be inside it again.

With care, he and Tavros got Kerac situated in his bed, covered him up and lowered the lamp wick to keep only a soft glow to the room. Kerac didn't stir, so after five minutes of fussing with Kerac's blankets and stroking his hair, Valis allowed Tavros to lead him by the hand out of the room and across the hall to the sitting room where their friends waited.

"How is he?" Aenali asked.

Valis sat on the couch next to Tavros with a deep, pent-up sigh. Aenali claimed his lap, climbing up without hesitation. She wrapped herself around him, just as she had wrapped herself around his heart when he'd first come to this monastery. He shrugged as he pressed his nose into her auburn curls and tried valiantly to smile when she turned her worried green doe eyes up at him. "He's as well as can be expected, I guess. He's still unconscious."

"It may have just been exhaustion coupled with his emotions," Zhasina said. She pushed her tight, black curls from her face and smiled knowingly at him, the warm cocoa color of her skin glowing in the firelight from the hearth. "He may not be as strong as you to deal with such emotions while exhausted."

Valis huffed a laugh. "I've never been that exhausted before. I hope I never have to go through that."

Zhasina shrugged, unrepentant. "Perhaps, but my point stands."

Seza clapped her hands, startling everyone. "So, let's come up with a rotation." She looked around, meeting each person's eyes in turn. "We need to get Valis's mind in the right place, and we need to know our schedules so that we can rearrange our duties to accommodate them."

"I can help, too, right?" Aenali asked. "I can run to get Firil just as well as you guys can."

"Yes, Aenali," Valis said, hugging the little girl. "You can help. You're often more level-headed than any of us, anyway."

"I know I am. It's about time the rest of you figured that out." She huffed and nestled against Valis, knowing he needed her close to keep him grounded, knowing that right now, her biggest advantage was her warmth and weight when Valis needed her most. And she only piped up a few times during the discussion to let them know when they were being obtuse, and to let them know her normal schedule and when she could fit Kerac's care into it.

Once they got the watch rotation schedule hammered out, Valis thanked everyone and watched them leave to get back to their duties. He thanked all the gods in succession that his own duties had been lifted for a few days due to Kerac's return and his medical state. It would also give his students a few days to process their lessons and practice on their own time. ...Or sleep in. The classes Valis taught were all before dawn, so he wouldn't begrudge anyone taking a few days to catch up on sleep or anything else they needed to do.

The moment they were alone, Tavros tugged Valis back into the sitting room and onto the couch. He sighed, nuzzling into Valis's hair. "Tell me how to help you. You're shaking."

Valis glanced down at his hands and groaned. He hadn't realized how bad his shaking was until Tavros mentioned it, but now he felt the tremors all throughout his body and his hands were the worst. He clenched them to try to get them to stop, but Tavros rubbed his tight fists until he relaxed them. "None of that. Tell me."

"I'm not sure," Valis admitted. "Truly, I don't know. I just..."

Tavros nodded. "I understand." Then he shook his head and stared into Valis's eyes with such intent that Valis almost cringed away. "You're exhausted."

"Just a bit, yeah."

His husband pressed a kiss to Valis's temple and gave him a nudge. "Go lie down with him. Just make sure to get some sleep instead of staring at him the whole time, okay? That won't help either of you."

Valis wiped a hand down his face and nodded. "I know."

"Then go on. I'll stay in here and wake you when it's time for the next watch."

With a heavy sigh, Valis stepped into Tavros for a sweet kiss then headed for the bedroom. Kerac laid just as they had settled him, his breathing soft and even in sleep. Valis didn't want to risk waking him, so he slipped off his boots at the door and tiptoed through the room until he stood on the opposite side of the bed. It took him a few minutes to gather the courage to lay down, but the moment he was horizontal, he rolled and cuddled up to Kerac's side. Before he realized what was happening, he was asleep.

The next thing he knew, Valis felt fingers in his hair and woke to see Kerac staring down at him with a soft frown.

"Papa? Are you okay?"

"No..."

"Can you talk about it?"

Kerac twitched his head to the side, his eyes filling with tears. "No..."

Valis reached for his papa's free hand and gave it a squeeze. "I swear it, Papa. I swear, if he's still alive, I will find him, and I will bring him home to you. You have my word."

Kerac's breath hitched in a sob, making Valis's heart ache.

It hurt that all Valis could do was make promises he wasn't sure he would keep, but that he would give anything to make happen. It hurt that he couldn't see Kerac's smile, because Kerac was too broken to do more than whisper single-word answers. And it *hurt* that he didn't know where Darolen was, or even if he was still alive, anything to give Kerac some semblance of a reassurance.

"I love you, Papa. Tell me what you need."

Another hitched breath, and Kerac whispered, "I just... wish I could..." He cleared his throat of the phlegm that clogged it, making his voice warble. "Wish I could hear his voice... just once more. Just once..."

Valis leaned up and pressed a kiss to Kerac's forehead. "Give me just a minute. I'll be right back."

He carefully extracted himself from the bed and raced to the sitting room. Tavros was there, book in hand by the fire. He glanced up when Valis threw the door open and set the book aside. "What is it?"

"Can you bring my phonograph and the record? Kerac wants to hear Darolen's voice."

"He's awake?" A smile broke out on Tavros's face, warming Valis's heart. "Good. I'll be back with it. Leave the doors open for me."

"Always."

While Tavros went to fetch that, Valis went and grabbed a glass and filled it with cold water from the tap. He carefully sat Kerac up and helped him drink, surprised that he tried to chug the entire glass in a single swallow. "Easy, Papa. I can always get you more. Are you hungry?"

With Kerac's nod, Valis helped him drink the rest of the glass and wiped down his face and neck with a cool cloth. "Once Tavros gets here, we'll get you some food. You may not like it though. You're on a liquid diet until your stomach is strong enough for solid food again."

"That's fine," Kerac whispered. "Anything will do."

Valis kissed his brow and smoothed back the flyaways that had escaped his braid. Just as he was thinking about brushing it out and re-braiding it, Tavros entered with the phonograph and set it up across the room. Without a word, Tavros wound the crank, set the needle down, and the room filled with Darolen's deep bass rumble singing The Journey.

There were so many reactions Valis thought Kerac would have, but none of them prepared him for what actually happened. Kerac stiffened in his arms. His breaths came out in short stuttered gasps that wrenched Valis's heart in a visceral way. His bony fingers clutched at Valis', and for as weak as Kerac was, the strength of that trembling grip surprised him.

"Shut it off," Kerac croaked. "Please... shut it off!"

Tavros raised the bell of the phonograph, removing the needle from the record with a soft hiss as the record continued to spin on the table. When silence descended, Kerac's entire body started to shake.

"Papa?"

Kerac hiccupped, his breaths coming faster. "That... that..."

"What is it, Papa?"

"I—I can't—"

"He's turning pale," Tavros said as he crossed the room in quick strides. "Lay him down."

"I'll take care of Papa. You go fetch Firil. Papa's hungry. And he may need something for anxiety. I think he's having a panic attack."

"He's—I—I can't—"

Valis took care in turning Kerac around and guided his face into the curve of Valis's neck. "Shh. It's okay, Papa. It'll be okay."

Kerac sucked in a sharp breath and whimpered. "It will never be okay. Never."

"Don't you have any faith in me?" Valis nuzzled into Kerac's hair. "Not even a little bit?"

"I—"

When Kerac didn't seem like he would finish that thought, Valis nuzzled until his lips found Kerac's ear and murmured, "I will ride to the ends of this earth until I find him, Papa. Nothing and no one will stand in my way. Do you hear me? Do you understand? I will not rest until Father is brought home to us. If he was alive when you last saw him, he's not given up. He's still alive, and I *will* bring him home."

He squeezed Kerac to him and rocked as his papa wept. "Just have faith in me. I'm not leaving until I know you're truly on the mend, and I still have many things I must do before Tavros and I can leave."

Kerac's hands clawed, clutching Valis's tunic. "I don't want… You can't leave me. Please. Not you, too."

Valis pulled Kerac back just enough to look deep into his golden eyes. "Trust in me, Papa. Trust in me, and I can do *anything*."

CHAPTER FOUR

IT TOOK AT LEAST an hour to calm Kerac down. Once he was
calm, Firil fed him, again using the tube to make sure he ate
enough with as little discomfort as possible. Seza and
Zhasina came to take up watch so Valis and Tavros could go
on and do other things, but it took all of them ganging up on
him before Valis allowed Tavros to lead him out of Kerac's
suite.

Now, he stood in his own suite's bedroom at the side
table, his scrying bowl before him. He needed to clear his
mind, but every time he thought he could scry, Kerac's voice
whispered through his mind, "You can't leave me. Please.
Not you, too."

Every time those words floated through his mind, it
broke Valis's heart all over again. It left him gasping, trying
anything in his power to get that broken whisper out of his

mind so he could concentrate enough to solve the problem that had broken Kerac in the first place.

He needed to find Darolen. And the sooner the better, so he could start planning his rescue mission, because no matter what, no matter *who* tried to stand in his way, he *was* going after his father.

You are so very determined, my son, Roba said, and Valis didn't even hear a bit of sarcasm in his tone. *Give yourself some slack. You have had a tumultuous and emotional few days between your joining night and finding one of your adopted fathers. You are* allowed *to grieve. You are* allowed *to have a muddled mind.*

Thanks, Dad. Valis blew out a breath and pinched the bridge of his nose before rubbing his finger and thumb into his tired eyes. *I just really want to scry after Father so that I can at least settle one of our main fears. If he's alive, that will help both of our mental states.*

Then get away from that bowl for a moment and calm down. Drop and give me one-hundred pushups, then you can return and try again.

Valis smirked but backed away from the table and his scrying bowl and dropped to the floor. It was true though. After the first twenty-five pushups Valis's mind started to calm. After fifty, he found a bit of clarity. After seventy-five, his mind felt almost numb. And after one-hundred, he felt calm enough to scry.

Sometimes Roba *did* have good ideas. They were just usually laden with snark and sass.

I will show you snark and sass, you little whelp!

Laughing, Valis disrobed, dropping his sweaty uniform into the hamper, took a cool cloth to his heated skin, and redressed. When he stood in front of the scrying bowl again, he came to it with a blissfully blank mind and a fair amount of hope.

As he stared into the still water, Valis focused his mind, remembering Darolen's voice, his scent, the ever-patient expression on his face, and commanded the water to show him his father.

Images swirled in the water, fast and cloudy. With the intent on showing him where Darolen was *now*, the images all turned to darkness. Valis sucked in a breath but waited for long moments until the darkness became overwhelming.

If only he could have sound. Was this darkness where Darolen was, or was it a representation that Darolen was dead?

Wait.

Could he get sound through a scry?

Thyran had never said if it was possible or not. It was worth a try. At least, Valis thought it was. If it failed, at least he'd know, or could ask more pointed questions when he next saw Thyran.

Valis took a deep breath in through his nose and blew it out through his mouth. He could do this. He'd proven many times over that what others thought was impossible was very much possible. He just had to believe in himself and use his intent to get the job done.

So as he stood there, staring down into inky blackness, he tweaked his iron-held intent to include the demand for sound. And what he heard made his heart stutter.

Gagging came through the bowl. When the wet splashes and retching stopped, Valis heard the soft, wheezing voice. "Phaerith, please let him be okay. Please... Kerac must be okay. He must. Phaerith... please... I—"

Hard, hacking coughs echoed up from the bowl, cutting Darolen's prayer off. But as soon as he had his breath again, he resumed, still in that quiet wheeze. "Give me a sign. Please, give me a sign that my husband and son are alive..."

Valis gasped and scratched at a tickle on his cheek only to realize that he was crying. He sniffled and wiped his nose on the sleeve of his tunic as he strained to hear anything else.

Keys rattled in the distance. Darolen's voice cut off abruptly as soon as he heard them, and the resulting silence seemed so tense that Valis could almost feel his father's dread increase with each jostle of those distant keys as they neared until they jangled right outside the room. Lamplight flickered from under a doorway, lighting filthy, trembling feet in a dim orange glow. Valis swallowed hard when he saw that each ankle was encased in heavy iron shackles anchored to the floor.

Memories of his vision when he had fallen off the back of a wagon in Lyvea rushed back to him. He had been on a rescue mission, intent on getting the Kalutakeni caravan back to the safety of Cadoras. During a moment of respite, Valis had been speaking of his worry over his fathers with

Tavros and fell to a vision. He remembered being in what he believed to be Kerac's body, sitting in his own filth, retching and cold and sick while Darolen, just as sick, tried to comfort him, apologizing for getting sick.

Now he wished he hadn't had that vision, so he could block the memory of those wretched smells from his nose as he watched the scene. He knew that shiny liquid surrounding Darolen's legs was vomit, urine and diarrhea. He knew that Darolen had sores from sitting in his own filth. He knew those sores were getting infected. How long had he been in such a horrid state?

Valis mentally urged the vision around so he could see his father's face. But the moment he got a glimpse, he wished he hadn't. Darolen's hair was long now, scraggly and matted with filth. The collar around his throat was too small, digging into his flesh to create ugly sores that trailed blood and puss down his naked chest. His wrists were also bound, held high up on the wall so that he couldn't relax without the iron biting into the raw, tender skin.

The worst thing, though, was how thin Darolen had become. Just like Kerac, he was mostly just loose skin over bone. His muscle mass had melted away as his body absorbed everything possible to keep him alive. Did his captors feed him at all?

When that door swung open, Valis saw his father's eyes for the first time. The dark brown depths didn't hold the anger and defiance he *knew* his father would hold in the face of the enemy. Instead, he looked grim and defeated, almost lifeless as if he knew he would die in that cell.

As if he *wished* for death.

Valis dismissed the scry as he recoiled from that look. Darolen would never have wanted Valis to see him looking so hopeless. And Valis had to shake himself free from the horror. He had to believe that Darolen would pull through. He wouldn't give up. Darolen wasn't one to give up on anything.

But, still… that defeated look in those beloved eyes broke Valis's heart, and he stumbled away from the scrying bowl, his hand clutching at his tunic over his heart. He tried to get his breaths to come even and deep, but each breath came as tortured gasps that barely filled his lungs. The sensation of drowning nearly sent him to the floor, but Valis staggered to the door and threw it open.

"Tav…"

He could barely croak the word, but somehow Tavros heard him and came running from the sitting room. He caught Valis on his way down as he sank to his knees. Tavros took one look at Valis's face and his own expression crumbled. "Oh, Valis…"

"I saw him," Valis said between gasps. "I saw him…"

"Let's go see Thyran. Come on."

He helped Valis stand and once he had Valis stable on his feet, guided him from their suite and up through the monastery to the temple and into the reliquary where Thyran was normally found.

By the time they got into the reliquary, Valis had his breathing mostly under control save for the odd sob that escaped him. And just like when Tavros had first seen him, Thyran turned from the book he was reading, took one look at him and frowned. "Valis... what is it, my boy?"

It took every ounce of Valis's strength not to break down into a sobbing mess. He let Tavros lead him to the table and push him into a chair. And as Tavros massaged Valis's shoulders, he relayed to Thyran everything he'd learned from his scry, and what little Kerac had been able to tell him.

By the end, tears streamed down his cheeks and neck and he wanted to bury his face in Tavros's throat to sob out all his grief, but he took a deep breath, blew his nose on the kerchief Thyran handed him and shrugged. "It matches my vision pretty well. Only in my vision, Kerac was with him."

"You say you were able to get sound in your scry?" Thyran asked.

Valis nodded. "Yeah. It took a bit, but I did manage."

"Well done!" Thyran grinned at him so hard that dimples pitted his cheeks. His blue eyes shone with his pride, making him seem younger than his salt and pepper hair let on. "Getting sound with a scry is advanced training, Valis. You did extremely well. Congratulations."

Valis shuddered and leaned his elbows on his knees so his open palms could support his face as he sagged in his chair. "It was horrible and horrifying, Thyran. The whole time he wheezed prayers to Phaerith, and all I wanted to do was comfort him. But, I can't, and I think that's what hurts the most. I couldn't give him any hope. I couldn't answer his prayers to tell him that Kerac made it here alive and that he's safe. I couldn't tell him that *I'm* safe and that I'm progressing well."

His throat clogged and Valis coughed into his shoulder, squeezing his eyes shut as he tried to swallow down his heart. "I couldn't tell him anything."

"Are there any shiny surfaces where he is being held?"

Valis looked up at the historian with a pained grimace. "The pools of filth all around him, but there are no sources of light unless someone comes into his cell, or wherever it is they're holding him."

"That may be enough for him to hear you," Thyran mused. "Though, you would have to learn how to communicate through scry. It is very tricky because normally in training the one you are contacting is awaiting your scry. In this case, you will need to push through the barrier to force a scry, to project yourself in such a way that your intended recipient can see and/or hear you when they are not expecting your call."

Sitting up straighter, Valis looked his friend in the eye and squared his shoulders. "I'm ready to learn. If I can give him hope, if I can do anything to give him a fighting chance, a *reason* to stay alive at all cost, I'll master it."

Thyran's grin widened, and he nodded. "I had a feeling you might say that. You know where to go."

"What must I do?"

The historian tilted his head. "Just open a scry, and I will interfere with it. You will *feel* my interference due to the concentration and focus you put into the scry. Once you have a good handle on that feeling, use it to try to interfere with my scry. That is the basis for two-way scrying. Once you have mastered that, we will focus on how to force a scry, even for someone who has no experience in the art."

Valis took in a long, deep breath and rolled his shoulders to try to get some of the tension out. "Right. The faster I get it, the faster I can—"

"Do not go down that road, Valis." Thyran's grin dimmed down to a paternal smile, and he reached out to grab Valis's hand. Somehow that firm touch grounded Valis, cleared his mind. "If you go down that road, your mind will fill up with doubts, insecurities, and myriad other things that do not belong. Focus on one thing at a time so you don't get over-whelmed like you tend to do. Can you do this?"

Valis swallowed down his arguments and nodded. "Yeah. I can."

Thyran smirked, giving his hand another squeeze before letting go. "Do not think you are fooling me, young man. I can almost hear your arguments."

Shoulders drooping, Valis groaned and scrubbed his hands over his face. "Impatience. Sorry."

"I am aware. But at least you are, too. Now, get your backside in the scrying alcove."

Like he was headed to the gallows, Valis stalked off to the dreaded alcove where he'd spent so many agonizing hours with headaches and gritty eyes while trying to learn how to scry, dragging his feet the whole way. The last thing he wanted right now was to stand in that dusty space between two tall shelving units full of ancient, moldering books and scrolls while staring at a bowl of water. But if he wanted to give Darolen any hope, he had to get it done. With that in mind, he forced himself between the stacks and stared down into the bowl with a desperate plea to Sovras ringing in his mind that he *get it* as soon as possible so he could move through the lessons at a steady pace.

The first scry, Valis only sought to check on Kerac. It was easy, because he knew exactly where Kerac was, what his environment looked like, and other prominent things to help guide him. Only five minutes into the scry, he felt something strange, as if someone was tugging at his mind—at his *focus* —and redirecting it. Fighting it became painful, and the moment he stopped fighting, Thyran's face appeared, his fierce blue eyes shining with pride.

"Excellent work, Valis. Do you think you can pick apart how I accomplished this?"

Valis bit his lip and sighed. "My mind is mush, Thyran. Can you just tell me? I know you tugged on my focus some-how. As to how you did it… I'm not sure."

Thyran gave him the wickedest grin Valis had seen on his face yet. "What have you been teaching your students?"

Sighing, Valis rubbed his eyes. "Cast by intent alone. Never use prayer because it's costing you valuable time."

"In this case, prayer has little to do with it as much as it is mental mechanics. But, I believe, with your skill set, you should be able to accomplish your task with simple intent. If you have trouble, we will go over the complex mechanics."

"Keeping it simple would be best," Valis muttered on a groan. "I really don't have the mental capacity for anything complicated."

"Just as well," Thyran said with a wink. "Give it a go and we'll see how you do."

With that, Thyran's face disappeared from the scrying bowl, and Valis had the sudden urge to throw the damned thing at the wall. If he didn't know for a fact that the frustration came from his own impatience and his need to see Darolen again and comfort him, he might have followed through with that impulse. Instead, he took a steadying breath and peered back into that dreaded bowl with the intent to see Thyran's face.

A moment later, clouds formed in the water like they sometimes did during a scry. Valis could hear Thyran's soft breathing as if it came from the bowl, and with a nudge of his focus, he mentally reached into the bowl and latched onto those sounds. When he tried to jerk them back, he heard Thyran's surprised shout from across the reliquary a moment before Thyran's wide eyes appeared in the bowl followed by the historian clearing his throat.

"That—" He cleared his throat and tried again, "Perhaps, Valis, in the future... you try not to be so violent, yes? But, well done."

Valis rubbed the back of his neck. "Sorry. I never did have a good grasp of subtlety."

Thyran snorted. "Liar. But you succeeded. Now, come back and let us work on something easy for a bit so I can regain the wits you scrambled for me."

For the next hour, Thyran taught him how to scry using different kinds of reflective surfaces, which to Valis's surprise, wasn't as intuitive as he thought. After using a fluid medium for his scrying since he began, anything less flexible gave him a strange echo, as if the surface of the objects he used reflected his visions back at him, instead of just showing him images. He had to totally retrain his focus in order to keep the images straight and the sound from warbling.

But, as they wrapped up the lesson, Valis rubbed his chest with one hand and gripped his golden pocket watch in the other. He had managed, and Thyran said the skill would only strengthen with time and practice. And until Kerac was healed and he could get things organized for a rescue mission to save Darolen, Valis had nothing but time to train and practice.

"Thyran?"

"What is it, Child?"

Valis smiled slightly at the endearment. Thyran had said at Valis's birth anniversary that he could no longer call Valis "Child" anymore, but still did on occasion. "I think it's safe to call off the search party. Darolen isn't lost in the wilderness or fields."

"Yes. I imagine that is the case."

Still, Valis's heart ached. "I *will* find him."

Thyran squeezed his hand and pushed him toward the reliquary doors and into the hall of communion. "Of that, my dear boy, I have little doubt. Now, go on to bed, the both of you. This has been a trying day, and you need rest for what is to come."

CHAPTER FIVE

THE NEXT MORNING, Valis thrashed awake from a nightmare about Darolen, and he found he woke up early with a restless energy he couldn't quiet. Waking up at this time had been routine for so long that he simply couldn't sleep anymore. His body decided it was time to wake up, and nothing he did could persuade it otherwise. So instead of wallowing around in bed in the heat of Tavros's arms, he got up, and kissed his husband's forehead. After he bathed, dressed, and donned his armor, he left Tavros a note on the nightstand next to his head, and Valis headed out to round up his translocation students.

He checked the arena first, but finding it empty, he groaned and started wandering the halls, knocking on doors and rousing his students. The guards he passed, he ordered to rouse the reliquary guards for their training in a few hours. If he was going to do this, he may as well take on both classes. No sense in half-assing things. If he had to be up and miserable, so did everyone else.

And then he felt like shit for making his problems everyone else's problems, but the damage was done. He'd already begun and had woken six of his students from their respite.

"Help me wake the others," he said to the group who followed him around like ducklings.

"I thought you were off for a few days," one of the women groaned. "We were supposed to be able to sleep in."

"Things changed." Valis ran his hands over his face. "There's little I can do for my father at this time, so we might as well get back to our normal routine. He needs rest, and we need to train."

By the time everyone made it to the Arena, Valis had finally worked out some of his nervous energy and was able to concentrate on the faces staring back at him. They all seemed tired but alert. Hopefully the tiredness didn't equal disaster.

"Today, you're going to be learning how to phase with a person in tow."

"Phase?" Averni asked with her brows drawn in confusion.

Valis nodded. "Phasing is just another word for translocation. It's what Thyran sometimes calls it, and it's easier."

"Ah, okay."

"Any other questions?" Valis asked as he glanced around the room.

When no one spoke up, Valis waved a hand. "Pair up and get in line. You're going to phase across the room with your partner, then your partner is going to phase back with you. It's just like before. Intent is everything. If you truly believe you can do it, there isn't much you *can't* do with magic."

"What are the things we can't do?" Stavlen asked.

Valis shrugged and leaned against the wall at his back. "Bring someone back from the dead. Make someone love you. Phase to somewhere you can't visualize correctly in your mind. Heal infections." He shrugged again. "I'm sure there are more, but that list is small compared to the vast list of the things that are possible if you put your mind to it."

Shyvus chuckled. "Are you certain even those things are impossible?"

Valis studied his reliquary guard friend seriously. Shyvus's blond hair extended down his face in a neatly trimmed beard, a new fashion for him. His blue eyes danced with mirth. But, Valis felt no joy in that moment. "Truthfully? Some of those, I wish weren't impossible. Some of them should never be attempted."

"Raising the dead," Kogar said, just as seriously.

"Exactly." Valis let out a sigh. "We are getting vastly off topic. Shyvus, you and Kogar go first. Shyvus phases to the other end, Kogar phases you both back. Begin."

As the class got underway, Valis watched for any mishaps with his mind churning.

I believe, Roba started, then hesitated. He took a moment of thought before continuing. *Healing infections is not quite impossible. If I can eradicate poison from your bloodstream as I did with that poisoned arrow you were shot with back in Urkori when we were attacked, you should be able to eradicate infections from blood and tissue. It may be worth it to try when you next have the time available.*

Good to know. Thanks, Dad.

You are always welcome, my son, Roba said gently. *It may not be possible, but there is no harm in trying.* He sighed and Valis felt his spirit grow restless. *I have taken much from you. It is time I start giving back in any way I can.*

Valis felt a smile tugging at his lips as his heart swelled. *Love you, Dad.*

I love you, too, my son.

Translocation training progressed with no casualties, and as Valis dismissed one class, the reliquary guard class started filtering in, grumbling amongst themselves as they bemoaned their lost sleep. Valis smirked at them, knowing their pain all too well.

"Valis, you shit, we were supposed to have a few days off!" Phalin muttered. His raven black hair looked like he'd rolled out of bed with just enough brain power to throw his armor on and stagger through the halls. His bloodshot brown eyes glared at Valis but held no heat. "I will get revenge. Do you hear me?"

Valis chuckled. "Loud and clear, you grumpy ass. Get in line."

Even though his own energy wasn't all that high, Valis kept his back straight and his shoulders back as the reliquary guard force lined up with their partners in neat rows, twelve abreast. It took that long for Valis to figure out what to teach them today. Now that they had all become adept at using intent instead of prayer, it was really getting to the point where Valis was pulling topics out of thin air and praying the men and women didn't think him stupid or repetitive.

But they needed to train. They all needed to keep their confidence high because Valis had a gut feeling that they would need these skills fresh for the days and weeks to come. He didn't know where that feeling came from, but everyone told him repeatedly to listen to his instincts, and he was starting to take their demands to heart.

"How is your father doing?" Kaltani asked.

Valis glanced at the brunette woman with a sad smile. "He will recover. Papa is the strongest man I know."

"Is there anything at all we can do?" Netai, Kaltani's wife, asked. Her hazel eyes shimmered with unshed tears, which was rare for the redhead.

Valis's heart all-but melted. "Whoever is close to him may visit him and even help in his supervision when the rest of our watch needs help. He is resting in his suite with the around-the-clock supervision from myself and Tavros, as well as my closest friends, and receives continued care from Firil. If you wish to visit him, make sure it is one or two at a time if you go with your partners. But if the watch on guard turns you away, please keep in mind that their first priority is Papa's care, and they wouldn't turn you away if he needs the rest or is receiving treatments."

Netai nodded. "Kerac's care is more important than our need to see him. We will all respect your wishes and the guards you have posted. Thank you, lad."

"So, what do you have planned for us this morning?" one of the other guards said with a knowing smile. Everyone else relaxed, seeming to know Valis needed a change in subject if he was going to keep his composure.

"More training against my black magic." Valis rolled his shoulders and cracked his neck. "Since I drained what little there was from Aryn and Tavros, as well as the Qos adherents who escaped their cells, I've expanded my power pool, and the more experience you all get in defending and attacking a stronger opponent, the better off you will all be when this war escalates."

"And where is Tavros?" Phalin asked.

"Tav is still sleeping since he hasn't come yet. He's been dealing with my thrashing and nightmares at night, so I let him rest. I left a note by his head, so he may yet show up."

Valis received more knowing looks. Everyone knew of his anxiety, so it probably wasn't a large leap to figure out that his anxiety would trigger nightmares and fitful sleep with the trauma of finding one of his adopted fathers half-dead.

Still, it took long minutes for Valis to clear his mind enough to start the exercise. Without Tavros there to keep him grounded, Valis needed to be extra alert so he wouldn't become a danger during the mock battle.

By the time they were done, Valis itched to go see Kerac, but he impatiently waited until the last group left in case they had any questions. Then he all-but sprinted through the halls to his fathers' suite. He opened the door as quietly as he could, but the moment he ventured inside, he saw Aenali slipping out of Kerac's room.

"How is he?"

Aenali brightened and skipped over to hug him around the middle. "He's awake. Since you're here, I'm going to go get Firil. Kerac's hungry and probably needs medicine."

Valis hugged her tight and ruffled her soft auburn curls. "Thank you, dollface. Neither you nor Firil need to knock when you return. Just come on in."

"Okay!"

Even before the door shut behind the little girl, Valis was in Kerac's room. He carefully sat on the edge of the bed closest to Kerac's side and removed his gauntlets, setting them on the nightstand. He suddenly wished he would have had the forethought to have removed his armor so he wouldn't accidentally injure Kerac when hugging him.

Kerac took in a soft, shaky breath as he opened his eyes. "Oh, Valis... You look stunning in your armor."

Blushing, Valis ducked his head with a grin. "Thanks. I've finally stopped growing, so I can stop getting it augmented."

Kerac's snort turned into a hacking, rattling cough. When

he calmed down, he looked at Valis with so much love that Valis's breath hitched. "You have grown so much since I last saw you. You are so much taller and broader than you were when we left, your hair longer and an even paler blond, and your face has become so much more defined. We missed so much…"

"Everything I've done," Valis whispered, "was to make you and Father proud. Every single thing. Now, everything I do going forward is to become stronger in body and magic so I can rescue Father and retrieve the lost god jar."

Kerac's lower lip wobbled. "You believe Darolen yet lives?"

To tell him, or… Valis placed his hand on Kerac's chest. Kerac deserved to know. "I scried after him last night, Papa. He's alive. Sickly, but wheezing prayers for your safety. He's staying strong, and I *will* bring him home. You have my word. No matter what I have to do, I *will* bring your husband home."

"I believe you," Kerac murmured.

His voice warbled with unshed tears and Valis plucked a kerchief from the drawer of his nightstand to dry his eyes. "No tears. I can't imagine how much pain coughing or blowing your nose would cause."

Kerac sniffled and nodded. "Fair point." Then he looked up at Valis intently. "And what of you? Have you found your Ezhav? Tell me of your adventures since I have been away."

Sitting back, Valis smiled and told Kerac all about his journey to retrieve the Kalutakeni caravan. He detailed Qeraden's capture and the resulting Battle of Tigak. Then he lent excitement to his voice as he spoke of teaching the reliquary guard force and his translocation students.

By that time, Firil had come with Kerac's liquid food. Valis stood aside, regaling him about his excellence in his scholastic studies and war training while Firil fed Kerac through a tube. As the Master Healer put Kerac through his physical therapy, Valis spoke at length about the death of his first horse, Chath, and the intelligence and love of his new horse, Rasera, a gift from the Kalutakeni tribe. Kerac chuckled when Valis spoke about Rasera's antics during the bonding hours Valis went out to the stables for every day.

He saved the best for last. When Firil finished up with Kerac's care, he wheeled his cart out and left them alone again. Valis sat on the edge of the bed and grinned. "And yes. I have found my Ezhav. Tavros and I had our joining night just a few days ago on the twenty-eighth of Spirituality. Today is Mobility second."

"Four days…" Kerac sighed and closed his eyes. "If I had only gotten here sooner…"

"If you'd gotten here sooner, you would have been in fits because of all the drama that went down during the two weeks leading up to the event," Valis muttered. "Truly. It was best this way given your condition."

"What happened?"

Valis groaned and told Kerac the brief version of events where Aryn had used scrying to project lifelike hallucinations to Valis and Tavros, trying to break off their engagement because of Aryn's toxic jealousy. He left off with, "Aryn is in prison, but I drained the black magic from him and Tavros, and Aryn will be getting intensive mental therapy. If it goes well, which I think it will, he will be released from prison in short order."

Kerac let out another long, gusty sigh that wheezed with his chest infection. "Life has not been dull for you."

"Not in the least."

"Just as well," Kerac murmured. "You never could sit still."

Valis grinned and patted his chest. "True." He winced and turned serious. "And things are only heating up. Things are escalating at a rate where I think this war will be over very soon. But my first priority is Father. Can you talk about it now? The more information I have, the more I can help him."

With the way Kerac shifted and looked away, Valis almost told him not to worry about it. But he needed to know. And he needed to trust that Kerac would let him know if he couldn't talk about it. He wasn't a child, and he knew his own mind. Just because his body was currently frail didn't mean Valis could treat him as if his mind was addled.

After a few moments of Kerac breathing heavily—probably gathering his courage, Valis thought—Kerac shuddered and gripped Valis's hand in a tight, bony grip. "It happened so fast."

He choked on a breath. Valis waited for him to get his wheezing under control, and a thought hit him. Or, rather, Roba gave him a mental shove toward the thought that he could possibly eradicate the infections plaguing Kerac's body.

While Kerac fought for breath, Valis drew on his magic and, with the intent to gently burn away all the infection in Kerac's blood and tissue, sent it flooding into Kerac.

Almost immediately, Kerac started breathing better, and he relaxed, closing his eyes and letting out a soft sigh of relief. He looked up and furrowed his brow. "What are you doing?"

Valis murmured, "Attempting to get rid of your infections. The Master Healer doesn't know how. But I might." He stared into Kerac's eyes and offered him a small smile. "I can listen while I work. Go on with your story if you're up for it."

Nodding, Kerac took a shuddering breath and closed his eyes as if he couldn't bear to look at Valis while he recounted the story, or as if he was reliving it. "It happened so very fast. We had been chasing a nest of Qos adherents to the southeast. They led us out of Arlvor and into Aspar. It almost seemed as if, for every person we killed or put into stasis, four more would take their place. Their forces were never ending."

He struggled to lift his hand, and Valis paused in his hopeful treatment of the infections to gently rub Kerac's eyes for him. "It's okay, Papa. Take your time."

Kerac shivered. "It was a mess. We had a moment of success when we found a crop of way stones. One of our commanders herded us into the center of the circle, and we defeated many by using the gaps between stones to funnel in our adversaries. But that was a ruse. They actually sacrificed many of their men and women to lead us further into Aspar toward the center of the country."

His lips pressed together as tears welled up in his eyes, making the amber turn to liquid gold. Valis took a moment to wipe away the tears with a soft kerchief and stroked Kerac's cheek. "Go on. It's okay."

"There were explosions everywhere," he whispered. "Many of us were caught or killed. Darolen was knocked unconscious, and I fought, trying to protect him. But I *failed*." His voice broke on the last word.

Valis couldn't help himself. He leaned in and pressed a warm kiss to his brow. "You didn't fail. You can't be held accountable for being overrun in a trap."

"It feels like I failed…"

He shuddered and went on a bit stronger. "I was knocked unconscious soon after. Or maybe put into stasis. Either way, when I woke, Darolen and I, as well as a good number of men and women, were naked, chained to the floor and walls by our wrists, ankles, and throats, left to sit in our own filth, starved and beaten.

"And then they started taking us out. One by one. And those who left never returned. I don't know how Darolen did it, but one day when the door opened for them to take out another of us, he broke free of his bonds, killed the guard, and used his keys to set a number of us free. He found our armor and forced me into mine, donned his, and as weak as we were, we fought our way out. He found our horses, threw me on mine, tied his to my saddle, and smacked their rumps hard before turning to fight, screaming at me to return to Avristin and get help."

Valis squeezed his hand and brought it up to his lips to kiss his palm. "Help will be on its way as soon as possible, Papa. Do you remember where you were held?"

Kerac shook his head. "No. I was delirious with pain and sickness and fatigue, both magical and physical. Someone found me, gave me medicine, but I continued on. If it hadn't been for my horse instinctively following the pull of Cadoras, I don't know where I would have ended up."

Finished with his attempt at healing, Valis pulled his magic back into himself and took both Kerac's hands in his and squeezed. "I will find him, Papa. I have enough information to get started."

"You can't go," Kerac whispered. "I can't lose you, too."

Valis leaned in until they were almost nose to nose and held Kerac's gaze. "You won't lose either of us. Not if I have anything to say about it."

He pressed a lingering kiss to Kerac's cheek and sat up, pulled the covers up to Kerac's chin and tucked him in. "Rest now. I've got to get back to my duties, but I'll be back soon to check on you."

"I love you, sweet boy."

"I love you, too, Papa."

CHAPTER SIX

As Valis closed the door to Kerac's room, his stomach let
out a loud growl that made two passing female Aesriphos
giggle. One grinned at him. "Go eat. Breakfast is still being
served."

Valis smirked back and rubbed his angry stomach. "Yes,
ma'am."

Not one to lie, and too hungry to argue, Valis headed
down the hall and grabbed a hearty breakfast from the
serving line. To his surprise, his friends and husband still sat
around their usual table.

"Valis? Why are you so late?"

Valis took his usual seat and gripped the back of Tavros's
neck in greeting. "I went to see Papa after training my
translocation and reliquary guard students."

"You're supposed to be taking time off, love," Tavros

griped. "I woke up alone, and it wasn't pleasant. I missed you, and all I got was a *note*."

"At least you knew where I was." When Tavros grumbled and attacked the remainder of his breakfast, Valis leaned in close and whispered, "I'll make it up to you tonight." He sealed his promise with a sweet, chaste kiss before starting in on his mountain of food. Thankfully, his friends gave him a few minutes to sate his immediate hunger before they started in with their questions.

"Why didn't you wake us up for training?" Zhasina asked. "We should have been there with you. We need to know these things as much as the reliquary guards."

Shrugging, Valis took his time to chew and swallow his current mouthful before answering. "You didn't answer your door, so I figured you were exhausted. It was a spur-of-the-moment thing because I was restless and didn't want to wake Tav, so I knew neither of you would have gone to bed early simply because we didn't." He shrugged and speared another bite of sausage. "I'm sorry. I'll try harder next time if it happens again."

Seza leaned forward with her mug clasped in both hands before her. "What did you teach? Anything new?"

Valis shook his head. "Since my power has grown with the recent events in the dungeon and with Aryn, I had them attacking and defending against more powerful black magic. It was more training than teaching."

"Then I'd like you to repeat that training with us when

you're not busy," Seza said in a tone that brooked no argument. "We all need that training."

"Of course."

"When do you think you'll be free?"

Valis thought about it for a moment as he sipped his spiced milk and grimaced at her. "I need to have a scrying session, get my physical training out of the way, spend some time with Rasera, and a few other things. I might possibly have some time after lunch. Actually, after lunch might be our best bet, anyway. I need to recharge after that training session. I had to be extra careful because I didn't have Tavros there to keep me from succumbing to the darkness. It was kind of harrowing, and I'm still a little shaky."

Seza gave a firm nod and sipped whatever graced her mug—probably tea. "We'll have Aenali take an extra shift while we train during that time." She glanced over at the little girl. "That all right, 'Nali?"

"That's fine," Aenali said. "Though, I'd love to watch you guys train sometime. But," she shrugged, "Kerac is more important, and I can get some of my studies done while I'm watching over him. And I have Valis's papers to grade from his lessons, so I can spend extra time with Kerac if you guys want, since it will take me a while."

Valis nodded. "Thank you, dollface." He sighed and rubbed the back of his neck. "Speaking of Papa, he's more alert now. Talking. I need to give Thyran a report about what he told me, but that can wait for the time being. He told me about his capture and escape."

"How did he escape without Darolen?" Maphias asked.

"Darolen smacked his horse's rump and fought the enemy back so Kerac could get away," Valis mumbled. "He never intended on escaping. His only priority was Kerac. But, if he hadn't sacrificed himself, Kerac would be there with him, and they might both be dead right now. They had been taking people out of the cell on occasion, according to Papa, and those people never returned. So, out of those Aesriphos who were captured, I think Papa and Darolen are the only ones left alive."

Silence descended on the table as everyone let that sink in. Finally, Valis took a deep breath and used their silence to inhale another large portion of his plate of food. He forgot just how hungry he was with the weight of the conversation. Now, he was ravenous, even after eating a good amount during the conversation.

The others let him finish his breakfast, but the tone of their quiet conversation remained somber. When he set his utensils down, Valis stretched, let out a soft belch, and leaned in to kiss Tavros's cheek. "I'm going to visit Aryn. Did you want to come?"

"Why don't we all go?" Zhasina asked. "It might help his mental state if we all show our support."

"As long as you're all nice, I don't have a problem with it," Valis said with a smile.

Seza nodded. "I'm in."

"Me, too," Jedai said.

Maphias shrugged. "I'll go."

"And me!" Aenali said. "Though… that leaves no one to look after Kerac."

"Who's there now?" Tavros asked.

"Papa is sleeping at the moment. Firil has already been in for his breakfast and physical therapy, so he should be fine. I'm sure it won't be a problem to get a guard to watch over him while we're visiting Aryn."

"Then let's go since you're finished with your breakfast," Seza said. "Then we can all get on with our duties before we resume our watch schedule for Kerac."

Nodding, Valis chugged the rest of his spiced milk and set the mug on his breakfast tray. Everyone got up as a unit and tendered their dirty dishes to the kitchen, sent a guard to watch over Kerac with instructions for his care, and filed down the halls to the prison in the lowest halls of the monastery. Below ground, Valis almost felt the entire weight of the massive building pressing down on him, but it was comforting in a way. All that weight consisted of people who were family, who would do anything to help each other, so the weight left Valis feeling warm and content in a way that he hoped he would never take for granted.

When they got into the holding cell with Aryn, the boy's eyes widened to see the whole group there. He tucked his lower lip between his teeth, chewing on the flesh as his eyes filled with unshed tears.

"What…?"

Valis smiled at him. "Everyone wanted to come. I hope you don't mind."

The tears spilled down Aryn's cheeks as he shook his head and whispered, "I don't mind."

For long minutes, everyone took turns going to the tiny cell to stick their hands through the bars, doing their best to hug him and say encouraging words, extracting promises for him to give his best in therapy. And when it was Valis's turn, he drew Aryn close and pressed a kiss to his forehead. "You got this, Aryn. You're strong, and your incarceration is only temporary. I know you can do it."

"I can do anything for you," Aryn whispered thickly. "Anything."

Valis shook his head. "No. Do it for *you*, Aryn. You're always doing things for others. It's time to do things for yourself. Believe that you deserve to get out of here. Believe that you deserve to heal. *You* are *worthy* of loving yourself. We all love you, but it doesn't matter what we think or feel if you don't love yourself. It never will. It will never be enough."

Aryn ducked his head, his fingers gripping the bars so hard his knuckles blanched white and his arms trembled. He looked up with wet, wounded eyes, a darker gray than his brother, Tavros'. "I don't know how. I just... I don't know how..."

"Give yourself permission to be *broken*," Valis whispered. He covered Aryn's hands with his own and rubbed his thumbs along his knuckles. "Give yourself permission to *not* be okay. Give yourself *permission* to be *scared*. Then, tell your therapist *everything*, Aryn. Hold nothing back. Don't lie to *yourself,* or to your therapist, and take their advice to heart." He squeezed Aryn's hands and gave him a reassuring smile. "And give yourself permission to be okay with your brokenness. Because if you shun it, it will only grow larger. It will only shrink as you heal."

"I'll try, okay?"

"That's all anyone can ask of you. And just by trying, you're making us all proud."

Aryn chewed his lip again, his eyes closed and his breathing ragged. "How do you know all this?"

Valis smiled. "You. I learned it from *you,* and from the others. You didn't tell me these words, but you all showed me that it was okay to be broken, and you showed me how to love myself by showing me love and helping me through my anxiety. But you helped most of all, because when you could, you protected me, and when you couldn't, you showed me how to protect myself, and gave me the pushes I needed to get better."

Aryn stared at him for a long moment. "I'll do my best."

"You'd better. We all miss you and hugging you through iron bars isn't comfortable."

The boy chuckled and rested his forehead against the bars. "Thank you."

"We love you, Aryn. Never forget that. We're still your friends."

All too soon, the guard opened the door to tell them their time was up. No one wanted to leave, but they all followed the ladies out of the prison and back into the Duty Captain's office. And the moment they left and ascended the stairs to the main areas of the monastery, Valis was itching to get to work. He needed to scry after Darolen. If he could get it right, he could at least put his father's mind at ease, and perhaps get some important information about the compound. If nothing else, it would at least give Darolen hope, or so Valis wished with his entire being.

His heart thundered as he and Tavros broke off from his friends and headed toward their suite.

"It's going to be okay, Valis."

Valis glanced at Tavros and gave him a small smile. "Thanks. I just hope I'm able to reach him."

Tavros frowned, and it was only then that he remembered he hadn't told Tavros about his success in two-way communications via scry. He took in a shaky breath and laced his fingers with his husband's and told him everything about that discovery, what he saw when he scried after Darolen, and what he had planned once they reached their suite.

"May I sit in while you scry?"

"I'd like that." Valis squeezed Tavros's hand and walked a little closer as they traveled through the halls, careful not to hurt his unarmored husband with his pauldrons. "It might help calm my nerves if it doesn't go as planned."

Their hands tightened on each other. Tavros knew how hard it was for Valis to concentrate when he was stressed or impatient. Hopefully, his steady love would make this endeavor easier than his past tries. Especially when he had first learned how to scry. It had taken him so long to learn that Valis thought he would never get it. Now, at least, he had some successes under his belt and felt a bit more confident.

Once they entered their suite, Valis went to fill the scrying bowl and brought it back to their bedroom. He didn't know why, but the bedroom always felt more appropriate for scrying. Or, perhaps not appropriate so much as more calming to his overactive mind. It was a place where he knew he could relax, where he knew that the only stresses would be great sex and calm words.

He set the bowl down and took a moment to just breathe as Tavros laid warm, wet kisses to the back of his neck. It worked to settle his nerves, and he turned around in the circle of Tavros's arms to thank him with a shared kiss.

"You can do this, Valis," Tavros whispered against his lips. His cloud-gray eyes darkened to storm colors as he stared into Valis's soul. "No bad thoughts. I know you can do this."

Valis nodded and lightly rubbed their noses together. "I'm more afraid of what I'll see. But, it needs done. Father deserves to know that Papa is safe. He needs his hope renewed."

"Get your armor off first." Tavros drew back and started work on Valis's pauldrons. "I want to hold you when you're done, and it'll just get in the way."

Chuckling, Valis helped shed his armor, and once they had it arranged neatly on his armor stand, Valis gave Tavros another quick kiss and left him sitting on the foot of the bed while he went and stood in front of the scrying bowl.

"Do some deep breathing exercises," Tavros suggested. "I can already see your shoulders tensing up."

Valis nodded and took a couple slow, deep breaths until he felt his shoulders relax and lower down from around his ears. Once his mind was clear, he stared down into the bowl and focused his mind. After only a few moments, the blackness overtook the bowl, and with another push, he could hear Darolen's wheezing breaths between whispered prayers to Phaerith.

The sound broke something deep inside Valis. Something more than his shattered heart. His breath hitched. His eyes watered, but he wiped the wetness away and redirected his focus. He had a mission, and he had to get it done before he broke down.

With a mental shove, Valis fought to break that barrier. He knew Darolen wouldn't be able to see him in the blackness of that cell, but if he could get it to work, his father could at least hear him.

Another shove, and Darolen grunted. Did it work? Valis swallowed his fear and whispered, "Father?"

"Valis?" Darolen croaked. "No... no, I'm going mad... No..."

"Father, it's me. I promise it's me. I'm contacting you through two-way scry from the filth around you. It's the only way I could think of."

"Valis..." Darolen made a pained sound, something between a whimper and a groan. "Valis, my boy... Gods, your voice... It has been so long, *too* long." He inhaled a raspy breath and coughed. "Keep your voice down, son."

"I will," Valis whispered quieter. "Can you still hear me?"

"I hear you more in my mind than I do from anything else. But..."

"I understand, Father. I don't want anyone to hurt you because of this. But I have news."

"Please..."

Valis shivered at the urgent plea. He didn't keep his father waiting. "Papa made it home. He's very weak. Sick, malnourished, and devastated to have left you behind, but he's home, he's alive, and he's getting around-the-clock care. *He made it home.*"

Darolen sobbed a breath. "Thank the gods!"

"I heard you praying for us yesterday," Valis said. "It broke my heart. It took a while, but Thyran took pity on me and taught me how to communicate via scry so I could answer your prayers. We're all fine, and Papa is getting better every hour. Your horses were in bad shape, too, but they're receiving the best care from the stable master."

Sniffles rose from the scrying bowl, and Valis wished he could reach through that barrier and pull his father into a tight hug, to pull him out of that place. If only he could see the room clearly so he could phase in and get him out of there, but... he had little hope of that happening. He would have to do it the old-fashioned way and break into the compound.

"Can you tell me where they have you captive?"

Darolen cleared his throat softly. "No. We were in stasis when they brought us in. I didn't see much when I freed Kerac. I was so focused on getting him out that I don't even remember the layout of the compound." His voice broke, and Valis's heart broke a little more with it. "I just know it's at the base of a mountain."

"I can work with that, Father."

"What?"

Valis set his mouth into a grim line. "It may not be as soon as I like, but I *will* get you out of there. You have my word."

"No. No, Valis. You must stay away! Do not come here!"

"That's not up for debate. I'm coming, and you'll just have to deal with it."

"No! Please, Valis—"

Valis gentled his whisper and sighed. "Father, please don't argue with me on this. Please. Papa is distraught. He is worried about you, *for* you. I am, as well. Trust that I'm strong enough, that I've done nothing but prepare for this. And trust that I'm not stupid enough to go alone."

Darolen let out an explosive sigh. Valis heard a thud and guessed it to be his father thumping his head against the cell wall at his back. "Damn it, son…"

Grinning, Valis leaned closer to the bowl. "I'm a stubborn man, Father. You can't out-stubborn me."

Darolen's soft laugh meant *everything* to Valis. "So I'm learning. Just… just be careful, Valis. Freedom will mean little if you aren't there to share it with us."

"I promise."

"Listen," Darolen whispered urgently. "Do not contact me again. It isn't safe. If they hear me talking, they could discover your scry and possibly trace it back to you. Do you understand? It could put both of us in danger."

Even though Valis's entire soul rebelled against that order, Valis nodded. "I understand, and I promise. I won't let you down, Father."

"You never have, son. Never."

CHAPTER SEVEN

"WHAT ARE YOU DOING?"

Tavros's exasperated tone made Valis glance over at him with both brows raised. "Writing a list."

"You've been stuck in your own head since you finished the scry with your father. Are you even going to talk about it?" Tavros pulled a chair up beside Valis at the desk in their bedroom and sat down facing Valis. "I know how much it hurt when he told you not to contact him again."

Valis shrugged and reached over to squeeze Tavros's hand to let him know he appreciated his support and care. "It did hurt, yes. But I also know why he demanded it. And I agree with him, so I'm not as bothered by it as I would be other-wise. Besides, I have plenty of things to do between now and when we go after him."

"You're intent on a rescue mission?" Tavros asked. "You know that's a suicide run…"

"Not if we're smart about it." He sighed and toyed with his pencil. "And not if we're more prepared than our enemy. They won't be expecting us to launch a direct attack on their stronghold. They will be expecting us to fall into their traps, to waste time with their nests. I plan on going straight for the heart, free my father, and everything else will fall as it falls."

After a moment of loaded silence, Tavros sighed and leaned forward to rest his chin on Valis's shoulder. Valis glanced over and could see the change of subject coming before Tavros even opened his mouth. "What kind of list are you making?"

"A supply list," Valis said. Truth be told, he was glad for the minor subject change, because speaking about that aspect of the rescue mission had started setting off precognitive explosions in his guts. He turned his head and kissed Tavros's chin, the tip of his nose, and then his plush lips, silently thanking him for knowing just what Valis needed. "As I told Father, I will be smart about it. And part of that is early, thorough planning. We need to make sure we'll have everything we need, and as much food as we're able to carry, while still being able to travel at a good pace."

His husband frowned as he studied Valis's face. "When did you plan on leaving?"

Shrugging, Valis jotted down another item onto his list and blew a puff of breath up to get a lock of hair out of his face. It didn't work. "I'm not sure yet. It depends on when the priests allow us to go. I'm hoping they'll let this be our first mission as Aesriphos."

Something in Tavros relaxed, and he sagged a little, closing his eyes when Valis reached over and carded his fingers through his shaggy black hair. He did it again just to revel in the softness as it pulled through his fingers. "I'm not going into this half-assed, Tav. I promise you that." He leaned close so they shared breath. "And I promise you another thing: I won't leave without you."

Tavros growled and nipped Valis's lower lip. "You'd damned well better not."

Grinning, Valis gave him a quick kiss and turned to note another item on his list. "Never, Tav. Never."

Tavros went quiet for a while as Valis started organizing his list into columns on another sheet of paper based on item type like food, clothing, money, and other necessities, and studied the result. There were things he was missing, but this list would get him pretty far if he started buying things today. He could squirrel them away with the Kalutakeni tribe where they had their caravan parked on the opposite side of Cadoras lake from the island. He also needed to commission a few wagons because the Kalutakeni would have to leave theirs behind due to the snow and necessary speed of travel.

That brought on another thought. He had to alert the Kalutakeni and mercenaries about his plans, and give them money to purchase their own supplies, making sure not to bother with excess food until he had a definite departure date.

The entire plan started formulating in Valis's mind until his head spun with all the things he needed to have in place. And hopefully he would need it all in place in short order because he wouldn't stop until the priests allowed him to go.

"Love…"

Valis sighed and turned in his chair to hold Tavros's hands. He'd been ignoring Tavros for a good hour before this conversation started and going off in his own mind again wasn't fair to him. "I'm sorry, Tav."

Tavros squeezed his hands and brought them up to kiss his palms. "You realize we have to go through the proper channels, right? It may take months before we're allowed to go anywhere. They may not sanction a rescue mission but send us elsewhere where we may be needed."

Valis's stomach instantly soured. "No. I have to rescue Father. I promised, and *no one* will make me break it."

He'd stressed those two words so vehemently that Tavros's eyes widened. "We'll do our best, okay?"

Sighing, Valis softened and closed his eyes. "I'm sorry. It's just—"

"I get it, Valis." Tavros cupped Valis's face in both hands and leaned their foreheads together as he stroked his thumbs over Valis's cheekbones. "I get it. And I will do everything in my power to help you keep those promises. But we need to be realistic about this, and we need to do it according to *protocol.* Can you do that for me? Can you take a step back, take a deep breath, and focus your energy on getting this sanctioned the right way, instead of browbeating the clergy into letting us go?"

The last sentence made Valis chuckle. "Well, I wasn't planning on *browbeating* anyone, but now that you mention it..."

"Don't you dare," Tavros growled. He punctuated it by lightly biting the apple of Valis's cheek. "Don't you even think about it."

With a devilish grin, Valis leaned in and stole another kiss. "Got anything to re-route my thoughts, husband? I may need persuading."

Tavros shivered and the possessive growl that emanated from his throat made Valis's insides liquefy. "Get naked and get on that bed. *Now*."

If nothing else, getting his ass plowed would help distract Valis enough that he could let go for a while, and just *be*. He slowly stood from the chair, making sure the tent in his pants brushed against Tavros's chin, and turned to stalk toward the bed. He took his time removing his belt and tunic, slowly dragging the hem up his torso, doing his best to tease and torture.

When he slowly untied the drawstring, Tavros growled again. When Valis glanced behind him, his husband was already naked and stroking his impressive, gorgeous cock while staring at Valis's ass.

"If you don't get those off *right now*, I swear to the Nine I will shred them."

Valis grinned and hooked his thumbs into the band at his back and inch by teasing inch, worked the pants over his hips as they swayed from side to side in a sensuous rhythm. "I think you're bluffing," Valis rasped. "I think you like the show."

Tavros's eyes darkened until they were almost black. He stalked forward like Valis was prey and dropped to his knees. He didn't shred the uniform pants, but he jerked them down and dropped them to flutter down to Valis's ankles. And before Valis could form another thought, his husband roughly grabbed both ass cheeks in his hands and stuffed his face between them.

His hot, wet tongue lapped at his anus twice before he nuzzled in closer and scraped his teeth across the puckered flesh. And with that rough graze, Valis's knees almost gave out on him.

He dropped forward, planted his hands on the end of the bed and stuck his ass out, shoving it against Tavros's face with a deep, guttural moan. His knees shook, threatening to send him to the floor, but he fought. Tavros still had a firm grip on his ass, and his tongue had moved from languid lapping from his perineum to his lower back with firmer licks centered on his hole, to short, sharp jabs that had Valis's anus clenching and releasing, trying to suck him in.

"Tav... Tav, please... *Please!*"

Tavros's throaty chuckle vibrated his tongue as it wriggled against his pucker. Fuck. If he kept that up, Valis might come and he didn't want that to happen. Not just yet, anyway.

Tavros finally worked his tongue past the ring of muscle. He swirled and twisted it until Valis rocked, humping his face with a steady keening whine streaming from his throat. He didn't even recognize himself anymore. All he was was sensation and sound.

Tavros released one cheek as he pulled back and smacked his ass. "On the bed." The order came with another swat at Valis's ass, making the flesh burn in the best of ways.

With his knees still shaking, Valis crawled up toward the head of the bed, making his ass sway with each shift of his legs. The bed dipped behind him, and Valis shivered as he felt the heat of Tavros's body cover his back. His hot breath puffed over his spine, trailing up from his lower back to his shoulder blades, leaving his sweaty skin chilled in his wake.

When his mouth reached Valis's ear, his husky whisper made Valis's cock leak. "Face down. Grab the edge of the mattress. Arch that beautiful back for me."

Valis didn't comply fast enough. With a gentle but commanding hand on the back of Valis's neck, Tavros pushed him until his cheek was flat against the mattress. Valis's hands grabbed the edge on reflex and gripped the sheets in his fists.

"That's it. So beautiful, Valis." Tavros's rough, gravelly praise had Valis's balls retracting tight against his body, drawing another moan from him.

Tavros's hands squeezed both of Valis's shoulders before

slowly trailing down Valis's back, then again to follow the profusion of gooseflesh he left in his wake. "Fuck, Valis..."

The metallic sound of the jar lid opening echoed through the room, breaking the tense silence filled with only their panted breaths. And this was *everything*. The buildup was almost more erotic than the act itself, and Tavros was drawing it out just how Valis loved it when they had time for more than a quick fuck.

But slow and sensuous could only last so long. Tavros's lubed finger circled Valis's anus, signaling the near end of the torture. After a few passes of that finger, massaging Valis's prostate with each withdrawal, he added a second and started pumping faster. When he added the third, Valis arched his neck and let out a harsh groan, spreading his knees wider on the bed as he humped back onto those fingers. "More. Tav..."

Tavros scissored his fingers open as wide as they would go within the tight ring of Valis's ass and drew them out with a wet sound. Almost immediately after, his slick cock pressed to the ring and pushed in.

After that, it was all sensation. Tavros thrust in deep, his balls slapping against Valis's perineum. Unable to help himself, Valis pushed up onto his hands and knees and as Tavros thrust forward, Valis shoved his ass back to meet him. Every grunt out of Tavros's throat spurred Valis on until he fucked himself on Tavros's dick like a madman.

Tavros leaned down and licked the sweat from between Valis's shoulder blades, trailing his tongue up to bite the back of Valis's neck before using his ponytail to pull him up. He wrapped his arms around Valis's chest and took over, fucking into Valis at a furious pace that pegged his prostate in ways that made Valis see stars.

"Fuck… Fuck! Kiss me, Valis. Gods, I need you."

Valis turned his head and Tavros gripped his chin, twisting him just that much farther until their lips met in hungry, tongue-dueling kisses that stole Valis's breath.

He jerked his head away with a feral growl but kept his hold on Valis's jaw. His hips slammed into Valis's ass and he stilled, gripping Valis's hip with his free hand to keep him still. "Are you going to browbeat those poor priests?"

Valis whimpered at his demand. "No! Please, Gods, don't stop fucking me!"

"Promise me, Valis."

"I promise!"

"What are you going to do?"

Valis was half crazed out of his mind with lust. It took him a moment to let the question sink in. It didn't work. "Huh?"

"Instead of browbeating the priests, what are you going to do?"

Whining, Valis ground his ass against Tavros's pelvis. "Follow protocol as best I can."

Tavros hummed as he slowly withdrew and pushed back in at a glacial pace that drove Valis mad. "I think you might be humoring me, so I'll let you come."

Valis wriggled his ass, making Tavros hiss. "I promise I'm

not. But I also promise I'll flip you over and take what I want from you if you don't fuck me right now, Tav."

His husband grinned and slammed forward, sending Valis to his hands and knees again with a cry of ecstasy. He clutched at the bedsheets, fighting to hold on to his sanity as Tavros drove them both closer to oblivion.

Valis's orgasm took him by surprise in a blinding flash that whited out his vision. His arms gave out, and Tavros followed him down onto the bed, fucking him through it, chasing his own climax. Valis whined, his hole overstimulated, but then Tavros roared as he came and collapsed over Valis's back, shaking and shuddering and mumbling nonsense as he petted Valis's sides with gentle, trembling hands.

They stayed like that until their breathing evened out, and Tavros carefully pulled out to flop onto his back beside Valis. "Okay. I believe you."

Laughing, Valis turned and scooted over, burying his face in Tavros's throat. "I'm so glad."

"So, did I dickstract you well enough?"

Valis choked on his snort and muffled his laugh against Tavros's sweat-damp skin. "Dickstract, huh? Yeah. I guess you did fairly well. We might have to try harder tonight though."

"Mmm... but you're back to training in the predawn hours, and I don't want you to accidentally kill one of your students... or yourself."

"You'll just have to protect them and me," Valis

murmured. "I'm sure you'll be up for the job after plowing my ass through the mattress."

"Doubtful. Very doubtful." Tavros pressed a kiss to the top of Valis's head and sighed, his breath warming Valis's scalp. "Maybe directly after dinner so we're not both half-dead during training."

"We might be able to make that work." Groaning, Valis shifted on the bed and grimaced. "Okay. Bath time and then we need to change the bedding. I'm sticky, the sheets are gross, and we need to get into Cadoras for supplies, and talk to the Kalutakeni and mercenaries."

Tavros sat up and perked a brow at him. "Why the talk?"

Valis sat up, too, and shrugged. "If there's a chance we're given permission to leave for this mission, I want to let them know. Because they both factor heavily into my plans. It wouldn't be right to spring it on them with little time for them to prepare."

"And if you're not given permission?"

Valis stared at him like he'd gone mad. "I said I wouldn't browbeat, Tav. I never said anything about backing down."

His husband let out this deep, long-suffering sigh and hung his head. "I was afraid you'd say that. You're going to make them all miserable until you get your way."

"Nope." Valis slid off the bed and headed toward the lavatory, turning to look over his shoulder when he made it to the door. "I plan on using cunning, logic, and perseverance. Now, get in here and bathe with me. We still have things to do today."

"Like?"

Bending down, Valis turned on the tap for the tub and sighed. "I need to put you, Seza and Zhasina through the training you missed this morning, tend to Rasera, go to Cadoras for supplies, talk to the Kalutakeni and mercenaries, visit Papa, have a chat with Brother Bachris, get in some physical training—"

"Shit, Valis… you can't fit all of that into a single day? At least not in what we have left."

Valis tested the water and slipped into the tub, reaching for Tavros who stood there with both hands firmly on his hips. Though, after a moment, he broke and let Valis help him into the steadily rising water.

"I'll fit in what I can," he promised. "We'll just have to prioritize. Now, enough about that. I want to spend some quiet time with you while I can now that we're thoroughly sated. We don't get many moments like these."

"No," Tavros whispered. He pulled Valis to him and held him close. "No, we don't."

"Think you can find a way to make the most of it?" Valis teased.

Tavros pressed a warm kiss into his neck and reached for the wash cloth and soap he left on the edge of the tub. "Well, I had planned on showing my husband just how cherished he is with a thorough washing, and then maybe brush his hair out until it's dry and my darling husband is comatose."

Valis shivered. Having Tavros brush his hair was one of the fastest ways of getting Valis calm, and Tavros had started using that tactic to get him to sleep some nights. It was both sensual and relaxing in a way that turned Valis into a boneless heap that Tavros could simply scoop up and pour into bed.

"You know," Valis murmured, "that might not be conducive to getting anything done for the rest of the day."

"Or, you could take a nap after, and actually be refreshed for the rest of the day," Tavros said against his ear as he drew the soapy cloth down the length of Valis's back. "You've been so stressed, love. You need to take some time for yourself."

Smiling, Valis leaned back just enough to capture Tavros's lips and rest their foreheads together. The rest of the day would go as it would. He would make it into Cadoras for shopping, take gold to the Kalutakeni and mercenaries for their own supplies, visit more with his papa, and have a chat with Brother Bachris. If there was any time left, he could deal with everything else when it happened.

Right now, his husband wanted to take care of him.

And Valis, for all his talk of priorities, would always put his husband's love and care at the top of every list.

CHAPTER EIGHT

WITH A LITTLE EFFORT and a lot of running around like a chicken with its head cut off, Valis managed to make it to the monastery's vault and retrieve a massive amount of gold with only a few raised eyebrows. Then he dragged Tavros to the mercenaries inside Cadoras walls, and the Kalutakeni caravan on the other side of the lake bordering the city and drop off hefty bags of gold with the help of their (very happy to get out of the stables for a ride) horses. And since their horses were so happy for a ride, Valis kept them out and used them to carry loads of non-perishable supplies to the caravan for safe keeping now that he'd received permission from their leaders, Vodis and Venabi.

Once they finished, Valis spent time with his black Kalu-takeni stallion, Rasera. And once he put his horse back into the stable master's care, he and Tavros headed back into the monastery with roaring stomachs. A glance at one of the wall clocks they passed showed it was dinnertime. Valis's stomach gurgled again, and he rubbed it.

"Did you want to have dinner with Kerac?" Tavros asked.

Valis tilted his head. "Probably not. It might upset him that he only gets a liquid diet for now, and we're eating solid foods in front of him. It wouldn't be fair, and it would make us all feel bad. Instead, let's eat with our friends, and then spend time with Papa before we go to Brother Bachris."

"You're worried about that meeting, aren't you?"

Valis made a face and groaned. "A little. I want it to go well, and I want to get underway as soon as possible. But I'm not going to dwell on it until we get there."

"Wise choice."

After dinner with their friends, they all split up again and Valis let Tavros lead the way to his fathers' suite. Valis's over-full belly felt so distended that he rubbed it and let out a soft belch trying to make more room. It made him drowsy and ready for a nap. Tavros glanced back at him with a soft chuckle. "One of these days, you're going to eat a normal serving and not nod off after."

"Maybe. Can't help it that physical training turns my stomach into a bottomless pit."

His husband snorted and opened the door to Kerac's suite. They thanked and dismissed the guard on duty who sat in Kerac's sitting room, and Valis led the way into the bedroom with hope in his heart that soared when Kerac opened his eyes and smiled at them.

"You look like you need a nap, Valis. You must have just eaten."

Tavros snorted again and laughed. "Some things never change, Kerac. He put away more than he weighs and went back for dessert."

Smirking, Valis patted his bloated stomach. "Hey. I'm still growing!"

"You'd better not be," Tavros growled. "You're already an inch taller than me, and you need to stop bothering the armorsmith with augmentations."

His smirk turned into a shit-eating grin. "Might not be growing taller, but I'm bulking up from training. Growth is growth."

Tavros's eyes roamed over Valis appreciatively. "Fair enough."

"Just be careful that you don't grow horizontally now that you've stopped growing vertically," Kerac teased.

Dropping the banter, Tavros pulled a chair up to the side of the bed while Valis sat on the edge and took Kerac's hand. His eyes roamed over Kerac's face before he murmured, "How are you feeling, Papa?"

Kerac's smile was bright but strained. "Much better than yesterday. Firil is rather astonished. He said that while my infections are not gone, my lungs are much stronger, and I seem to be stronger overall. When I told him of your attempt to rid me of the infections, he smiled and assured me that while you were valiant for trying and failed, your work was not in vain, and indeed helped me overall with my recovery.

He asked me to thank you for your assistance and said that if you could perform a similar task daily, it could give my body the strength to help my immune system fight off the infections naturally. He also asked for a report on what exactly you did so he can add this technique to his repertoire of healing spells."

Valis grinned and ducked his head. "I'll be sure to visit him with a report sometime today or tomorrow when I have time. Or better yet, I'll spend some time training him so he can, in turn, train his assistants."

"Where did you learn how to perform such magic?" Kerac asked. "It is a wonder."

"Yes. It really is." Valis sighed and decided now was probably a good time to tell him the truth about another "adventure" he'd had since Kerac and Darolen left.

"Your face just drained of all color," Kerac whispered. "What is it?"

Valis took a deep breath and met Kerac's gaze. "Roba's dead, but he's still with me."

Kerac's face grew red with rage. "What?"

Rubbing Kerac's chest, Valis leaned in and kissed his forehead. "Calm down and listen, okay? It's not as bad as it sounds."

His papa didn't look happy, but he nodded and Valis went on. "On my twenty-first birth anniversary—and that's another story for later—Roba killed himself, shoving all his power, magic, and life force into me, expanding my power pool exponentially. In essence, he made me as powerful as a High Priest of Qos."

Kerac shuddered and gripped Valis's hand as tight as he could. "Oh, Valis..."

Smiling, Valis shrugged. "In the fight before that, he had cast a spell on Tavros that was killing him. But I found out that Roba's consciousness had been shoved into my mind along with his power and magic. He helped me save Tav. Since then, he's... he's become so much more, Papa. Somehow, his soul has become purified. We aren't sure if it's because he's free of a corrupted body and his black magic, or if being linked to me has purified him, but... he's become the father I always wished he had been."

Kerac glanced away, and when Valis saw the sheen of tears, he urged Kerac to look at him with gentle fingers on his chin. "He'll never replace you and Darolen. Never. But... now I have three fathers, Papa—you, Father, and now Dad. And, he's said he's glad that I've had you and Father in my life. He doesn't want to replace you. He's dead. He can't even try. But... he's helped me so much, *taught* me so much, and has done all he can to make up for the years of abuse he'd put me through. He's the one who taught me that nothing is impossible and helped me become a more competent mage than the reliquary guards to the point that I now train them."

Kerac's eyes widened. "Truly? You train the reliquary guards?"

Valis nodded, his chest puffing up with pride. "Every

morning before dawn. And before that class, I train other students in the art of translocation."

"His scholastic proficiency is coming along nicely, as well," Tavros added.

"And Dad has been teaching me other languages when I need something to re-route my mind from anxiety," Valis admitted. "He taught me Urkorian on the way to and from rescuing the caravan, and he's begun with Noldworian and Gessian lessons lately because of the mercenaries I've allied with. He considers it penance along with teaching me all he can about the Qos army and their tactics."

"He's expressed remorse, then?" Kerac asked, and Valis was glad to hear the curiosity in his voice instead of scorn.

"Yeah. Quite a bit. Now he does everything in his power to help me achieve anything that makes me struggle."

Kerac nodded with a deep sigh that made Valis thrill with the lack of rattle in his chest. "I'll endeavor to forgive him. It may take some time, however."

"That's all anyone can ever ask," Valis said with a squeeze of Kerac's hand.

"Now," Kerac looked at Valis seriously, "tell me about you being older."

Valis ducked his head. "Dad had me on paper as younger, but when he poured his power into me, he said that I was twenty-one instead of nineteen. He kept me younger than normal through magic and locked my magic away to more easily control me. That's how I grew and advanced so quickly. My magic was working overtime to correct what

Dad did so that I'm at the size and capacity I was meant to be."

Kerac frowned and sighed. "At least that accounts for your emotional turmoil during that time, and your occasional lethargy." He brushed the thought away. "Let's speak more about your adventures. And I would like to hear more about Roba."

Tavros took the chance to change the subject and said, "One time, we were in Lyvea or Urkori returning from rescuing the Kalutakeni caravan and were ambushed. Valis suffered a poisoned crossbow bolt through his thigh and fell unconscious. Roba somehow got control of Valis's body and... while he was prickly and sarcastic as anything, he was, very obviously, doing his level best to be kind, and he took care of the arrow and poison, then showed Seza how to heal his leg. He didn't think he could do it himself because he didn't know if he could control Valis's gold magic without catastrophe."

Kerac shivered. He laced his fingers with Valis's and closed his eyes as if he wanted to escape the vision of Valis in pain. "Thank you, Roba."

He's very welcome, Roba said gently. *Though, I admit, it was for selfish reasons at the time.*

Valis chuckled and relayed the message. Kerac's eyes went hard and glinted like gold disks. "Selfish reasons?"

Giving him a gentler smile, Valis said, "He didn't want to die a second time. He doesn't know what would happen to his consciousness or soul if or when I die."

"I… can kind of understand that." Kerac shivered again and this time when he closed his eyes, he seemed more sad than anything. "I can only imagine…"

They spoke for a while longer, mostly about Tavros's progress and his trials leading up to his joining night with Valis. Then, when Seza and Zhasina came for the start of their watch shift, Valis kissed Kerac's forehead and promised to see him again tomorrow.

Now, they both stood outside Brother Bachris's office. Valis took a deep breath, trying to calm his racing heart.

"You okay?" Tavros asked. "You're pale."

"Just nervous." Valis rolled his shoulders to release some of the tension and knocked. "Let's get this done."

Brother Bachris opened the door after only a few moments and looked from Valis to Tavros and back with his usual paternal smile. "Greetings Brothers Valis and Tavros. Are you both well? You seem… determined."

Valis offered what he hoped was a reassuring smile. "We are. We just need to talk for a moment. Do you have time?"

"Of course." The older Patron Priest smiled kindly at them, his blue eyes shining as he opened the door to his office wider. He adjusted his tunic on his lanky frame as if trying to look more presentable, combed fingers through his head full of thick chestnut curls with the white frost at his temples and motioned them to the seating arrangement near the fire. "To what do I owe the pleasure?"

"I want to talk about possibly acquiring our first assignment as Aesriphos," Valis said as he and Tavros took seats on the comfortable couch. "It's important to me."

Brother Bachris hesitated before taking his own seat in the well-worn chair across from them. He rubbed at the deep furrow between his brows but nodded. "I am listening."

With Tavros's steady presence by his side and their fingers linked, Valis felt steadier and met his friend's eyes. "I want to set up a reconnaissance mission to rescue Darolen. I've scried after him and spoke to him. He is alive, and I—"

The Patron Priest's jaw set and he sat up straighter. "Absolutely not."

"But—"

"No, Valis," Brother Bachris said adamantly. "You have not finished your Valiant training, and it would be a suicide mission. I cannot, in good conscience, send you out to such a place. Especially since we don't know where it is! Have you managed to figure out the location?"

Valis's stomach churned, and he frowned. "No. But it's only a matter of time before I do. I do know the general area, however. It is east of Aspar's center at the base of a mountain."

"That is not good enough." With a deep sigh, Brother Bachris rubbed his forehead. "It is not nearly good enough. How many men and women would you take across the country, searching for the compound where Darolen is held captive? How many men and women would you send to their deaths for a mission where you not only do not know an exact location, but aren't yet ready to take on such a duty?"

Gritting his teeth, Valis fought to calm down. Getting into an argument, getting visibly upset wouldn't do him any favors. If he wanted to get through protocol and do this right, he needed to keep a level head. But the sense of betrayal that rose in his chest hurt in a way that not even Aryn's betrayal had.

Once he was certain he could speak without growling or raising his voice, Valis unclenched his jaw. "I've not only been training *heavily* for this, but I have been training others. My time every morning is spent training translocation students, followed by an intense class with the reliquary guards. Because I'm so *advanced*, Tav and I, as well as Seza and Zhasina have already finished our Valiant training, and we're all extremely diligent when it comes to physical and magic training every day."

He sighed and sat back in his chair, gripping Tavros's hand tighter. "How are we not prepared? We've already been on an assignment, rescuing the Kalutakeni caravan. We didn't know the exact location of *that*, either. Zhasina's map was useless, and the caravan wasn't where it was supposed to be. We just had a general direction that they would be traveling from Plorvas to go on. And during that mission, I've proven myself, capturing Qeraden and an entire nest of Qos adherents, who I killed single-handedly when they escaped their prison cells. I've made allies of the mercenary band who had attacked the caravan, earned the caravan's loyalty, and have proven myself a capable leader. And, I have made allies of the entire town of Tigak by freeing them from the Qos adherents' tyranny."

He shrugged and stared at Brother Bachris defiantly. "Tell me again how I'm not ready."

The Patron Priest let out a long-suffering sigh and stood to pace before the fire in stiff strides. "Before I even consider letting you go on any mission, you need a clear destination in mind, Valis. You need an army, and I'm not about to assign other Aesriphos to such a quest, knowing that no destination is forthcoming, because you cannot find such a thing via scry. It isn't possible!"

"Yet, I've shown this monastery that most of the things you all find 'impossible' are, in fact, very possible," Valis countered. "Just today I surprised Firil with a new spell to help strengthen the body during an illness so it can more easily fight off infections. I've taught the reliquary guard force how to cut their reaction times in half or more by casting by intent rather than with prayers. And, I've shown that we can utilize shields in a whole new way, by blocking shots as they come, rather than keeping a dome shield up at all times. They now know how to make their shields into complete spheres, to turn their shields invisible, and to mold their shields to their body for better ease in fighting. There's so much more, but... Brother Bachris, we *are* ready. I promise you."

"But that does not answer the fact that you have no idea where the enemy compound resides!" The Patron Priest sighed, looking anywhere and everywhere but Valis's eyes. "It would be useless!"

Valis lifted a brow. "How, exactly, would it be useless? All I would have to do is follow the trail the Aesriphos paved during their mission, which I can accurately do based on the courier marks on the letters they sent. Then head east. By word of mouth from the villages, towns, and cities we pass, we will be able to locate Qos nests, take them out, and search the holdings, question our prisoners until we find the compound." He sat forward and clasped his hands between his knees. "It isn't impossible. It's actually very, very possible."

"No, Valis," Brother Bachris muttered. "It isn't that simple. I forbid it."

"You *forbid* it? Is there more you aren't telling me? Because your objections aren't making any sense."

His friend and mentor grunted and shook his head. "No. There is nothing else. But, my point stands. Unless you have an exact location, I refuse to consider such a reckless request. If you somehow *do* find out where this compound is, we may revisit this discussion, but as it stands, I will not allow it. It is a *foolish* endeavor. I—"

Valis stood and balled his fists at his sides. "Are you telling me that rescuing my *father* is *foolish*? Are you telling me that his *life* means *nothing* to this monastery?"

Brother Bachris paled and raised his hands in a placating gesture. "Now, Valis, I—"

"No," Valis growled. "I won't accept that. All lives matter,

Brother. *All of them.* The other Aesriphos who were with Papa and Father are dead, but they're keeping Father alive for some reason. I *will* rescue him. I *promised.*"

The elderly priest let out a resigned grunt and sank back into his chair. "That was not your promise to make, my boy. You are not ready, you don't have anywhere near enough experience for such a mission even if you *did* know the exact location, and I will not budge from my stance on this. Please, return to your duties and put this out of your mind."

"I refuse," Valis spat. "You can't ask me to put my *family* out of my mind."

"No," Brother Bachris conceded. "No, I cannot. Nor would I ever ask such a thing. But, you need to put the idea of a rescue mission out of your mind." He gave Valis a pointed stare. "You are dismissed, my boys. Go back to your evening duties."

"I—"

Tavros tugged on his hand and forcefully drew Valis toward the door. "That's enough, love. Let's go."

Valis fumed as they left the office. He wanted to stay and argue, but Tavros's grip on his hand was like iron, and Valis reluctantly let his lover drag him away. He knew the last thing he needed was to make Brother Bachris angry, but his instincts kept telling him to fight.

"It will be okay," Tavros said, keeping his voice calm and reassuring. "We'll try again in a few days when you've both had time to calm down and see reason."

Valis struggled to swallow down the betrayal as it sent

bile up into the back of his throat. He never thought Brother Bachris, who had always been so kind and helpful, would betray him in such a vile way. And that thought rankled the most. He *knew* how much Kerac and Darolen meant to Valis.

He groaned, unable to hold it in. Tavros frowned, releasing Valis's hand to wrap his arm around his shoulders. "Breathe, love. Arguing with him more than you already did would have been pointless. We need to be smart about this."

Now that they were a few hundred yards away from Brother Bachris's door, Valis's anger went from full fury to a simmer that threatened to burn him alive. Even Tavros's steady presence did little to calm him down, and he could only feel his irritation rising.

And with that rising irritation and anger, Valis started forming a plan. He could raise his own army, Brother Bachris be damned.

"Why don't we go spar for an hour or so?" The question tore Valis out of his thoughts. Tavros glanced over, his clear gray eyes shadowed with worry. "It isn't healthy for you to be this angry."

Sighing, Valis nodded. "A spar might be best, yes."

"Then let's go. We have a while yet before bed. Let's get sweaty."

CHAPTER NINE

BY THE NEXT DAY, Valis was still seething. The spar only did so much to help curb his anger. It helped just enough to enable him to sleep, but nightmares woke Valis in a pool of sweat with a scream echoing in the room. Tavros's eyes that morning were wide and worried as he pulled Valis to his chest and murmured words of comfort and love, stroking his sweaty hair and rocking until Valis calmed.

After Valis finally calmed from the nightmare of Darolen's painful death, the anger swarmed him again, suffocating and hot enough to make him want to claw his own skin off. The more he thought of Darolen sitting in his own stinking filth, starving and bleeding from his bonds, the more Valis wanted to rip Brother Bachris's face off for denying him the right to search for his father, friend or not.

And the fact that Brother Bachris *was* his friend felt like the vilest of betrayals until Valis struggled to just breathe.

He'd almost thrown his hairbrush at the mirror after his bath, but Tavros massaged his hand until he released it, and took over brushing Valis's long hair, being as gentle as possible to try to calm Valis's ire.

Unlike normal, it didn't work as planned.

"You have to calm down before you train the reliquary guards," Tavros murmured. "It's dangerous for all of us if your anger makes you fall into the darkness."

Valis rested his head on Tavros's shoulder and groaned. "I know. Perhaps we'll work on speed with raising partial shields instead of anything to do with black magic. I can't risk it with as pissed as I am."

"You're shaking." With Tavros's quiet whisper against his ear, he smoothed his hands down Valis's back and around to massage his trembling hands. "I've never seen you this angry before."

"He just... *dismissed* the idea of rescuing Father," Valis muttered. "Like his life doesn't matter. Like he's *nothing*! How could anyone, especially a *priest*, be so... so *heartless*?"

"I don't know, love." Tavros wrapped his arms around Valis and held him like a treasure, his embrace warm and secure, his hands rubbing up and down Valis's spine in slow strokes that did, somewhat, alleviate some of Valis's tension, if not his anger. "I wish I did. He has his reasons, and we'll try again later, okay?"

Valis let out an explosive breath and tucked his face into

the curve of Tavros's neck and shoulder, huffing his husband's scent. "It feels like I'm failing Father, you know? Like this is a test, and I'm failing, and not because I'm not prepared, but because *one person* won't let me succeed."

Tavros's sigh tickled Valis's neck, and he shivered. "You're not failing anyone, Valis. It's just a bump in the road. We'll keep trying. In the meantime, we'll keep preparing, just in case."

"Yeah." Valis sighed and clutched the back of Tavros's tunic. "Yeah. We'll keep trying."

AFTER TRAINING WITH THE TRANSLOCATION STUDENTS AND reliquary guards, Valis's anger had become slightly more manageable. At least he hadn't barked his orders at them. He'd had enough control to keep his voice level and calm for the most part, and everyone seemed to understand when he lost his composure the few times his control slipped.

When the last reliquary guard had left, Valis ate breakfast with a few of his students, as well as Tavros, Seza and Zhasina. Then they were off to visit Aryn. It seemed like a whirlwind of required engagements loomed ahead. But when he sat in his fathers' suite with Kerac's hand in his, he thought he might have some downtime.

Then Thyran came in, and Valis groaned.

"You seem unhappy to see me," Thyran said, his tone amused.

"I'm just trying to calm down and have some time to myself," Valis groused.

Kerac chuckled and patted Valis's thigh. "Tough morning?"

"You could say that, yes."

Thyran drew closer and squeezed Valis's shoulder. "Things will even out. But, for now, I would like you to accompany me to the temple for training. You have been lax since before your joining night, and we have a bit more to go before you are competent in your scrying skills."

"But—"

Another rusty laugh from Kerac and he waved Valis away. "Go on, son. You can come back and keep me company when you have more time. I think I should rest, at any rate. I find I'm quite tired."

Sighing, Valis stood and kissed Kerac's forehead. "Fine. I'll see you sometime this afternoon."

"You'd better." Kerac winked and settled, and Valis tucked the covers up near his chin.

When his papa was comfortable, Valis forced himself to turn around and follow Thyran out. He smiled slightly when Tavros waylaid him with a kiss and whispered near his ear. "I'll keep watch over him until the next watch arrives. Then I'll find you."

"Sounds good," Valis murmured.

As Thyran led Valis from the suite, Valis rubbed at his tired eyes and sighed. "So, what's on the agenda for today?"

Thyran smiled back at him and waited for him to catch

up so they could walk side-by-side. "First, I wish to teach you how to keep others from interfering with or listening in on your scrying sessions. Then, you need to learn how to block mental attacks. It has little to do with scrying, but is useful, nonetheless. After, we might have a bit of fun, but only if the first two lessons go well."

During the long walk up through the monastery to the temple, Valis tried to calm himself down. Teaching others while he was in a pissed-off rage was one thing. Learning anything in this state could either be disastrous or completely useless. Thyran had better things to do than teach someone who had their blood boiling so hot that they were only capable of lashing out at others.

"Your mind is rather tumultuous today," Thyran remarked. "You should let the anger go, Valis. Nothing good will come of it, and you will be better able to achieve your goals with a calm, level head."

"Yeah. I know," Valis muttered. "I've just never really been *this* angry before. At least, if I have, I don't remember it. It's *consuming*, and I feel like my blood is about to catch fire."

"Things will settle down. You'll see." Thyran nodded to the Aesriphos at the doors to the temple and the women pulled them open, revealing the bright Hall of Communion within. Thyran shaded Valis's eyes from the Light of Phaerith with a chuckle, and Valis forced his eyes down to follow the sapphire blue runner that led the way toward the back of the room and the reliquary beyond.

When Thyran was certain Valis wouldn't get lost in the

Light, he lowered his hand and guided Valis by his elbow until they entered the reliquary. The doors boomed shut behind them, echoing in the space, though Valis still had no idea how with as full of books and shelves as the room was. But, the sepulcher quiet of the room let Valis relax, almost as if the familiar room with its familiar scents and artifacts were more *home* than the suite he shared with Tavros.

Almost.

"You seem to have relaxed," Thyran noted. "Good. Perhaps the lessons will go by swiftly for you."

Valis shrugged and scratched his chest, having removed his armor before he went to see his papa. "Coming in here kind of muted my anger. Not sure how or why, but I'll take it."

"Excellent. Let's get started."

Thyran raked his hands through his salt and pepper hair and headed to the long table that bisected the room length-wise. As he leaned on it, he clasped his hands in front of him and smiled. "You have proven that you can do almost anything that you set your mind to, even with minimal—if any—training. I am fairly certain that the reason you were so unsuccessful with your scrying is because Aryn had somehow blocked your ability to do so, whether by force of will or by accident. So, I want you to put that temporary failure out of your mind and focus today. Can you do that?"

Valis rolled his shoulders and nodded. "Yes, sir. I think you're right about Aryn. Once I broke through his hold, I was able to scry easily for the most part. And I think I was only able to break through because of how weak and exhausted he had become."

"I believe so, too." He motioned to the stacks where Valis had spent way too long attempting his scrying lessons, and Valis instinctively groaned. "Go ahead and get situated. There is already water in the scrying bowl. We will begin with the first lesson: learning how to block others from listening in or tampering with your scrying. To do this—"

"I just need to shield my mind and the bowl," Valis muttered. "Make it impenetrable from any attack, physical, mental, or magical."

Thyran raised both brows. "Perhaps. Let us see if it works in practice. If it does with great success... we may disseminate that tactic to the rest of the monastery."

Valis tilted his head. "That's not the way it's usually done?"

His mentor chuckled, and his blue eyes flashed with pride. "No. It is not. However, your way would be much faster, as well as likely stronger than the other way, especially for those who lack the ability to focus as hard as others."

He lifted a finger. "But... it would have the drawback of not allowing two-way communication."

Valis shrugged and smirked. "Unless I add to the shield that anyone with gold magic can penetrate the scry for any reason."

"You and your surprises!" Thyran snorted and waved to the stacks. "Get back there and show me what you can do."

An hour later, Thyran called a halt to the training and

when Valis exited the alcove, he found his mentor and friend wiping sweat from his brow. "Excellent work," he said in a raspy, tired voice. "I think that went better than I expected."

"You think?" Valis teased.

"Hush, imp." Thyran smirked and rubbed his eyes. "You've given me quite the headache. What did you do?"

"I added a parameter to the shield that any outside force trying to interfere with my scry would receive a shock to interrupt their own scrying and focus."

Thyran grunted. "It worked. A little too well."

A pang of worry hit Valis in the chest and stomach. "I didn't hurt you, did I? I didn't intend for the shocks to hurt."

"They were more annoying than anything," Thyran assured. "I will be fine. But, I think that is enough scrying training for the day."

"And the mental attacks?"

Thyran gave him a look that asked if he was insane. "I think you have that down, as well. It would be the same principle for you."

"Yeah. I thought as much." Valis rubbed his shoulder and cracked a yawn. "So, what's next?"

Thyran grinned, this evil thing that made Valis's insides clench. "I thought we might have some fun."

"I don't trust that grin," Valis muttered. "Evil shit."

"Oh, you might be surprised. Today, I had thought to teach you levitation."

Valis perked up at that and stared at Thyran with a

perked brow because he already knew how to levitate things. Apparently, he never told Thyran. "Really?"

"Yes. Come on. We have little time to spare."

Ah, well. It wouldn't hurt to learn a new way of performing the task, and humoring Thyran wouldn't hurt anything. And with the way his gut pitted, he knew it would be stupid to fight it.

Fortunately, Thyran wasn't privy to his thoughts. His grin never dimmed as he guided Valis out of the reliquary and down through the halls to the arena. Once they arrived, Valis watched as Thyran took in the few people who trained within. Some wielded wooden swords against training dummies, while others sparred amongst themselves, either in bare-hands combat or with their own wooden swords.

After a moment, Thyran clapped his hands, the sound echoing loudly through the cavernous room. "Attention, please. May I have your attention?"

Everyone stopped mid-swing and turned toward Thyran. "What can we help you with?" one of the men asked.

Thyran smiled and motioned to Valis. "I must ask you all to vacate the arena. I have a very destructive training session today with Valis, and it would be much better if there is no one here but us so there are no casualties. Please give us at least 2-3 hours before you return, for your safety. And please send a pair of Aesriphos to stand guard to keep anyone from entering during our allotted time."

"We'll stick around for guard duty," Cassavin said, motioning to her partner, Nevesar. Valis glanced at the two, nodding his thanks. They were two of his best students in the reliquary guard force, attentive and quick studies, so he felt safe with their guard and nodded his approval.

She continued with his acceptance, giving him a small smile. "We were almost done training, anyway, and our next duty doesn't begin for four hours."

"Excellent. Thank you, Cassavin."

The women nodded and filed out with the rest, only they took up post on either side of the entry in the hall. Valis waited until the last person left and wrinkled his nose.

"Why is it so dangerous?"

Thyran turned to him and shrugged. "If you remember the time I showed you with the pillow, it is a multi-directional push and pull. If you don't exert enough push and an equal pull, you can make whatever you levitate explode. And, it is rather disastrous if done with people or animals."

"Oh, gross."

"Indeed."

"So…"

Thyran moved deeper into the arena and laid a hand on one of the straw and wood training dummies, just like the ones Valis had destroyed during his magic training. "In order to levitate something, you must push from the bottom, while pulling from the top. Push from the side opposite where you wish it to go and pull from the side where it is going. Plus, push on either side to keep it from toppling over."

Grunting, Valis stepped up and regarded the training dummy. "That sounds like an awful lot of work for a single spell. And Tavros and I didn't do it that way when we levitated the shield full of fish out of the river and onto the magical litter. And we levitated the litter from the river back to the Kalutakeni caravan for food."

"You... did what?"

Valis shrugged. "We didn't think about it. We just did it. Intent is what matters, more than logistics or training. It was laughably easy."

"But—"

He took pity on his mentor and motioned to the training dummy. "I want to learn this way, too, though."

Thyran furrowed his brows. "Whatever for?"

Another shrug and Valis glanced down at his boots. "I don't know. It feels precognitive, so I'm just going to go with that. I need to learn it, and I'm willing to give it a shot."

"Very well."

As Thyran took a moment to regain his composure, Valis stared at the training dummy. He had been casting via intent for so long that he wasn't sure he could cast any other way again. But his gut said he had to try. Every time he thought the word levitate and looked at Thyran, his gut pitted again, and he ended up rubbing it to try to get that awful feeling to abate. At least it wasn't making him physically ill. But he knew it was important just the same.

"For this, Valis, you will be calling upon Dapen, the Goddess of mobility, direction, and journey. You must have the directions firmly in your mind, concentrating on the correct push and pull to achieve the height you want, as well as its final destination." He patted the training dummy and stepped away behind Valis. "Shield us and move the dummy across the arena."

Valis snapped up his shield, then made it invisible so that its golden glow wouldn't interfere with his concentration. When Thyran gasped, Valis chuckled.

"You need to quit surprising me, young man," Thyran muttered. "I'm getting too old for this."

"And I'm a layman," Valis teased.

Still laughing, Valis tried to calm himself and when he managed it, he cast up a prayer to Dapen with his destination and height in mind. He tried to visualize the push and pull he needed on each side, but as the training dummy started to lift, the entire thing began shaking. Valis managed to move it two feet before the shaking became so violent that straw fell from it like fall leaves. Then, before Valis could do anything to salvage the situation, it exploded in a spray of splinters and straw dust, coating almost every inch of the arena floor in a catastrophic mess.

"You do realize you will be on clean-up duty after this, yes?" Thyran teased. "Try again."

Groaning, Valis tried again. This time, he got the training dummy a foot and a half before it exploded, just the same as the first.

After twenty-three dummies, Valis was ready to give up. He rubbed his forehead, wiped away the sweat that slicked his face and ran down his temples. "Fuck."

"What is the problem?" Thyran asked in that fatherly tone he sometimes used. "You seem stressed."

Valis grunted and wiped the sweat out of his eyes. "Brother Bachris."

"Ah."

"It's driving me insane. He's acting like my father means nothing. He said trying to rescue him was *foolish*, for fuck's sake! And I can't sleep well, because I keep having nightmares of Father dying, and wake up screaming in the mornings, scaring Tavros half to death. It's just… I'm so angry that I'm afraid I'm going to combust or explode like these fucking dummies!"

"There is little you can do for now," Thyran said. He squeezed Valis's shoulder and looked him in the eye, his expression oddly serious. "Give it time."

"Father doesn't *have* time!"

"He may have more than you imagine." With a soft sigh, Thyran rubbed his own furrowed brow and glanced around at the mess Valis had created. "I know you are angry, and your anger is valid. But, use it to your advantage, instead of letting it rule you."

"And how am I supposed to do that?" Valis threw his hands up and started pacing, his boots crunching in the splinters. "He won't listen!"

"And you are a very resourceful young man," Thyran reminded. "Keep that in mind and put your anger aside. You said you had a precognitive feeling in regard to this training, so set it aside and let us continue."

Blowing out a breath, Valis nodded and went through a few moments of breathing exercises to try to calm himself down. When he was no longer shaking with his anger and frustration, Thyran patted his back and gave him his most paternal smile.

"Try again," Thyran said, completely shifting focus. "You got it five feet this last time! You're getting better!" He patted Valis on his shoulder, grimacing at his soaked shirt. After wiping his damp hand on his own tunic, Thyran motioned to the storage closet at the end of the arena. "Go get more dummies and let us continue."

Valis crunched across the arena toward the closet. Every inch of the floor was littered with wooden splinters and coated in so much straw and burlap dust that every step brought up a puff of the stuff and clogged Valis's nose until he sneezed so hard, he saw stars. It took three more sneezes before he had the great idea of putting a shield around his nose and mouth.

Eighteen more training dummies, and Valis finally made a successful transfer from one side of the arena to the other without an explosion. The dummy made it intact, and Valis was dripping with so much sweat from the exertion that he sloshed in his boots.

"How on earth do you work up such a sweat when wielding magic?" Thyran asked. "You are quite the mess."

"Shut up before I hug you," Valis groused. "And you're getting the dust pan and bin for this mess while I sweep."

Thyran let out a soft sound that could have been a groan

and followed Valis to the storage closet. "This was supposed to be your job."

"It was mostly your fault."

"True." Thyran sighed. "True. Let us hurry so you can throw your smelly self in the bath."

Gods, Valis wanted a bath. But more than that, he wanted food.

"Deal."

CHAPTER TEN

"Dɪᴅ you really *have* to destroy the arena while training?" Cassavin asked. She stepped further into the arena and tossed her waist-length auburn braid over her shoulder before planting her hands on her armored hips. As one of the reliquary guards, she gave Valis a respectful nod, but still kept a stern, motherly look on her oval face and in her hazel eyes as she stared him and Thyran down. "This place is a disaster. I swear, you two ought to be ashamed of yourselves. You were never this messy when you first came to the monastery, Valis. You used to be such a tidy boy!"

"It's his fault," Valis whined playfully as he pointed at Thyran's chest. "He made me do it."

Cassavin snorted and rolled her eyes. "Let me get more hands in here to help clean this shit up. Some people need to actually train today. We can't very well do that if the place looks like someone decimated an entire forest in here."

Her partner, Nevesar, smirked and shook her head as she looked around. She stood half a head shorter than her wife, but was bulked with a bit more muscle. She tucked her black hair, cropped short to her chin in a straight bob, behind her ears and headed for the supply closet. "You round up hands to work. I'll get started with the clean-up. Leave it to the men to destroy the place."

Valis gaped at her, but she winked at him and gave his shoulder a playful shove as she passed him. "Keep working. We'll get this mess sorted quickly so you can go about your day. Hopefully with a bath first. You're rather rank, Valis. What did you do? Get sprayed by a skunk?"

Valis lifted his arm and took a sniff of his armpit and groaned. "No. That's all Thyran's fault. He worked me to death."

"Just as well. Let's hurry before your stench scares away the others before they even get here."

An hour and a half later, and with the help of fourteen Aesriphos, they managed to get the arena back to normal. And by that time, Valis's back and arms hurt so bad from sweeping that all he wanted was a hot bath and food.

His stomach growled loud enough to make the six women giggle. The men teased him mercilessly, calling jeers about the beast he carried inside him. Their joviality helped keep him from falling over, but only by a small margin.

Actually, perhaps food first... that way he could sit down and rest.

"You stink, my boy," Thyran said. "Bath first. Your friends shouldn't have to plug their noses while they eat. It would be rude to subject them to your odor."

Groaning, Valis stowed away his broom and thanked all the gods in succession that other Aesriphos had agreed to take out the bins full of splinters and straw and burlap dust for burning. If he'd had to do that, he would probably collapse on the way back, if not on the way to the furnaces. Then even more people would be "subjected to his odor" when they had to move him from wherever he fell to his suite.

"Go bathe," Thyran said in a kinder voice. "I will meet you in the dining hall for lunch. Just make it quick. I fear you falling asleep in there and drowning."

Waving a rude gesture in Thyran's direction, Valis shuffled off, staggering through the arena and nearly colliding with the wall beside the entry.

After a quick bath, Valis wanted to soak, but knew he didn't have time. And as Thyran had feared, Valis thought his chances of falling asleep and drowning were too high to chance it. Instead, he drained the tub, dressed, and after brushing his hair and tying it back, headed to the dining hall.

His friends all sat around their usual table. Tavros took one look at him and perked a brow. "What the fuck happened to you? Your eyes are all red and puffy, and so is your nose. Please don't tell me you're coming down with an illness..."

Valis rubbed his nose, and promptly sneezed, barely covering his face with his elbow in time. "Burlap and straw dust from training. Please. Just feed me."

"He had fun exploding things this morning," Thyran supplied helpfully. Then he motioned to the serving line. "Go get your food and quit complaining. At least you smell better. Now fill your stomach so you can work on your personality."

Grumbling, Valis went and got a tray of food, purposely not heaping it as high as normal so he wouldn't dive head-first into food coma. When he sat down, Tavros wrapped an arm about his shoulder and pulled him in to kiss his temple. "You look awful."

"I'm exhausted, and I wanted to soak, but I figured Thyran would come yank me out of the tub if I did. That, or I'd drown like Thyran predicted."

"You are not far wrong, Child. I was tempted to peer into your mind to see what was taking you so long."

Snorting, Valis tuned him out and started in on his plate, barely tasting anything of the rich steak and gravy with creamy, buttery mashed potatoes, roasted vegetables, soft, steamy buttered rolls, and crisp salad with some kind of zesty vinaigrette dressing. It looked good, smelled great, but he was so tired, the taste barely registered as his mind blanked out into white noise.

"Valis?"

Valis grunted.

"Valis!"

Someone shook him, and Valis glanced up with bleary eyes. "What?"

Tavros chuckled and rubbed his shoulder. "Finish eating. Then you're going to take a nap."

A nap sounded wonderful, but Valis tried to figure out if he had the time.

"We'll make the time," Tavros said in a tender tone. "Everything can wait for two hours."

Groaning, Valis nodded. He barely managed to finish his plate of food without falling asleep in it, and when he finished, Tavros excused them and dragged Valis away. Before he knew it, his husband had them both undressed and in bed, Tavros cuddled behind him. And that was the last thing he remembered until Tavros gently shook him awake.

"Love, it's time to get up."

For once, Valis didn't remember dreaming. He rubbed his eyes and rolled onto his back to look up at his lover. "Now I don't want to get up."

Tavros chuckled and leaned in for a kiss. "Too bad. I promised you two hours, and it's been three. Get up. What did you have on your agenda until dinner?"

Sighing, Valis glanced at the clock. "I want to do a bit of scrying practice. Then perhaps some endurance training."

"With as tired as you are lately," Tavros said hesitantly, "why not skip anything strenuous? One day of rest won't ruin all the hard work you've put into your body." He leaned close and cupped Valis's jaw, stroking his thumb over his cheekbone. "I'm worried about you. You've been running ragged since we found Kerac, and it isn't doing you any favors. You need to pull yourself back together before you mentally fall apart."

Valis thought it over for a moment, but it was the worry in Tavros's eyes that made Valis nod. "All right. Nothing strenuous. But, I will do some scrying training. Then, I'll spend some time with Papa before dinner, and perhaps have an early night tonight."

The slow smile that brightened Tavros's face was worth every concession Valis had just made. He reached up and wrapped his arms around Tavros's neck and pulled him down for a slow kiss. "I love you," he whispered against Tavros's lips. "I'm sorry I've made you worry."

Tavros shook his head. "We'll make it through. You just need to rest. I wish I could have let you sleep longer, but then I feared you wouldn't sleep tonight."

"Good call."

With a yawn, Valis slowly sat up and dug the heels of his palms into his eyes, rubbing the sleep from them. "Scrying training, and then I'll let you lead me wherever."

"Sounds good. Do you need me to leave for your training?"

Valis thought about that for a moment, then shook his head. "No. If that changes, I'll let you know."

He stepped to the chair where he'd tossed his uniform and redressed. Once he had his scrying bowl filled and settled at the side table, he cleared his mind. He needed to find the exact location of the enemy compound where Darolen was being kept. That was the key to getting Brother Bachris to let him go on a rescue mission. Everything hinged on that one piece of information.

"You're thinking too hard," Tavros said from his seat on the corner of the bed facing him. "You've gone absolutely rigid. What has you so tense?"

It took a few breaths to force his muscles to relax. "I just want to find Father. Every thought keeps circling back around to him."

"Are you looking for him?"

"In a way, yes."

"You're looking for his exact location, then," Tavros guessed.

"Yes. One way or another, I *will* make Brother Bachris sanction a rescue mission."

Tavros sighed and gave him a nod. "Just don't tax yourself too hard. You're already exhausted."

Truthfully, after that nap, Valis felt a bit rejuvenated. Yes, he was still tired, but nowhere near as bad as he had been at lunch. Now that he'd had a nap, he was rather pissed at Thyran for making him work so hard with that levitation spell, needed or not, because he could have used that energy now in his scrying attempt.

But, it was what it was, and Valis knew he had to let go of petty excuses.

With a deep sigh that rippled the water in his scrying

bowl, Valis worked to clear his mind as best he could. He pulled his focus in, concentrating on just one thought: Find Darolen.

The water in the bowl swirled with dark clouds. They changed color and texture several times before the image stilled to an inky blackness that Valis was almost certain was the cell in which his father was kept. He didn't want the cell. He wanted to see the exterior of the compound, so he tried again.

Just as before, the bowl roiled with multicolored clouds. But every time he tried to nail down an image, it always came back to that blackness and the sound of Darolen's wheezed breathing.

Valis broke off his concentration to rub at his eyes, only to find that his hands ached and his palms bore half-moon indents from clenching his fists tight. He shook them out and when he rested his hands back on the side table, he noticed his fingers trembling.

He needed to calm down if he was to have any success, but the harder he tried to find the location of the compound, the more his frustration built. And the more that frustration grew and churned inside him, the harder it became to focus at all.

"Are you making any headway?" Tavros asked quietly.

"Not at all," Valis muttered. "It just keeps showing me blackness filled with Father's wheezes. No matter what I try, I can't see the outside of the compound."

"Do you think they might have something going on like

what happened with Aryn? The way he kept you from scrying?"

Valis rubbed his forehead and leaned heavily on his hands, letting his head hang low toward the bowl of water. "I don't know. They could have some kind of anti-scry shield up, but then how would I see Father in his cell? It's not making any sense to me!"

"Calm down, love." Tavros came up behind him and rubbed his shoulders, digging his fingers and thumbs into knotted muscles just hard enough to release the tension and make Valis groan. "Maybe think of a different tactic. Have you used the same one throughout this exercise?"

"I—"

Did he? He kept trying to intend to see the enemy compound where Darolen was kept. In every scry, he had Darolen at the forefront of his mind. Groaning, Valis straightened and leaned back to rest his head on Tavros's shoulder. "Yes."

"Then switch it up. It will come to you eventually."

Valis could only hope. With any luck, he would get it today so he could relax before he confronted Brother Bachris again tomorrow.

This time when he tried, he concentrated on seeing the route to take to the compound. Then he tried looking for the mountain that loomed over it. But, everything Valis tried either showed him nothing, or it showed the blackness of Darolen's cell. He always knew the cell because of Darolen's harsh breathing, or his hacking coughs, or the wet splashes as he created more waste on the cell floor.

And the more he heard his father's misery, the angrier Valis became until his head pounded with his heartbeat and his pulse raced. His entire body shook with his restrained rage. When he looked up, even his vision pulsed with his heartbeat from the tension and strain of his anger.

He took a deep breath, but it didn't help.

"Valis?"

Valis roared and punched the wall behind the side table, leaning against his fist while he heaved for breath. He needed to get his shit together before he hurt himself, or worse, Tavros.

He heard footsteps approaching. Tavros's hands came to rest on his shoulders again, and Valis shrugged him off. "Give me a moment. I'm... I—"

"I understand," Tavros murmured. "Tell me what you need."

"I just... Give me a moment to calm myself down."

Gods, his voice was such a low growl that he almost didn't recognize it. His entire body shook and he squeezed his eyes shut tight, trying to block out the pulsing darkness in his periphery, trying to block out the way his entire body felt like a throbbing, festering open wound.

It was strange, too. During the scrying, itself, he had felt almost normal. But the moment he pulled back from it, the sheer fury was still there, growing to unmanageable levels that he didn't know how to deal with.

His hand throbbed. He shook it out with a curse and stared down at his swelling knuckles. After a breath to regain some semblance of control, he filtered golden magic into the area with the intent to heal before it became too painful, and thus add to his anger and misery.

"What happened that time?"

"Same as before," Valis growled. "Just swirling clouds and the blackness of Father's cell. I don't know what else to try."

"What does Roba have to say?"

Valis glanced over his shoulder at his husband with a perked brow. Roba had been quiet the entire time, and he hadn't even thought to consult him on how to find the compound via scry, or if he might know the location off the top of his head.

No, Roba said, his tone full of regret. *I fear I do not know the location. I haven't been to any of the compounds or outposts for Qos on the eastern side of the continent.*

Do you have any idea how I can find it through scrying?

His birth father went quiet a moment, then let out a ghostly sigh. *Unfortunately, as I've said in the past, scrying was my main weakness. I never was able to do long-distance scries without help or a relay, and anything specific that had nothing to do with a person with whom I was familiar was beyond my capabilities. Whether it was because I didn't have the ability, or because I lacked the aptitude for learning it correctly, or whatever other reason there may be, it was something I never had been able to grasp past rudimentary skill. You are already so much more advanced than I ever was.*

Sighing, Valis roughly scrubbed his hand over his face now that his knuckles were healed. "Fuck."

"Bad news?"

"I forgot Roba had told me that scrying was his worst skill. And he says he doesn't know the location because he's never visited any of the compounds or outposts on the eastern side of the continent."

"Well, shit."

"Yeah."

"Are you at least calmer?"

Valis shrugged. "I'm less likely to bite your head off, if that counts for anything."

At that, Tavros came up behind him and wrapped his arms around Valis's chest. He pressed a gentle kiss into the side of Valis's neck and rested his forehead there. "I wish I could help."

"You are helping," Valis whispered. "Just being here helps. Wanting and trying to calm me down helps."

"I know. I just wish I could help in your searches."

Groaning, Valis turned in Tavros's arms and settled his hands on his husband's hips. "What if it's really impossible like Brother Bachris said? What if I can't find the location at all?"

Tavros went quiet for a few moments, his breath washing over the side of Valis's neck in soothing waves. "I don't know," he finally said. "Even if you did see the outside of the compound, it wouldn't tell you how to get there. And I'm not good enough at scrying to see as much as you are, so I don't even know where to begin in helping."

Valis closed his eyes and buried his face into the curve of Tavros's neck, hiding there in the hopes that his husband's scent and strong arms would help to banish the rest of his anger and frustration. He couldn't see Kerac like this. His papa didn't need to have that kind of worry when he was still so frail and sick. And if his friends saw him like this, they'd swarm him, and he didn't think he could handle that right now. Not without blowing up at them.

"I know what you need," Tavros whispered.

"What?" Valis mumbled into his neck.

"You wanted to soak in the tub earlier. Think that would help?"

He honestly didn't know if it would or not, but he'd never turn down a chance to be naked with his husband. "Let's find out."

"And no more scrying today?" Tavros gave him a squeeze and turned Valis around to give him a gentle shove toward the lavatory. "You can try again tomorrow. We won't give up, Valis. I promise."

CHAPTER ELEVEN

FIVE DAYS. It had been five days, and Valis's disgust only grew. He paced his room, tugging at his loose blond hair as he muttered to himself, racking his brain on how to scry *differently* than he had been so he could find an exact location to throw in Brother Bachris's face. Anything to get his trip sanctioned.

Nothing had worked. And Valis had been trying for *five days*. The worst thing was, he felt no closer to a breakthrough than he had when he began. At least in the beginning he'd had determination and hope. Now, all he had was a growing sense of despair that gripped his heart and shredded it every time he looked into Kerac's eyes and saw the hope shining in their golden depths.

Valis had made a promise, and for the first time, he wondered if he'd be able to keep it. Would he be able to rescue Darolen? The only thing that kept him stranded in the monastery was his sense of duty. He had promised his fathers that he would become an Aesriphos and devote his life to the monastery's cause. He had friends here who he didn't want to disappoint, Brother Bachris included. His husband desperately wanted him to get the mission sanctioned, so they could enlist other Aesriphos for a more unified approach to the journey.

And all Valis wanted was to run recklessly across the country in search of his father.

It wasn't fair. But, Valis knew from his years under Roba's abuse that life was rarely fair.

He stalked around his room now, ignoring the scrying bowl that sat, taunting him, on the side table. Every time he glanced at it, his stomach churned. The anger he'd held before had turned into pure frustration that he couldn't escape. Resigned, he struggled to find a new way of convincing Brother Bachris to sanction the mission.

Nothing he came up with measured up. The only thing he kept coming back to was abandoning the monastery completely and heading off with the mercenaries and the Kalutakeni, knowing they would follow him out of loyalty if nothing else. He had their support after only a few months of travel, but the monastery he had spent well over a year in, that he had come to love, that finally felt like *home*, wouldn't budge on its stance.

They were abandoning his father, and that thought made Valis sick and struggle not to see red like he had when he'd killed the bandits in Sithera on his way from his childhood home to the monastery and his cellmates from his time in the prison on his first day here. Now, it threatened to throb into his vision. Not because of his anger, but because his frustration was so high that he wanted blood, wanted to destroy.

And that wasn't like him.

"Love, what can I do?"

Tavros stood by the open door to their bedroom when Valis glanced up from his glaring at the floor, watching his feet take step after step in his pacing. He sighed and rubbed the back of his neck, trying to ease the tension that kept building until his entire back, neck and shoulders felt like steel.

"I don't know."

Tavros hesitated in the doorway before striding over to Valis and cupping the sides of his neck with both of his strong hands. "Let's go spar. It will help release some of this aggression."

Valis relaxed somewhat with Tavros's fingers kneading the back of his neck near his spine, his thumbs gently rubbing along his pulse points. He closed his eyes and tilted his head forward, reveling in his husband's touch.

Over the last few days, Tavros had done all in his power to make up for the times he was an ass when Aryn had been torturing them both. Valis kept telling him he understood, that Tavros didn't need to make up for anything. But his husband wouldn't be deterred. Tavros remained attentive and loving, giving Valis what he needed when he needed it. Though, to be fair, Valis loved the attention, had begun craving it like a drug which amused Tavros to no end.

"Come on. No armor. Just scrapping until this aggression bleeds out or we're unconscious and need scraped off the floor by passing guards."

Valis snorted but nodded. He needed *something* to get this feeling inside to abate so he could think clearly. "Yeah." He sighed and gave Tavros a chaste kiss. "Thanks. Let's go."

On the way to the arena, Seza stopped them in the halls, Zhasina at her side. Both women stared at Valis as if he'd just risen from the dead. "What the ever-loving fuck is wrong with you? You look like you're about to murder an entire village."

Valis ducked his head and sighed. "I kind of feel like that, too."

"We're about to head for a spar," Tavros said, squeezing Valis's hand. "He's frustrated and needs a release."

"Just like old days," Seza muttered. "Though, to be fair, that one time was to get *you* to stop being an ass, Tav."

She studied Valis for a moment and shook her head. "We'll go with you to keep you both from killing each other. Neither of you have much in the way of restraint when you get going in a spar."

Zhasina glanced at her wife with a raised brow. "They are that bad?"

Seza laughed. "Just wait and see. Though, I guess we

could get in our own sparring practice while keeping an eye on them in case of trouble. We need it."

"Indeed, we do." Zhasina looked Valis over, her golden eyes boring into him. "Perhaps not as much as Valis, but we will make do."

"What did you two have planned for the day?" Tavros asked as they started walking again, Seza and Zhasina flanking them.

Zhasina shrugged. "We just returned from spending time with the caravan and letting Zorar and Rasera spend time with their brothers in the Kalutakeni herd." She reached out and squeezed Valis's shoulder. "I did not think you would mind."

Valis reached up and squeezed her hand in thanks. "I don't mind at all. Thank you for thinking of him. My mind and schedule have been a mess of late."

They made it into the arena shortly after they all went quiet. Valis shucked his shirt, tossing it with Tavros's on a bench along one of the walls. He rolled his shoulders and glanced around at the others who occupied the space, wondering if any of them would try to put a stop to the spar, because Valis didn't think he'd be able to stop until he was near unconscious.

"You need to quit thinking so hard," Zhasina murmured. "Relax and let your body do what it needs."

"Relaxing is near impossible," Valis said on a sigh. "That's why we're here."

"Fair enough." She patted his back and headed to a bare

spot where Seza waited for her. Soon after, they began throwing punches and blocking each other's shots.

Valis turned away from them and focused on his husband. "How do you want to do this?" Tavros asked. His eyes were so shaded with worry that Valis wished he could comfort him but knew that the only comfort would come when Valis could think straight and perform normal tasks without wanting to throw things and scream his throat raw.

"We'll figure it out along the way." Valis rolled his shoulders again and took his stance. "No holding back. Let's give Firil something to marvel over when we're done."

Tavros snorted and cracked his neck. "As you wish, my love."

Valis shivered. He'd never get tired of hearing Tavros call him that. But, he put that thought aside and launched himself at Tavros the moment his husband got into position.

The first punch missed Tavros's face as his lover dodged to the right. Tavros always was the faster fighter. Five punches hit Valis's ribs and armpit in rapid succession, but Valis breathed through the pain and leaned into the onslaught. He grappled with Tavros, getting into his personal space. For the first time in days, his mind went blank, and Valis let his body lead.

With relative ease, Valis kneed Tavros in his side, swept his legs out from under him, and when they both tumbled to the floor, they rolled around, both trying to get the upper hand. Valis became relentless.

Then hands hauled him up off Tavros. Valis glanced back

to find both Seza and Zhasina giving him worried glances. "You okay?"

"Yeah," Valis said, rolling his neck. "I'm fine."

"My fault for letting that cheap trick work," Tavros muttered. "We're good."

The girls released Valis, and he cupped Tavros's neck. "You sure?"

Tavros grinned. "We're just getting started. You backing out now?"

"Never."

"Then get into position and let's get sweaty."

Now that they were out of their body lock, Valis started to feel the bruises forming. The pain brought much needed clarity, and he stared at Tavros as they got into their stances. His husband had his hands balled into loose fists, protecting his face just like Valis. He bounced on the balls of his feet, waiting for Valis to strike first, and all Valis wanted to do was lock bodies and grapple.

Maybe that was just his libido talking. He had to get his head back into the game. This fight was to help his aggression and frustration, not to make him horny.

But maybe sex would also help with the aggression and frustration…

Then again, they'd tried that the last few days, and it hadn't worked. And as they started throwing punches, blocking, dodging, and landing powerful kicks to ribs, thighs, backs and abdomens, Valis wondered why fighting was helping so much when more enjoyable practices failed.

Tavros landed a hard punch to the side of Valis's head, knocking his vision out for a brief moment. When it came back, he tried to shake off the triple vision. It went down to doubles, and when he could see only a single Tavros before him, he roared and redoubled his efforts, landing a good four solid punches and two kicks before Tavros knew what hit him.

"That all you got?" Tavros taunted when he regained his balance. He wiped the blood from the corner of his mouth and grinned, showing bloody teeth. "You're holding back. Quit it."

Valis tongued the split on the inside of his cheek and nodded. The aggression still bubbled in his gut like poison, and he needed to get it out to be anywhere near productive in the coming days. Already a plan was formulating in his mind, but it was just the bare bones. He needed to flesh it out.

Raising his fists to protect his face, Valis took position again. This time, Tavros became the initial aggressor and threw a series of quick punches that Valis easily dodged and blocked. He caught Tavros in the armpit with a powerful kick that knocked him off his feet. Valis helped him up, and they went at it again.

Sweat dripped down the length of Valis's spine, soaked his hair. He didn't dare wipe it off his forehead or temples for fear of getting knocked out by Tavros's solid fists. He ducked a right hook and leaned into the next punch, landing two to either side of Tavros's ribs.

And as he lost himself in the fight, as the arena faded away into a soft haze, Valis found his center. Everything faded away. The noises from the others training in the arena bled away into silence only punctuated by the gasps, grunts, and heavy breathing coming from himself and Tavros. The lights dimmed except for where he and his lover fought. His muscles burned in a pleasant way. And every bruise that bloomed on his skin and in his muscles brought his clarity to new heights until Valis felt like he was in another world altogether.

Valis became aware of nothing except the fight, almost like a meditation. He focused on the next flex and release, the next step of his feet, the next punch.

And as the fight wore on, Valis barely noticed the aggression slipping away. The frustration faded. All that mattered was the pain and victory. In this moment, Valis had nothing to be frustrated about. His aggression had a clear outlet. His mind had nothing to stew over, nothing to overthink, nothing to obsess over.

Tavros landed another punch to Valis's sensitive ribs, and Valis caught him in the side of the head with a left hook. They traded bruising blows like they did kisses in the night as they drifted off to sleep. It was almost holy, a dance between lovers that made everything that Valis had been carrying around release their grasps on him and leave him calm and sated.

A hard kick to his calf nearly sent Valis to the floor. He staggered and came up with an uppercut to Tavros's jaw as he closed the distance, trying to get Valis on the floor. They almost went tumbling when Tavros staggered forward, his wits momentarily scrambled. Valis fought for control enough to stop the fight, just long enough for Tavros's eyes to quit rolling.

He steadied Tavros with hands on his shoulders, keeping him from staggering around half the arena. "You okay?"

"Just fine," Tavros grunted. "Give me a minute. The room's still spinning."

"I think it's time to call a stop," Seza muttered.

Valis glanced over, and her face was swollen. Zhasina fared no better. He swung his gaze around to look at Tavros again, and noticed that his swollen lips were split, both eyes were swollen and starting to blacken, his nose was bloody, and he had red marks all along his torso. Valis feared what was below the belt hidden by his uniform pants.

And Valis wondered just how bad *he* looked. If his lover was any indication, he must be a sight to behold.

"Firil is going to have a field day," Zhasina said as she wiped a trail of blood on the sleeve of her tunic. "We're all a mess. Especially you, Tavros. I think Valis proved his point, yes?"

Tavros shrugged and winced. "Probably."

"Come on, brutes," Seza said. "Let's go get patched up before we can't stand anymore. I think the only thing keeping you two upright is adrenaline and two brain cells."

Valis limped along behind her. "You're not far wrong."

He headed to the side wall and retrieved his and Tavros's

uniform tunics, passing Tavros's to him. Neither dared to raise their arms high enough to put them on. They carried their shirts and belts over their arms, walking through the halls like they were two breaths from passing out.

When he looked over at Seza and Zhasina, they both seemed only a hair better than Valis felt. And everyone who passed them in the halls gawked. A pair of ladies let out low whistles. "Did you have fun?"

Tavros gave them a rude gesture, making them giggle. "Don't die on the way to the healer's ward!"

"Promise," Valis muttered.

When they finally made it to the healing ward and entered the sterile room, Firil came out of his office and looked at them with eyes so wide it was almost comical. "What on earth happened to the four of you?"

"Sparring sessions," Zhasina mumbled. Her swollen lips didn't allow for more coherence than that. "They went well."

"So I see," Firil muttered. "Get on the cots. Gods, you're all a mess. How bad are the injuries?"

"No idea," Valis admitted. "We've got above and below the belts."

"We at least managed to keep ours above the belts," Seza said. "We were the smart ones."

Firil rolled his eyes and went to wash his hands in the basin in the corner. "That is entirely debatable, young lady."

Seza snorted a laugh and all-but fell onto her cot. "Figured."

The Master Healer disappeared into a door at the back,

and soon he was flocked by seven assistants. He rolled his wrist toward the four of them and sighed. "We have work to do. Please ensure you update their charts. Seza, Zhasina, Valis, and Tavros."

"Yes, sir," one of the women said dutifully.

Then the healing began, and Valis lost consciousness twice. When he woke up the last time, no one stood over him and the lights were dim. Then he glanced around to find Tavros in bed beside him. It took him almost five whole minutes to realize they weren't in the healing ward anymore. When he glanced around again and blinked the blur from his eyes, he saw the familiar surroundings of their bedroom.

Rolling over, Valis stretched and let out a contented sigh. Tavros still slept on, and Valis wondered if he could make his mind blank out to follow suit.

Then his lover's eyes fluttered open and zeroed in on him. "You're awake."

"It appears so, Mister Obvious."

"Wait. How did we get in our room?"

"Not a clue," Valis admitted. "I only just woke up."

Tavros stretched and flopped onto his back. "Did it work?"

Valis took a moment to search his thoughts. The frustration was still there, but it was greatly diminished. The anger seemed just out of reach. His body felt blissfully tired, sated in a way that sex couldn't always accomplish. Closing his eyes, Valis rolled over and rested his head on Tavros's shoulder. "I think so."

"Good."

"We should get up."

Tavros pressed a kiss into Valis's hair and made a negative sound in the back of his throat. "No. Sleep, Valis. We should rest before lunch." He glanced over to the clock on their nightstand and sighed. "We have two hours. Let's make the most of it."

"Are you going to tie me to the bed?"

His husband stared at him seriously for a moment, his left brow slowly climbing toward his hairline. "Don't make me. I'm exhausted, and I want to nap with my husband."

Chuckling, Valis let his body go lax. "How can I say no to that?"

CHAPTER TWELVE

THE LONG NAP did help to erase a good bit of Valis's exhaustion. When they woke, he let Tavros lead him into the bath to scrub away the dirt and sweat from their fight in the arena. Neither of them wanted to subject their friends to their stench after such a vigorous spar. And he had to admit as he lowered into the steaming water that the bath was a great idea. His muscles all turned into putty as he submerged up to his neck and cuddled to Tavros's side. It was almost relaxing enough that he wanted to go back to sleep, but Thyran's worry that he'd nod off and drown rose in his mind and made him chuckle.

"What are you laughing about?"

Valis shrugged. "I'm still tired, and the bath feels good. I remembered Thyran's worry about drowning in the bath."

Tavros let out a snort and shook his head. "No sleeping in the bath. We need to get clean and get to lunch. Your stomach is getting noisy."

It really was. He rubbed it as it roared again. "Okay, so that's a good idea."

"All my ideas are good ones," Tavros muttered.

"Yeah. We'll go with that."

Tavros glared at him. "You think differently?"

Shrugging, Valis dunked under the water to wet his hair and started soaping it when he rose again. "Well, there was that time you had the idea to send me to prison for bearing the Mark of Qos. And when you thought I was evil because I wield black magic. Then there was the time—"

"Okay! Okay, I get it," Tavros groused. "I'm sorry."

"Long forgiven, my heart."

What was supposed to be a quick wash in the bath took half an hour because neither of them could make themselves stop soaking. Only when the water started to cool did they reluctantly get out and drain the tub so they could get dressed and change their nasty bedding.

At lunch, Valis glanced at Seza and bit his lip. The clarity that had come during the spar still shrouded him in its brightness, and he remembered the plan that had started forming in his mind after his confrontation with Brother Bachris. And that plan formed anew in his mind and grew with every breath.

"Seza, what do you and Zhasina have planned for after lunch?"

She chewed what was in her mouth and swallowed, then pointed her fork at his chest. "No more spars today."

Valis lifted both hands in a placating gesture and laughed. "Promise."

"Then nothing that can't be set aside, why?"

With a soft sigh, Valis looked down at his plate of food and tore apart his bread roll to butter it. "I want to have a meeting with the mercenaries and the Kalutakeni caravan."

She shrugged. "I'm in."

An hour later, Valis looked around the caravan. Mercenaries of all skin tones from fair to deeply tanned mingled with the darker-skinned Kalutakeni warriors. All of them looked to Valis with questions in their eyes.

"What brings you out?" Jintas, the leader of the mercenaries, asked. "You look… serious."

"This *is* serious," Valis said, squaring his shoulders. "It's a matter of life and death, and I need your help to get everything in place."

"What is it?" Venabi asked. The livid pink scar down her dark cheek pinched when she narrowed her eyes, pulling the corner of her lip up into a snarl. She was lighter than most of the Kalutakeni, but that scar was still a huge contrast, and made looking away difficult. "It is someone close to you, yes?"

Valis nodded and sighed, rubbing the back of his neck. "My father. Or, one of them. One of my fathers, Kerac, arrived home during the Autumn Festival. He was emaciated beyond belief, hanging onto life by a mere thread, and he's been tortured. I'm not at all sure how he made it home at all after what he's been through. But, my other father, Darolen, is still in that awful place. He's in a dank cell, sitting in his own filth. He's severely malnourished, and they're keeping him barely alive for some unknown reason while they've apparently killed all the other Aesriphos who were captured with him."

Jintas's face turned into a hard scowl and Valis's stomach clenched. "You mean to rescue him."

"You're damned right, I do."

The man raked his hands through his short red hair, his beard bristling with his frown. His grass green eyes stared into Valis's for a long moment before he nodded. "How can we help? Is that why you brought us all that gold?"

"Yes," Valis said. "It's to buy non-perishable supplies you'll need for the journey. The destination is somewhere east of the center of Aspar where they were captured. We're not sure about the exact location, but we'll no doubt find Qos nests along the way, and there are ways of extracting that information the closer we get to that country."

"Torture."

Valis glanced at Venabi and shook his head. "No. That isn't how I run things. But there are still ways to get that information, even if I have to enter their minds to dig it out."

"You can do that?" Vodis asked with wide eyes, the whites of his eyes stark in the midnight skin of his face.

Valis shrugged. "It came to me during a lesson with my mentor. He taught me how to block mental attacks, and I kind of learned that if I can block them, I can instigate them. And that leads me to believe I can create telepathic links with more than just my mentor if I try. It's something I have to ask him to teach me, since I believe I'm quite capable."

Valis sat on one of the newly made rough-hewn benches that surrounded a well-used fire pit in the center of the circle of caravan wagons. Since it wasn't raining, the tarp wasn't set up, and he looked up at the clear blue sky as Tavros sat beside him. Seza and Zhasina sat on his other side, Seza looking at him with a grim expression.

"You're thinking of doing this without a sanction?"

"If I can get this mission sanctioned, I'll be ecstatic," Valis muttered. "But after my meeting with Brother Bachris, who called it foolish and gave my father not a single extra spare thought, I don't have any hope for that at the moment."

She sighed and looked down at her clasped hands. "I'm with you," she whispered. "Just keep trying for a sanction, okay?"

"Definitely," Valis promised. "I want it sanctioned as bad as anyone because I'd really like to have help from more Aesriphos than just the four of us."

He sat back and looked around at the mercenaries and Kalutakeni as the leaders and most knowledgeable of the two bands of people filed into the circle and sat on the other benches ringing the fire pit.

"So we will be going into the heart of one of the enemy compounds?" Jintas asked. "Perhaps more than one?"

"Yes." Valis glanced from one set of eyes to the other and

noted the seriousness that had descended. There was no more curiosity. Now, it was all grim intent and focused attention. "I plan on infiltrating this place, rescuing my father, and if the lost god jar is anywhere near this compound, we'll add that objective to our mission.

"If we're extremely lucky—and I say this with a good amount of internal groaning—we'll run into several Qos nests on the way, and that will lead us to extracting an exact location to meet our primary objective which is rescuing my father. Anything else will be a bonus. I want to get Darolen to safety, get him into a condition where he can travel without further compromising his health, and get him home to his husband."

"We may need a bit more gold," Venabi said. "If we're leaving as soon as I think you mean to, we will be traveling in the heart of winter all too soon."

"You will have it," Valis vowed. "I'll make another withdrawal from my cache and bring it to you tomorrow or sometime within the next few days." He glanced to Jintas. "I'll bring yours here as well. I might as well just bring an entire crate. You can all divide it up how you wish. I don't expect any of you to fund any aspect of this mission from your own pockets, and I will pay you for your help."

That got the bulk of the mercenaries' attention. "Pay us?" one woman asked in a heavy Noldworian accent. "Truly?"

Valis perked a brow. "You didn't think I meant you all to go into danger for free, did you?"

"Well… we had, yes."

Valis gawped at her. "And you were willing to go, anyway?"

"Yes. Of course."

Blowing out a heavy sigh, Valis shook his head and fought back grateful tears. "Thank you. That means much. *So much.*"

"We have lived a comfortable life within these walls," Jintas said kindly. "We have enjoyed our time here. And we have made friends with some of the city's layman forces and a few Aesriphos. It has come to feel like home, lad. We have been offered permanence here with the provision that we join Cadoras's laymen forces, which we are more than happy to do since they are accommodating our strengths in war as assassins, scouts and warriors. And we owe it all to you and the kindness you showed us of letting us join you instead of throwing us all into prison where we rightly belonged."

Valis scoffed. "You didn't belong in the prison. You had no idea that Qeraden was a Qos adherent!"

"But your laws wouldn't have seen it as such without you coming to our defense. Your own Duty Captain said as much. Your voice carried the weight of our punishment from our shoulders and gave us a home. We owe you greatly."

Jintas shrugged and scratched his red beard. "And, you often come out to train with us. You didn't just abandon us the moment we were out of your care. Having you and Tavros come to train with us almost daily shows your true personalities and goes a long way to making us feel even more welcome here."

Valis shrugged. "It helps us learn different techniques than what we were taught, so it makes sense. And your group is fun." Then he grinned. "And I get to learn Noldworian better, so there's that, too."

Half the mercenaries laughed at that, at least those who understood Arlvorian did. Valis grinned brighter at them. "At least I'm honest."

"That you are, lad," Jintas said when he stopped chuckling. "Now, let us start planning. When did you want to leave?"

"That, I'm unclear on," Valis admitted. "While I want it to be soon, I also want to keep trying to get it sanctioned through the priesthood as an official mission. Father would be pissed if I did this without an official sanction, and frankly, as I said before, I want other Aesriphos to go with us to not only bolster our numbers, but to help in the fight against the Qos adherents since they're more skilled in fighting against black magic than I assume your men and women and the Kalutakeni are."

"You're right," Venabi said. "Our only Aesriphos is Zhasina. We came with her because we want to strengthen alliances with Cadoras and perhaps form a trade route to Arlvor in our country. We are unused to fighting against black magic, but we are skilled in war."

"Then yes. I'd definitely like to get more Aesriphos on board. We shouldn't go into this blindly, no matter how much I want to start our journey today. But I may need you all ready to ride at a moment's notice."

Vodis nodded and his deep, booming voice rose over the crackling of the fire that one of the other Kalutakeni had just fanned to life. "We can do this. But we will leave our wagons behind. They will slow us down. They are useful for traveling long distances at a slower pace, but with what you seem to be planning, speed will be paramount, and our wagons will do poorly in the snow."

"Then we'll need plenty of pack horses," Valis mused.

"That is taken care of," Vodis said as he motioned to their milling herd. "From all that have gone home, their horses still linger. They are strong and fast, and will be able to carry what we need."

Valis nodded. "Good. I'd also like you to ensure there is enough gold in our possession during the journey, so each pack horse should have a small stash, as well as the horses we ride. I don't want to be in a snow storm near to a village without enough gold to ensure our horses are stabled and we have warm beds and hot food in our bellies."

"You mean to travel as light as possible, then."

"Yes." Valis cracked his neck. "I want us to have food enough to reach the nearest city, clothing for both autumn and winter, bedrolls, tents, and the bare necessities. Anything else, my plan is to buy as we go. Though, if we do end up adding a band of Aesriphos to our numbers, that plan may change based on their input. If that's the case, we'll be hitching a few wagons to horses. That shouldn't slow us down much."

"No, it shouldn't," Vodis agreed. "The more provisions we take, the better prepared we are if we're caught in the open without a city when we most need it. We can prepare for this. Leave it to us."

"Thank you," Valis said with a sigh. "Truly, the journey back from retrieving your caravan was the first time I traveled with so many people. I admit that I'm unused to planning for this many people."

"We will get it done." Vodis glanced back as a stiff breeze kicked up, sending the fronds of the weeping whiptails to rustling loudly. He sniffed the wind and motioned to a group of the Kalutakeni. "Put up the tarp. Rain is coming soon."

Valis glanced at the sky. The bright blue held very few white, fluffy clouds. The sun shone bright, warming Valis's face even as the cold autumn breeze gusted, seeking the cracks in his cloak and chilling his body. It didn't seem right that rain would come soon, but he trusted Vodis's weather prediction skills more than he trusted his own.

"What do you know of the location?" Venabi asked as the Kalutakeni began raising the tarpaulin. "You sound as if you know more than you have told us."

Valis leaned back, resting his palms on the back edge of the bench. "I've scried after Father. He's in a cell, and I was able to communicate with him. All he knows is that he was captured near the center of Aspar, and that the Qos adherents had been leading them into traps due east. Another hint, is when he helped Papa escape, he said he saw they were at the base of some mountain, but he couldn't tell where."

"East of Aspar? There are a few ranges along the eastern side of the continent," Jintas said. "One that comes up through Ptheras and into the far east side of Aspar, and two that trail from the south of Endyer up through Vaynai and into Mosvol and Qhin. The one that enters Qhin branches off into a smaller range that leads up into Nonsi and Auskil."

Valis groaned. "Fuck."

Jintas shook his head and waved a negligent hand at Valis. "Relax, lad. If they were leading the Aesriphos army east, they were most likely heading for the mountains in Aspar or Endyer. There are several passes through the range in Aspar as they're smaller mountains and have carved roads throughout. The ones in Endyer are nearly impassible, however. We will narrow our choices down once we dispatch a few Qos nests as you had planned."

With that information, Valis let himself relax, even if only a fraction. He took a deep breath to calm himself and leaned against Tavros's shoulder for comfort. His husband wrapped his arm about Valis's waist and kissed the side of his head, making Valis smile.

"Thank you all for helping us," Tavros said. "We couldn't do any of this without you."

Venabi gave him a grin that looked almost sinister with the way the scar on her cheek pinched. "We're happy to help. And, I see you two have bonded. It's about time."

Valis laughed. "Yeah. We had our joining night two days

after Seza and Zhasina. I completely forgot to tell you all. I'm sorry!"

Congratulations for all four of them rose from the men and women sitting around the fire and standing behind the benches between the caravan's wagons. When they all died down, Venabi waved him away. "Go now. When you have news of whether your mission is sanctioned or not, we will discuss this further. In the meantime, we will be awaiting the gold cache so we can begin preparations in the city proper."

Valis stood with his friends, and after a round of good-byes, they headed back across the lake to the city. With Tavros at his side, the first thing Valis did was head to the vault and withdraw one of his gold caches, much to the surprise and scorn of the vault keeper. He chose the one he'd taken the bags of gold from earlier, leaving the full ones behind. Then, with the help of two passing guards, they got it outside the monastery and onto a cart.

"You're not leaving anything to chance, are you?" Tavros asked.

"Not a damned thing." Valis grunted as he shoved the chest farther back onto the wagon, then assured the wagon owner he'd be back with it before the rains came. "I want this mission to succeed and getting all the pieces on the board is the first step toward that goal."

"You've been spending too much time with Jedai," his lover mused. "You and that Harbinger's Way game."

Valis chuckled as he hauled himself into the seat at the front of the wagon and took up the reins. "Maybe. Now, get on. The sooner we get this chest to the caravan, the sooner we can get back and maybe have some time to ourselves before dinner."

He gave his husband a playful wink, showing just how much innuendo he'd packed into that sentence, because he intended to show Tavros just how much he appreciated his support today in as many positions as possible.

CHAPTER THIRTEEN

THE NEXT DAY, Valis woke from another nightmare, but this time he only woke up gasping instead of screaming, and he was able to come back to reality much faster than any night previous since he had scried and found Darolen in the darkness. Apparently, hashing out a plan with the mercenaries and the Kalutakeni had helped his mind heal some of the tears that Kerac's sudden appearance had caused. If he were honest with himself, hearing Darolen's wheezing prayers probably caused him more damage, but he didn't want to dwell on that. He was just grateful that he was able to get on with his morning without suffering through a grueling panic attack before he could start his day.

Tavros pulled him against his chest and kissed the back of Valis's neck with a lazy purr. "Another nightmare?"

"Yeah," Valis whispered. "It didn't affect me as bad as normal, though. I'm okay."

"Then can we talk a bit before we get up?" He played dirty by dragging his nose along the soft skin behind Valis's ear, knowing it would make Valis do anything he asked.

Valis let the delightful shivers cascade through him, then rolled over until he faced his husband and kissed him softly. "What is it?"

Tavros stared into his eyes for a moment and brushed a lock of hair off Valis's face, tucking it gently behind his ear. "You know I'll support you no matter what you do, right?"

Valis hesitated but nodded. "I do."

"And I don't want to see your father rot in a cell, nor do I want you to break your promises to yourself and Kerac."

Sighing, Valis snuggled closer to Tavros's front. He had to hold back not to burrow into his neck and hide from this discussion. "I know. And I know there's a 'but' coming."

Tavros smiled. "*But*, I would like you to try as hard as you can to get the mission sanctioned, no matter what happens. If Brother Bachris balks again, we can try going over his head. He's probably just worried because he's fond of you, among other things we might not know or understand."

"And if I can't get it sanctioned, no matter how hard I try?" Valis whispered.

His husband sighed and leaned in to kiss his forehead, another one of Valis's favorite things. "I'm with you no matter what, Valis. Always. I promised you before, and I promise again."

He shrugged and went on a little softer. "I just want you to try harder. And I'd really be happy if we could wait until you finish training the reliquary guards. But it was good to let the Kalutakeni know, and the mercenaries because they both want to help, and would probably be insulted if you didn't ask them to accompany you on this mission. But I think going behind the priesthood's back to garner support from others is a bit too underhanded for you. We need to do this right."

Valis let out another long sigh and closed his eyes. "I just want everything in place for when it does get sanctioned. I want as many pieces on the board as possible as I said yesterday. And to get that done, I'll do anything and everything in my power to make it happen."

Tavros frowned and cupped Valis's jaw, his thumb brushing over the shell of his ear. "What more do you have planned?"

"I want to have a talk with my translocation students and the reliquary guards today between their two classes before the translocation students depart for their other duties."

"And garner more underhanded support," Tavros said. He pressed his lips into a thin line until Valis kissed the expression off his face. "I don't like it, Valis. It doesn't feel right."

Valis shrugged and leaned their foreheads together, yet another one of Valis's favorite things. He draped his arm over Tavros's side, playing his fingertips along the bumps of his spine. "It feels right to me, though."

"A precognitive feeling?"

Another shrug and Valis nodded. "I think so, yeah. I feel like I'm being tugged down this path. Not the jerking like I get with the horrid stomach pitting, but like a gentle tug that stops when I make the right decision."

Tavros let out a long, drawn-out sigh that ended in a quiet groan. "All right. I won't argue if it's Phaerith's guidance. But, if we find out it's not, and things go sideways, we'll stop, right?"

Valis kissed him again and rolled out of bed. "Right. I don't want to put us in unnecessary danger," he said as he headed toward the lavatory. "I just want to be as ready as possible and have as many allies as we can scrounge up so we have the highest chance at success when we do leave, whether we get sanctioned or not. And," he added as he leaned against the door frame to the lavatory, "yes, I'm hoping just as hard as you are that the mission gets sanctioned, no matter what my actions might say to the contrary."

Tavros followed him into the lavatory and playfully smacked his bare ass. "You're going to turn me gray before I reach seventy."

"Only if you resist me," Valis promised with a wink. Then he proved to his husband just how he was going to make sure they both stayed young.

THE MOMENT VALIS'S TRANSLOCATION CLASS ENDED, VALIS took a deep breath and glanced at Tavros, who accompanied him. It was rare for Tavros to come to observe this class, but since their joining night, Tavros came more often than not. Now, his husband gave Valis the strength and support he needed to call on his students before they left, even if he didn't completely agree with Valis's reasoning.

"Before you leave, I'd like you all to stick around until all the reliquary guards get here. Those of you who are not Aesriphos may leave. Everyone else, please stay. Once the reliquary guards all file in, I'll have an announcement and a question for all of you, but I want to get it all done at once with as little confusion as possible."

His students all nodded. Shyvus, though, stepped forward and touched Valis's elbow. "Is everything all right? Kerac?"

Valis shook his head. "Papa is healing as well and as fast as can be expected under the circumstances. This is something else."

"Very well, then." Shyvus shook his blond head, his ice blue eyes searching Valis's face. "If I can help at all..."

"I know. That's why I asked you to stay."

With Shyvus's nod, they stood around to wait while the reliquary guards started filing in, pair by pair. Valis shucked his left gauntlet and reached over to pull Tavros's right off as well so he could link their fingers together, needing the comfort of that contact. Tavros turned a fond but concerned smile on him and squeezed his hand.

Even with the concern, Valis warmed with the show of

support. It helped him man up and call the Aesriphos to attention once everyone had gathered around him. "Please, quiet down. I have an announcement, and I would like absolute secrecy in this. Do I have your support?"

The room quieted immediately, and then murmurs of ascent rose in a quiet, respectful wave. Valis let out the breath he hadn't been holding and held onto Tavros's hand for dear life. "Thank you. This is a really sensitive subject, so your secrecy is appreciated. Please, tell no one outside of this room. If you want to speak of it, please feel free to come find me, or wait until the next class. I will always be willing to talk before and after each class, but you all know that already."

"What's wrong, lad?" Phalin asked. He stood next to his husband, Shyvus, and leaned his raven head against his lover's pale one in a brief greeting. "You look harried."

Valis shrugged. "Not necessarily harried. I'm just... doing my best. But, let's get into it." He rolled his shoulders, something he'd found himself doing often with the stress always creeping up on him. "I am trying to get a rescue mission sanctioned to retrieve my father, Darolen Jaund. He's being kept in a cell, sitting naked in his own filth, in an enemy compound at the base of a mountain somewhere east of the center of Aspar."

He let that sink in for a moment, taking in the anger and concern that raced across the faces of the men and women present. "I already have the Kalutakeni caravan who are stationed on the shore of Cadoras Lake on board, as well as the mercenary band who helped in the Battle of Tigak. But I want to make sure I have as many Aesriphos on board as possible. Because, no matter what, I *am* going, sanction or not. If I have to go alone, so be it. But I could greatly use your support."

"You mean for us to break protocol?" Xetar asked. He and his husband frowned, but Xetar's vibrant green eyes showed concern more than censure. "I cannot see the Grand Master Aesriphos refusing such a request, lad. Have you *tried* getting it sanctioned?"

Valis let out a loud sigh through puffed cheeks. "I went a round with Brother Bachris, and he was adamant that I not go. He called the mission foolish. So, I'm getting everything I can ready, just in case. Because I plan on going another round, or more, with the man. No one will keep me from finding my father. I will go through any trial, any heartache —I will go to *any length* to get him home safe and in his husband's arms."

Murmurs arose, and Valis's gut squirmed as he waited. Some of the Aesriphos present visibly balked at the idea of doing anything against regulation, but some were discussing heatedly between themselves in quiet whispers that echoed around the room in unintelligible waves. The dingy white walls seemed to close in as Valis waited for them to make up their minds. He hadn't really posed the question, but these men and women weren't stupid. They knew what Valis wanted without him spelling it out. And as Valis looked from face to face, he could almost see who was resolute, and who was still on the fence.

Tavros squeezed his hand again, and Valis pulled his shoulders from around his ears, forcing them down and trying to relieve the residual tension. With his armor on, it was almost impossible to let the tension go completely, but he tried, focusing on letting the muscles go as lax as he could manage while the Aesriphos in the room all talked amongst themselves.

"We will help," Vohan said. He shook his head, sending his short brown hair swaying around his face as he lifted his voice for all to hear. "No Aesriphos should be without their mate. *Any* Aesriphos captured should be immediately rescued if at all possible. That is in our *laws*, brothers and sisters."

He turned back to Valis and raised a brow. "The directions given are enough. We should mount a reconnaissance mission as soon as possible."

Valis gave him a solemn, thankful nod. "According to Father when I spoke to him via scry, the Qos adherents kept leading them deeper and deeper into Aspar into a trap. I'm almost positive, based on my precognitive feelings, that there are Qos nests along the way that we'll stumble across, and that we can get more information as to the compound's whereabouts along the way. The lack of an exact location is Brother Bachris's main complaint, but I'm not buying it."

"Then we should take it directly to the Grand Master Aesriphos," Kaltani said.

Netai, at her side, nodded her agreement. "The Grand Master Aesriphos is the one who has the final say. Brother Bachris would take the request to him in order to get it fully sanctioned. He could not give you a positive answer, no matter what. He would only act as a bridge to the true power of the Aesriphos force. He can, however, deny you by refusing to take the matter to the Grand Master Aesriphos for consideration, but as reliquary guards, we can do that for you."

Valis bowed at the waist in deference to their ranks. "Thank you. But, for this moment, I want to go through Brother Bachris. No matter what he's doing now, he's still my friend, and I'd rather not burn that bridge. But, if all else fails, I would greatly appreciate your support and your words reaching his ears."

More murmurs flooded the room, and Valis stood tall again, waiting for everyone to quiet down. Some were still visibly against the idea, but more had joined the group still on the fence, while others moved on to being visibly supportive if their focused attention on him with approval in their eyes meant anything.

When everyone had quieted, Valis swallowed hard. "I know this is a lot to ask of you. But I've already given a cache of gold to the Kalutakeni and mercenaries to start gathering supplies we'll need. All we need now, is for a greater force of Aesriphos to go against the Qos adherents we will come across, because no matter how much we want it to be otherwise, four against the horde will fail sooner rather than later."

Zhasina pushed to the front of the line of reliquary guards and the few Aesriphos from his translocation students, Seza trailing behind. They both stood with Valis, showing their support. "We have already pledged to Valis's cause."

"But you're just Valiants!" Kogar cried. "You can't—"

"Actually, Kogar," Shyvus interrupted with a raised hand, "these four have trained with the reliquary guards for a while, now. And they've passed their Valiant training before they even had their joining ceremonies. They're all at the base Aesriphos rank now. These four have been the most advanced Aspirants and Valiants I've ever seen, and they've earned their ranks."

Kogar sighed but acquiesced with a nod. "Very well."

Valis squeezed Tavros's hand and dropped it to clap for everyone's attention. "That's all I have for you. Translocation students, you're dismissed to your normal duties. Any of you, if you are willing to assist and go on this mission with me, leave a note in our suite with your name. And again, please keep this close. I'd rather not face Brother Bachris's ire when I'm still trying to convince him that this rescue mission isn't just a *foolish errand*."

Silence seemed to boom around the arena. Then the shuffling of feet echoed as the translocation students took their leave. Valis wasn't sure if any of them would be on his side, but from the looks on some of the reliquary guards' faces, there might be some hope with them.

"So," Phalin said as the silence stretched on too long, "what are we doing today?"

Valis shrugged. "Just more training against black magic. I think that's the most important thing at this juncture, whether you're with me in my quest or not. Any of you could get shipped out to a Qos nest at any time, and I'd like you all to be as ready as possible. I'd like to know you're coming back alive and in one piece."

"Then let's get on with it. I'm itching to try to break that shield of yours, you little rat bastard."

Laughing, Valis raised his hand. "Line up!"

CHAPTER FOURTEEN

"Burn these notes if you wish to retain secrecy. I am with you."

"If you can obtain a sanction according to regulations, I will follow."

"I am with you."

"None should be left to Qos. Count me in."

"Obtain the sanction, and I'm there, Valis."

"I'm in."

"Your fathers are great men, and it has been a privilege to call them my brothers. It would be an honor to help you in this endeavor."

"Get it sanctioned, and I would follow you anywhere."

"My sword and magic are yours if you obtain the sanction."

Valis rifled through the stack of notes with a heavy heart.

There were already dozens of them littering the low table in his sitting room. So many, but nearly all of them called for a sanction, and Valis wasn't positive he could acquire it. Still, the outpouring of support made Valis warm all over. Not one of these men and women felt like rescuing his father was a foolish endeavor.

Even thinking about those words from Brother Bachris's mouth had Valis tasting the lunch he'd just eaten searing the back of his throat. How could he have been so crass? How could he just throw away a life like that?

Valis's hands started to tremble as the familiar rage started to boil up again. It wasn't fair, and Darolen didn't deserve to be cast aside so carelessly.

But that was life, wasn't it? At least, that's what Roba had taught him before Valis ended up at the monastery and his birth father had committed suicide.

Sighing, Valis flipped through the stack of notes again, his heart sinking. Everything hinged on him getting Darolen's rescue sanctioned, and he hated it, but he couldn't blame any of the Aesriphos for that stipulation. Most of them had given hundreds of years to this monastery, and they were devout.

"If you keep staring at those pieces of paper, they're liable to catch fire," Tavros teased. He came up behind Valis and rested his chin on his shoulder. "Love, we're not done yet. Don't give up on the sanction, okay? You haven't confronted Brother Bachris again yet. Give him a chance to change his mind. And you *heard* the reliquary guards! If Brother Bachris keeps his stance, you have an entire group willing to go to battle for you to the Grand Master Aesriphos."

Valis leaned back against Tavros's chest with a groan and closed his eyes, enjoying the warmth of the hearth on his front, and the warmth of his lover against his back. "I know. I think the impatience is rearing its head again."

Tavros chuckled. "You never were a patient man."

"Nope."

"I—"

A knock on the door interrupted Tavros, and he pressed a kiss behind Valis's ear before pulling away to answer it. When he came back, all their friends followed him into the sitting room. Well, everyone except for Aryn. Having his former best friend missing rather felt like having a hole in his heart. But he covered his loss with a smile as he sat on the loveseat next to his husband. "Impromptu meeting?"

Seza nodded. "It's needed. Everyone deserves to know what we're getting ourselves into."

Valis huffed and rubbed his forehead. "Fair enough."

"So, what's going on, man?" Jedai pushed his red curls back away from his forehead. He needed a haircut, but the curls were rather endearing on the huge, muscular brute. "Seza has been cryptic as fuck."

"She's been sworn to secrecy," Valis said. "She was supposed to be cryptic. Or, rather, she wasn't supposed to say anything at all." Valis glared at her, but she stared back with a shrug, completely unrepentant.

"So...? What's going on?" Maphias asked. He wrinkled his nose. "This stinks like trouble."

"Oh, it's trouble, all right," Tavros muttered, "and it has Valis tied up in knots."

"Will *someone* just please say what's going on?" Aenali demanded. She sat on her elder brother, Jedai's lap, their auburn curls almost identical with as long as Jedai's had grown out. "Stop beating around the bush and spit it out, already."

Valis snickered at the little girl and smoothed his hand over his face. "Fine. I went to Brother Bachris the other day to get a rescue mission for Father sanctioned, and he was adamantly against it, calling it a foolish mission."

He told them the whole story, reiterating exactly—or as exactly as he remembered it—what was said during that meeting. Then he detailed that morning, asking the reliquary guards and a few base Aesriphos to stand behind him, recruiting them to his cause.

"And you have an army in the Kalutakeni and mercenaries you brought back with you from Lyvea," Jedai mused. "You *have* brought them into this, haven't you?"

"Of course, he did," Tavros said. "That was the first thing he did after Brother Bachris made his displeasure known. He's also given the groups an entire gold cache to split among them to gather supplies."

"Because, of course, Valis is going, sanction or not," Maphias muttered. "Of course, he is."

"You're not wrong," Valis said on a sigh. "You know me too well."

Maphias raked both hands through his brown hair and leaned his elbows on his knees while still holding his head. "You're going to end up getting expelled, Valis."

"I really don't care, so long as I rescue Father and retrieve the lost god jar." Valis looked around at each of his friends. "It's true that I needed the monastery to get to where I am now, to be able to wield the magic I do, to have grown my power base, and to find my mate. But..." He shrugged and held his hands out to the sides before dropping them back to his lap again. "I don't need the monastery to achieve my goals now. I just need the help of the men and women in it. I can't do it alone, but I don't necessarily *need* a sanctioned mission to complete my objectives."

He reached for the low table and tapped the neat stack of notes. "Each of these papers holds a message of support and the name of the supporter. Most of them are requesting the mission be sanctioned, yes. But they are also all willing to help me go above Brother Bachris's head in the chain of command to bring the matter up to the Grand Master Aesriphos. We're not done yet."

"I agree that it's best to get it sanctioned," Jedai said. "While you're working on that, I can start recruiting from the layman warrior ranks. Maph and I have garnered quite a few allies."

"Laymen?" Valis tilted his head. "But—"

Jedai cut him off with a hard stare. "Remember what I

told you when we first started playing Harbinger's Way? You *need* laymen. They pave the way, if for nothing more than to create diversions while you skirt around the enemy's lines of awareness to reach your goal. We're expendable, but we're necessary. And," he added, raising a finger, "most of your mercenaries are laymen, so don't try to dodge that tactic."

Sighing, Valis leaned back into the loveseat's cushions. "You have a point."

"Of course, I do."

"Then have them leave their names in here like the reliquary guards have started doing," Valis said. "Once we have enough names, I'll confront Brother Bachris again, and this time, he'll either listen, or we will go over his head."

Valis frowned and stared at the stack of names. "I'm done playing around."

ONCE EVERYONE CALMED DOWN, OR, RATHER, ONCE EVERYONE calmed *Valis* down, Seza dragged everyone through the halls toward the prison. "I hear Aryn's actually being good," she said. "We should reward that with more visits, don't you think?"

"Absolutely," Valis said. "Though, even if he wasn't doing well, we should still visit him more often. I've been so wrapped up with preparing for this mission and getting it sanctioned that—and I hate to admit this—I've forgotten all about him for the past few days."

She glanced at him from over her shoulder and smiled. "It's allowed, Valis. He's not your priority right now, and you have friends who can remind you. That's what we've done today, so don't beat your own ass over it."

Valis chuckled and gave her a solemn nod. "Yes, ma'am."

Once they got into the room with the holding cell and the door boomed shut behind them, Valis stared at his friend and sighed. Aryn was too pale, still too skinny though it appeared he had gained at least *some* weight while he had been incarcerated. The dark circles had disappeared from beneath his eyes, but he still looked exhausted and like he was about ready to give up. Valis's heart hurt for the boy, and when it was his turn in the line, he hugged Aryn through the bars as best he could and whispered, "Don't you give up, Aryn. You're stronger than this. Your incarceration is only temporary. Do you hear me?"

Aryn sucked in a sob and nodded.

"Is that face because we haven't come to see you in a few days?"

When Aryn's expression crumpled, Valis cupped his face through the bars and sighed, leaning in to press a kiss to his forehead. "I'm so sorry. Things have been so hectic, but we should have made time for you."

"It's okay," Aryn whispered. He used his braid to wipe his eyes and sniffled. "I—"

"It's *not* okay," Valis stressed. "And we *will* do better." He raised his voice just enough for the others to hear as he said,

"Even if we can't all come together, at least *one* of us will be here each day. Will that be better?"

The boy's shoulders dropped some of their tension and he nodded. "That would be great. Thank you."

"Now that that's over, how is your therapy going?"

Leaning back against the wall in his cell, Aryn scrubbed at his face with the neck of his prison uniform to dry the tears. "Sister Qisryn is my therapist. She's her usual self, and it's been going rather well. But... it's hard. I didn't know it would be this hard..."

"Any kind of therapy is hard," Seza said, though she kept her tone gentle. "Just think of what Kerac has to go through with his physical therapy to get his mobility back. And then there's therapy to get his stomach strong enough for solid food again." She shrugged. "It's hard work, but like any work, it will pay off by the end."

"Sister Qisryn says my therapy may never end," Aryn said in a small voice.

"That doesn't mean it won't get easier," Maphias said. "Just like with physical therapy. The more you do it, the easier it gets, but you'll still benefit from it in the long run."

"I guess..."

"No guessing about it, man." Jedai tapped the bars with his large knuckles and smiled. "You won't start believing it until you look back on all this and realize you actually *have* gotten better, and while you may not be fully recuperated, you're stronger than you were, and you'll have that huge boost to push you to reach higher."

Aryn snorted. "How do you figure?"

Jedai shrugged and tapped his chest. "I used to be a tall, scrawny twig with large bones that made me look ridiculous. It was hard as anything, and I hated it. But I put myself through trials. I did the exercises. I did the dead-drag. I ran. I ate right. And I did all that twice—sometimes three times—a day for years and still do today. And, well... look at me." He spread his arms wide, showing off his broad shoulders, biceps that strained his tunic, bulky chest, thick neck, and powerful thighs the loose uniform pants couldn't hide. "I'm not a twig, and I actually enjoy exercise now. It will eventually be the same for you. Just you watch."

Aryn still looked dubious, but he stopped arguing and conceded to Jedai with a short nod. "I'll keep that in mind."

"You'd better."

Valis smiled at his friends and rubbed his chest. For Aryn's sake, he hoped the boy did well. And then a thought hit him. "Isn't there anything positive you can think of about therapy? Something that you enjoy that you might not realize?"

His friend frowned and glanced down toward his feet as he thought. Then Aryn lifted a shoulder. "She always brings me a sweet, or 'sneaks' me in a cup of tea, though we all know the guards know full well she's got it." He sighed and glanced around the room, not settling on anyone as if what he was about to say next was something he wasn't proud of. "And she's motherly. She's always been nice to me, so I do kind of like spending time with her, even if she does ask me to do things that I don't like."

"Like what?" Zhasina asked curiously.

"Like going into details about my obsession with Valis, when I don't know them, myself. Or talking about Tavros. Just... she asks questions I don't always know the answer to, and when I do know the answers, she asks me to keep going, and... it's horrible. It hurts."

Valis went up to the bars again and reached inside, taking hold of Aryn's hand, making the boy look up at him. "Did you ever ask her why she does that, why she asks those questions?"

Aryn shook his head and bit his lip. "No. I figured it was punishment."

"Oh, Gods, no, Aryn," Seza said. "No, no, no. It's not punishment. She's trying to help you get everything out so you can work through it. You can't work through a problem if you don't know what the problem is. She's trying to help you find it so you can solve it. She's *guiding* you, not punishing you. I promise, Aryn. She would never do such a thing."

"I think that should be your assignment for your next therapy session with her," Maphias said. "Ask her to explain what she's doing and why. Because, the more you understand, the less you fight against change. It's always been like that since you came to the monastery. From getting up earlier to taking on new duties, you've always needed a *reason* to change."

Aryn cringed but nodded. "Yeah… You're right."

"I know I am, you shit. I still remember that black eye you gave Tav your first morning."

Tavros snorted and rubbed at his eye. "I remember that, too. It wasn't pleasant. I just wanted to hug my baby brother, but he punched me with his tiny, bony fist, instead."

Valis wasn't sure, but he thought he heard Aryn huff a small laugh. He glanced over, and Aryn's lips twitched as if he was trying to suppress a smile. Valis wanted to see a real smile, so he said, "Serves you right for sneaking up on a sleeping man. Ever heard of knocking. Some big brother you were."

Aryn covered a giggle with his hand and shook his head. "Oh, he knocked. I just refused to answer, hoping he'd go away. Then he came in and leaned over the bed for the hug, saying 'Good morning!' in this annoyingly bright, cheerful voice. It irritated me because I was still exhausted, and the knock gave me a slight panic attack, so when he tried for that hug, I did the only thing I could think of to get him to back off."

"It worked, damn it," Tavros muttered. "I've never touched him to wake him up since. I usually throw something at his head if he's needed before his normal waking time."

"Are your roommates good?" Valis asked. "Do they leave you alone?"

"Ugh." Aryn covered his face with both hands and groaned. "I had a panic attack my first night because I was in with three other men, and they wouldn't shut up and kept leering at me. So they put me in solitary. I... admit I like it better. It's the same kind of cell, just smaller and with a single cot. It doesn't have a bench like the multi-person cells, but I don't mind sitting on the bed, and there's enough room to move a bit."

He sighed and looked up to the ceiling. "I just wish they would give me something to read. I'm so bored in there."

"I'll see what I can do," Valis said. "That's a reasonable request. I don't see them denying it."

"Really?" And Gods, the hope in Aryn's eyes and voice shot Valis right through the chest, making his breath hitch.

"Yeah," he said. "Really."

"I know what kind of books you like," Aenali said. She shoved her way to the front so Aryn could see her. "I'll pick out two each day, and give them to the Duty Captain, and collect the ones you've read to take back to the library."

"Thanks, 'Nali." He blew a breath through his nose and glanced from one set of eyes to another. "Thank you all. But... why haven't they called time yet?"

Valis grinned. "The reliquary guards who guard the prison on rotation are in my class in the mornings as my students. I asked for extra time, and they didn't argue."

"You clever man."

Winking, Valis grinned. "Less clever, more resourceful." He stood up to his full height from where he was slouched down against the bars. "But, our time really is up. We should be heading up to get our afternoon duties done before dinner. Someone, though, will be by to see you tomorrow if all of us can't come."

"Thank you." Aryn's eyes filled with tears and he clutched at the bars. "Thank you…"

"Get better," Valis said, covering one of Aryn's hands. "Get better and get out of here. We'll all be waiting for you, brother. Always."

When they left, Tavros pulled him close, wrapping an arm about his waist. "Thank you," he whispered. "For giving my baby brother hope. I don't think I could have done it."

"We all need some hope," Valis murmured against his jaw, then kissed it. "If I have to, I'll have enough hope for us all."

CHAPTER FIFTEEN

EVER SINCE THEY got back to Valis's room, Valis couldn't shake the nagging feeling that he was missing something. But as he progressed through his duties, that nagging feeling started moving from his chest down to his gut. Was it gas? Did he have a massive amount of trapped wind? It didn't rumble in his gut, so he doubted it. One could hope though.

And then the pitting started. Ah, there it was. Valis groaned as he doubled over. He didn't miss that sensation whatsoever, and when Tavros rubbed the back of his neck, Valis almost wished he'd take a hint and guided Valis toward a bed where he could curl up in the fetal position.

"Gods, Valis. Are you ill?"

"I wish," Valis gasped between gulps of air. "Precognitive pitting. Gods, I forgot how much it hurts."

"They don't usually double you over like this," Tavros said. "It's *that* bad?"

"Not quite." Valis slowly rose to a somewhat more upright position and clutched at his gut. "It just took me by surprise. I thought I'd had gas."

Tavros erupted with peals of laughter until he leaned against the wall and wheezed. "Only you," he croaked. He cleared his throat and wiped the tears from his eyes. "Only you could think precognitive feelings are possible farts. Shit, Valis."

Valis shoved Tavros back into that wall. "Asshole." That just made Tavros laugh again. Unable to help himself, Valis started chuckling, too, and snatched Tavros's hand, trailing him behind like a banner in the wind on his way to the dining hall.

Even with the pitting dropping his gut through the floor, having this lighthearted moment felt amazing after all the anger and tension Valis had wrapped around himself the last few days. Laughing felt amazing, and he felt good going to dinner, like he might actually enjoy his food and his friends without his problems swamping him, precognitive pitting be damned.

Heading into the dining hall, Valis's stomach dropped through the floor again, and Tavros gripped his arm to keep him from falling on his face. "You okay, love?"

"It's getting worse."

"You shouldn't ignore it," he murmured, guiding Valis toward the serving line.

"I have no other choice." He shrugged, picked up a tray and started filling it with food, though not the mountain he usually ate. If his gut was going to keep doing this, he didn't want to waste a ton of food, and he could always come back for more.

"And I hate that you have no other choice," Tavros muttered. "It isn't fair that you get precognitive feelings and can't do anything about them."

"Tell me about it." Valis huffed and filled his mug with spiced milk, grabbed a set of utensils, and led the way to their table to join their friends.

Once he sat down, he doubled over and almost planted his face in his pile of mashed potatoes. His friends all stared at him wide-eyed, and all Valis could do was give them a small smile. "I'm okay. Or, I will be eventually."

"Precognitive pitting," Tavros told the group. "Too bad it's not a vision so we could do something about it."

Valis groaned. That was the last thing he wanted. Falling into a vision was something he didn't ever want to do at the dinner table. But he had to admit that Tavros was right. If he could see what was coming, the pitting might stop.

He got halfway through his meal when Seza gasped. "Oh, fuck."

"What is it?" Valis asked. He glanced up at her and that pitting sensation nearly made him lose his dinner. He swallowed hard to keep his food down. When he glanced over his shoulder to see what Seza was staring at, his stomach tried to rebel again.

Brother Bachris stormed through the room, his expression twisted with fury and his eyes locked onto Valis with such intensity that Valis wondered if he would soon burst into flames under that glare.

"Valis." His name from Brother Bachris's mouth sounded like an explosion. "I would like to speak with you. *Now*."

Thankfully, Valis was mostly done eating. His stomach couldn't handle much more with the precognitive feelings trying to send everything back up. But he'd have liked to spend more time with his friends. Still, Brother Bachris looked like he wouldn't wait, no matter what excuse Valis tried to make.

"Get up, boy," he demanded, his voice hard and loud. "Don't just sit there and stare. Come with me and be quick about it."

Tavros jumped to his feet, sending his chair skidding back with such force that it toppled over with a loud clatter of wood on stone. He rounded on Brother Bachris, his face in a determined scowl. "This is bullshit, Brother. If you're going to talk to Valis, you will do it after he has finished eating, and you will do it with *civility*. Do you understand? He isn't a dog. He is a *person*, and he is a respected mentor of this monastery's elite forces. He deserves enough respect for you to *ask* for a damned meeting. You don't just come into a crowded dining hall and spike his fucking anxiety by loudly demanding his obedience in front of his peers. Have you gone mad?"

Brother Bachris narrowed his eyes at Tavros, but before

he could speak, Valis grabbed Tavros's wrist and tugged until his husband looked down at him. Every eye was on them, and Valis had to appear in control and unaffected. "Calm down, Tav. It's fine."

"It is *not* fine! I'm tired of him treating you like you're nothing."

It took effort, but Valis managed to keep his thankful, affectionate smile from his face. "I know. We'll deal with it. Let's just go and hear him out."

Valis remained seated for only a breath more before he stood and followed Brother Bachris out into the hall. The moment he left the entry to the dining hall, the Patron Priest started in on him as if Tavros hadn't just tore him down in the dining hall.

"What is the meaning of this? Are you mad, boy?"

Tilting his head, Valis furrowed his brows. "What do you mean? What have I done?"

"You know full well what you have done!" Brother Bachris began pacing the width of the hall, from one wall to the other, his head shaking as if he couldn't believe Valis's gall to be so foolish in whatever he'd done wrong. "How dare you?" he went on. "How *dare* you start recruiting troops for this *foolish* mission? It's suicide, Valis. I will not allow it. And you know this. Yet you go behind my back, subverting me, ignoring my order."

He glared at Valis, stopping his pacing and advanced on him, pointing a finger at his chest. "You know I could have you tossed into prison for this."

No, Valis didn't. But he wasn't about to tell Brother Bachris that. He wasn't about to open his mouth for anything until the Patron Priest finished his tirade.

"You will cease this nonsense, Valis, and continue with your studies, training, and await *official* orders. Do you understand?"

Finally, Valis had had enough. He advanced on his friend, got up in his face. "Nonsense? *Nonsense?*" He balled his fists at his side. "Do you really believe that my desire to rescue my *father* is foolish *nonsense*? Because if you *do*, I really need to rethink our friendship."

The Patron Priest didn't back down. He was as tall as Valis even though he was thin as a reed. That bony finger wagged under Valis's chin as Brother Bachris went on. "You will stop this! You cannot just go around in secrecy and recruit this monastery's elite forces to your will! That is not how this institution is run, young man. That is not how you get a mission sanctioned. And, that is not how you rescue your father. Because, he is *gone*, Valis. You *must* accept that. He will be dead before you even get halfway to where he is being kept. There is no way that man will survive long enough for any sort of rescue attempt. It isn't possible. So, yes. It *is* a foolish endeavor!"

The only reason Valis hadn't interrupted him in that speech was because each word felt like they stabbed through him, rendering his heart and guts to shredded meat. How could he be so crass? How could he be so heartless? Trembling with the surge of betrayal and rage, Valis had to keep reminding himself that Brother Bachris was his friend, a mentor, and not his enemy. Because with every beat of his heart that red tinge he thought he had outgrown threatened to encroach on his vision.

"How dare you?" He hissed through his clenched teeth and advanced another step, making the Patron Priest back up. "Would you say that if it was Sister Qisryn who had been captured? Or you son? Maybe your grandchildren? Would you be so heartless then? Would you throw their lives away as *foolish* or *impossible* when you had assurances from Phaerith that it *was* possible?"

Brother Bachris paled but still didn't back down. "How do you know you have such assurances? That isn't possible."

"Isn't it, though? Or have you closed your ears when I told you I spoke directly to Sovras when I was knocked out of my body on our way back from rescuing the caravan? Are you calling me a liar now? Do you dare?" Valis perked a brow. "Thyran believes me, and he knew Sovras in life. But, you? You hadn't even been born yet."

He pressed in again, making Brother Bachris take another step back. "You can keep your disbelief all you wish, Brother. But I know it's possible because that's the only way Kerac could have ridden from that far in the state he was in. Slumped over the back of his horse the way he was, it wasn't just Cadoras's pull that brought him home. And—"

"That was just sheer luck, my boy. And Phaerith's blessing upon Kerac that he be spared!"

"Bullshit," Valis spat. "It's well known that mates don't

survive long after they're separated from their partners. It's documented. How long would Kerac survive after Darolen dies in that prison? We'd save him, rehabilitate him, and for what? Fatten him up and get him moving for him to die, anyway? Are you really that dense?"

"See here, young man! That's—"

"It makes sense!" Valis roared. "You're ignoring the obvious!"

"Your father would be ashamed of you." Brother Bachris tilted his chin up with a condescending sneer. "He would never approve of you talking to anyone in such a manner."

Hands grabbed Valis as he launched toward the Patron Priest. If they hadn't, he would have punched his friend and felt absolutely no remorse. The reliquary guards, Cassavin and Nevesar, held Valis at his sides, keeping him in place. "Easy Valis," Cassavin said. "Not here. Not now."

"You have gone too far, Brother Bachris," Shyvus said. "That was completely uncalled for, and *you* should be ashamed of yourself for treating an Aesriphos in such a manner."

Xetar growled from somewhere behind Valis, as if he were right behind him, looking over his shoulder. "Such complete disregard for the health and safety of one of us is a disgrace to our Order."

A warm, familiar hand brushed Valis's low ponytail over his shoulder and started massaging the back of his neck. Valis leaned into Tavros's touch with a soft sigh, doing his best to let go of his anger, but not really succeeding. He needed to calm down before he did something he would regret—before he did anything *everyone present* would regret.

Brother Bachris raised his voice, his face going red. "He is disgracing the Aesriphos order by subverting the chain of command!"

Valis tensed again, balling his fists as he tried to launch himself at the Patron Priest again. Cassavin and Nevesar never let up on their grip, keeping him back. "I was garnering support in hopes that you would change your mind when I asked for a sanction again! Almost every Aesriphos who has pledged to my cause made it clear that they wanted this mission sanctioned before they would lend their full support. Next time, get all the facts before you start in on your crusades."

"You insolent—"

"Enough!" Vohan's shout echoed through the hall, making even those eating in the dining hall go stone silent. "Valis is correct. He did say he was trying to get it sanctioned. He demanded secrecy to prevent *this*."

Valis strained against the women's hold. "I haven't ever felt this betrayed by one of my friends since Aryn, and he tried to kill his own brother, my *mate*."

Brother Bachris paled, and his hand fluttered to his throat before clutching his tunic at his chest. Apparently, *that* finally reached him. He sputtered nonsense for a moment before Phalin, Shyvus's husband, stepped between them. "I think it's best if you stop talking, Brother. Please."

Valis, still trembling with rage, shook off the women at

his side and moved Phalin aside to stare at Brother Bachris. "I *won't* stop. Not ever. I *will* get this sanctioned whether you like it or not. And if I don't? I will go alone if I have to. No one has the right to keep me from saving one of the first two people who gave a single fuck about an abused, terrified little farm boy who didn't believe in trust."

He sneered at Brother Bachris. "And you know, it's a good thing I have men and women here to remind me that that little farm boy was wrong, because you have seriously broken my trust, and I doubt you will earn it back anytime soon."

With that, he stormed off, Tavros swiftly catching up to stay by his side. If he hadn't left, he would have either punched the Patron Priest, or started crying from the intense emotions pummeling him.

Several footsteps followed, and Valis glanced back to see Cassavin, Nevesar, Vohan and Xetar following him. It seemed Phalin and Shyvus had remained behind to keep Brother Bachris from following and making Valis punch him. He vowed to thank them when he saw them next, figuring they wouldn't be far behind.

When he made it to the suite, Tavros guided him into the sitting room and onto the loveseat. He massaged Valis's fists until they relaxed, then held Valis's hands while the others filed into the room and took seats.

"Are you okay, lad?" Cassavin asked. "That was... intense."

"It was a clusterfuck," Vohan growled. "Shit, *I* almost

punched him. I'm surprised you had that much restraint, Valis. I'm proud of you."

Valis snorted and shook his head. "If Cass and Nev hadn't held me back, I'd have decked him twice. Thank you, ladies."

"It was self-preservation," Cassavin muttered. "We still need you to keep training us, damn it."

"I wonder what his problem is," Xetar said, almost as if to himself. "He's not one to be this crass or this stubborn. He is normally a very easy-going man, jovial and kind, quiet and unassuming. This evening, he was a terror, and in the worst way. He usually would never behave in such a manner, let alone say some of the things that came out of his face tonight."

Valis nodded. "I agree. That's not what hurt the most, but it was a close runner."

Tavros wrapped his arm about Valis's shoulders and pulled him into his side. His warmth helped Valis somewhat relax. Thank all the gods they had removed their armor and bathed before dinner. He shifted slightly, stuffing his face in the curve of Tavros's neck and breathed him in, closing his eyes and letting himself just get lost in his lover for a moment. Right now, Tavros was the only thing keeping him grounded, and he desperately needed to calm down so he could think through things rationally, instead of through the lenses of hurt and betrayal. Those lenses would do more harm than they would any sort of good.

A few moments later, someone knocked on the door to their suite, and Cassavin got up to answer. When she returned, Phalin pushed a cart in and started handing out plates. "Since our dinner was rudely interrupted, I thought we could all use a little bite in polite, *calm* company."

"That's amazing," Valis said. "Thank you. Now that I'm calming down, I *am* getting a little hungry."

"I figured," Shyvus said, a tease in his voice. "You always eat more than you weigh, and when I saw you in the serving line, you didn't fill your plate nearly as high as usual, and then you didn't eat more than a few bites of what you *did* have before Brother Bachris pulled you away and you both started shouting the place down."

Valis sighed and rubbed his eyes before accepting the silverware to start in on his food. He smiled when Phalin set a steaming mug of the creamy spiced tea that he sometimes indulged in on the low table before him. "Thank you."

"I noticed you drink it when you're stressed," Shyvus said. "I thought it might help."

"It will. Thank you. And thank you for keeping Brother Bachris from following. I really needed to get away from him."

"You are quite welcome, lad. Now eat up."

They all went quiet as they tucked into their food. No one spoke until Valis's plate was empty, and he'd stacked it back onto the cart. Even after he sat down again and cuddled into Tavros's side carefully so his husband wouldn't spill his food, the silence remained. But, it was mostly comfortable. Just the sounds of eating, and the crackling fire that Nevesar had stoked to life once she added a few more logs.

It was... *peaceful*, which felt strange after the tension of only a little while ago.

Then, his other friends, Seza and Zhasina, along with Maphias, Jedai and Aenali, filed through without a knock. Then again, they all knew they didn't need to. They were family.

"Well, that was an epic clusterfuck if I've ever heard one," Seza said. "Are you okay, Valis? That couldn't have been easy for you."

"Yeah. I'm getting there." He gave her a soft smile, and she must have taken that as good enough, because she nodded and took the other loveseat with Zhasina by her side.

"The entire dining hall heard that mess," Jedai muttered. "I'm so sorry that happened to you."

"Shit, the entire floor probably heard it," Vohan said around a mouthful of roll. "Neither of them were quiet."

"But, let's shelve that discussion for now," Cassavin said. "We're here to calm Valis down, not rile him up again."

Murmured apologies went around the room, and Valis's chest warmed. "Thank you."

"At least you got some food into you," Zhasina murmured. "You had barely even touched your plate. I was worried."

"All thanks to Shyvus and Phalin," Valis said. "They saved my stomach."

Zhasina smiled at the two. "Thank you for your kindness."

"Well," Shyvus said, "it was either that, or the lad would eat *us*, so it was more like self-preservation."

Laughing felt so good. When Valis glanced around at the faces in his sitting room, he sighed and leaned deeper into Tavros's side.

Sovras... thank you for my family. I couldn't have asked for better.

CHAPTER SIXTEEN

THE NEXT MORNING, when Valis was about to dismiss his translocation students, he called for them all to stop. "I'd like you all to stick around. If you have other plans for the next three hours, and they're important, you may leave. But I'd like those of you who are *not* reliquary guards to observe the reliquary guard class. You will all be learning these things eventually unless this war suddenly comes to an end and the need has been negated.

"But since that is unlikely, I would like you all to be prepared. You have all started training—or should have, at least—on how to cast via intent and how to do other things. What I now train the reliquary guards in is defending against, what we think is, the power of the Sovereign Priest of Qos."

"What?" Averni asked. "How?"

Valis shoved a ball of black magic into his left hand and raised it up. "From all the Qos adherents and Priests of Qos I have drained since my birth father gave me *his* magic and life force, essentially making me a High Priest of Qos in power, my power base has continued to grow exponentially with every bit of magic I draw in."

"And you unleash it on a regular basis at our faces," Netai muttered as she walked in. "One of these days, I'm going to best you, you little vermin."

Valis chuckled. "I eagerly await that day, my friend. That's what I'm training you for."

She gave him a solemn, respectful nod. "Fair enough."

Once all the reliquary guards entered, Valis straightened his spine and glanced around. "Translocation students, line up against that far wall for observation and erect a shield. I will also be shielding you just in case something catastrophic happens because mine are far stronger. Everyone else, into formation."

"That isn't giving me the warm and fuzzies," Stavlen groused. "Catastrophic?"

Valis looked at him seriously and nodded. "There is always, *always* a chance that I will succumb to the darkness. During this training, Tavros is always by my side because he knows how to bring me back into the Light. And I've gotten better at avoiding that fate. But, I'm not about to risk your lives by having no safeguards in place when that chance still exists."

Stavlen paled but nodded. "I appreciate that. Thanks."

Chuckling, Valis grinned at him and headed to his usual spot in the corner closest to the entry so he could stop the attacks if anyone appeared there. Then he cast the golden shield wall around his translocation students, broke it off from himself after giving it permanence, and rolled his shoulders. "You all know the drill. Let's begin."

Several hours later, Valis was about to call an end to the class. Everyone looked exhausted, and truly, Valis did put them through trials greater than he had in the past weeks. But when he opened his mouth, several reliquary guards winced and shuddered. Cassavin shook her head as if trying to rid herself of a mental fog. "Thyran requests our presence. You, too, Valis."

"Class dismissed," Valis called. "Good work today. Go rest for a bit and get breakfast."

Truthfully, Valis wanted to go straight to breakfast, but he'd never disobey direct orders from Thyran. He was one man Valis trusted with his life.

As he entered the reliquary with the eighteen reliquary guards who were telepathically summoned, Valis almost felt like he didn't belong. It wasn't a feeling he got from any of the people present, but something else.

He glanced at Thyran, and the historian smiled at him, his fierce blue eyes twinkling as merrily as usual, but there was a serious cast to his countenance.

"Am I here for scrying practice while you speak with these reliquary guards?"

Thyran shook his head. "No. You deserve and need to be here because you are the one who discovered the fact that there are anchors to Qos. These men and women are the anchor teams and will soon be dispatched on the mission to eradicate the three anchors remaining, so we can move ahead with our plans."

Something in Valis's chest eased, and he nodded. "Good idea."

"But, sir?" Cassavin stepped forward, a frown on her face. "Some of us made promises…"

Valis laid a hand on her armored shoulder. "This is just as important, Cass."

"No, Valis." She turned to him, fire in her eyes and a hard set to her pouty mouth. "It may be important, but so is what we all pledged ourselves to." Valis smiled at her as she tried so hard not to let on about the mission to rescue his father, doing her best to keep the secrecy.

"You can smile at me like that all you want, but I won't budge."

Thyran sighed and sat on the edge of the table. "I am well aware that you and many other Aesriphos have pledged to help Valis." He shrugged negligently and gave Valis an apologetic look. "I have had a vision, and according to it, I cannot interfere with that quest. And Valis is well aware that I can be in his mind, seeing what he sees and hearing his thoughts at any given time." He turned back to the reliquary guards and held his hands out to his sides. "I will do what I can with regard to the sanction, but for the rest of you, your pledges to help eradicate the threat to our world is more important. With Valis's help, we have a clear direction to take, and as some of the best Aesriphos we have, I need the eighteen of you to take on these three missions."

"Three?" Nevesar asked.

Thyran nodded. "Valis said there are four anchors. His birth father was one, and he is dead, as you know. Valis also found out that there is a short time between the death of an anchor and the appointing of another, so we need to attack as fast as we can to eradicate the other three. Only then can we go after our ultimate goal and rid the world of the Sovereign Priest of Qos, and in turn, find the last god jar."

Cassavin gasped and clutched her hand against the breastplate over her heart. "You mean this could all end soon? Truly?"

"It is possible, yes," Thyran said. "I will make no guarantees, but if things go to plan, then yes. It could, potentially, all be over within a year or so."

She closed her eyes and covered her face. "Gods. Yes..." Dropping her hands, she looked over at Valis, unshed tears in her eyes. "I am so sorry, Valis, but—"

"No," Valis said. "I get it. This is more important, and I have a ton of allies to help. If you finish this quest early, we can contact each other via two-way scry and you can meet up with us if I can get this mission sanctioned. It isn't over, Cass. It's just delayed."

She gave him a beautiful smile and nodded. "Thank you."

"Thank you for your support," Valis replied. "I can't thank you and the others enough."

Thyran clapped his hands and folded them on his lap. "Now that we have that settled, let us get this underway." He nodded to Valis. "Valis will spend some time scrying. I would like one of you to write down what he sees and hears, as if he is successful, these notes will become part of your orders. It is apparent that he sometimes sees what I cannot."

He slid off the edge of the table and picked up a parchment. "Cassavin and Nevesar, you and your team will be heading to Ges to take down Angas Braywar." He rattled off the rest of the names, assigning six reliquary guards to each of the three anchors: Angas Braywar, Carnis Doveran, and Valis's maternal aunt Ortima.

"Are there any questions?"

The silence spoke for everyone. Valis had a ton of questions, and he was certain everyone else did, too, but they were all too stunned and subdued to ask them.

No one stepped forward, so Valis cleared his throat. "I'm ready to start scrying whenever my scribe is ready. Let's get this done. I assume the anchor teams will be leaving in a few days instead of in the morning, right?"

Thyran nodded. "Yes. They will have enough time to say their goodbyes, get their gear packed, and give their final report on the lessons you have been teaching them. They will leave day after tomorrow."

Nodding, Valis glanced at the others. "Why don't you all take a seat and start writing that report now so that you have more time to relax and prepare before you leave." He glanced back at Tavros who had just entered and closed the reliquary door behind him. Valis smirked and held out his hand. "Tavros can be my scribe like he was when we were reading Roba's books."

"I think that is a fine idea," Thyran said. "You all can either stay to write your reports or go on about your business and I will summon you once your orders are finalized."

No one left, and soon the long table in the center of the reliquary had a butt in almost every seat. He watched them for a moment before shucking his gauntlets and laying them on a side table. Tavros followed suit, and they headed to the alcove where Valis's scrying bowl sat. Or, at least the scrying bowl that he used when he was here for training. His own bowl sat dry in his suite's bedroom. And honestly, he would have preferred to do his scrying in there where he wasn't hemmed in by stacks of books. But he needed to be here in order to pass along any important information the reliquary guards or Thyran might need immediately.

Still, he wished for the comfort of his own room where all he could smell was cool stone, Tavros, and *home*.

How strange that the monastery itself was home, but he felt more at home in a room he'd only had for a short time.

But, he pushed that thought aside and filled the bowl with the nearby pitcher of water. He had to clear his mind, get his focus honed so he could get this done and get to breakfast. Already his stomach was complaining noisily that he had expended a lot of energy and it needed fuel. Tavros quietly chuckled at his side, his eyes crinkled at the corners as he stared at Valis's armor-covered gut. "Do you want me to bring you something to tide you over?"

"No." Valis sighed and rubbed a hand over his face. "I want to get this done and have a real breakfast where I can sit down, relax, and enjoy my food. And, hopefully we'll be done by the time the others are up to eat so we can have breakfast with our friends."

"Sounds like a great idea. We don't get that luxury often anymore."

"No, we don't," Valis agreed. "We should start making it a point to have a snack after training the reliquary guards and waiting to eat a full breakfast with our friends while we're all still here."

"You really think you can get this mission sanctioned?"

Valis turned to look into Tavros's eyes. "Yes, I do. If I hadn't before, then what little Thyran said about his vision makes me believe that we have a very good chance at success."

"Then I'm with you," Tavros vowed, and punctuated it with a chaste kiss. "Always."

Valis smiled and kissed Tavros again, then focused on the bowl, clearing his mind and intent on the missions ahead for his students and friends. An hour or so later, Tavros had a good list, and Valis's eyes felt like they contained sand. He staggered out of the alcove, Tavros trailing behind, and almost missed the chair he aimed himself at.

"Rough time scrying?" Nevesar teased. "You look like ass."

"I feel like it, too." Valis rubbed his eyes again. Soon, someone pulled his hands away and tilted his face up. Cassavin pressed a kerchief into his hands and smiled down at him. "I'm going to rinse your eyes. It will help that sensation go away. Keep the kerchief to wipe up the mess."

Relaxing, Valis let her pry open his eyelids and drip a few drops of water from a pitcher onto his eyeball. He blinked several times, mopping up the run-off. After she did it to the other eye, and repeated it twice for each eye, Valis groaned from the relief. "Ugh. Thank you. That is so much better."

She patted his cheek and went back to her seat. Then, Valis sat back and relaxed as the others finished their reports. While they waited, Tavros added bits to his notes and handed them off to Thyran.

"You boys go on to breakfast," Thyran said. "I'm sure someone here will bring you news of their final orders when things are settled." He grinned up at Valis. "I could hear your stomach complaining all the way over here when you were scrying. Go feed it."

Valis laughed. "Yes, sir. Thank you."

They made it to breakfast just in time to get behind their friends in the serving line in the dining hall. Apparently Seza and Zhasina waited to eat with their friends, too, because they got in line behind Valis and Tavros.

"What took you so long?"

Valis glanced back at Seza and smiled. "I had to scry to help with orders for the three anchor teams. Thyran is sending out eighteen men and women in three days, six for each anchor. He wanted my assistance to give them a better chance at success."

She nodded and grimaced when Valis's stomach let out another loud peal. People from the surrounding tables chuckled at him, and Valis felt heat start to creep up his throat.

"I swear, your stomach acts like you never feed it," Seza said, knocking her knuckles on his breastplate. "It's always so noisy."

Chuckling, Valis filled his plate, got his spiced milk, and headed to their table. Aenali sat up straighter. Jedai set her tray in front of her, then went back to the serving line to get his own breakfast. When he left, Aenali pointed her small forefinger at him. "Why were you crying?"

Valis shook his head. "Wasn't crying. My eyes were so gritty from scrying that Cass poured some water in my eyes to rinse them out."

"Oh, okay. Your lashes were wet, and I was about to go off on someone."

Leave it to the little girl to make Valis's chest feel three sizes too small for his heart. He sighed and tucked into his food. Before long, he was so zoned into filling his belly, completely lost in the taste, that he didn't hear anything until Seza poked his cheek.

He blinked up at her. "Huh?"

She rolled her eyes and shook her head. "You and your food obsession. I asked if you were going to see Aryn today."

Valis frowned down at his food and thought for a moment. "No. Not today. I need to spend time with Papa and get some things done in preparation for the anchor teams leaving."

"What things?" Seza asked. She tilted her head and stared at him. "You're not planning to sneak off with one of the teams, are you?"

"Oh, no," Valis said. He waved that thought away with his fork and speared another piece of sausage. "I just want to make more notes on each of the anchors from what I remember of the visions so I can give them to each team. I also want to make sure they all have enough gold to see them through the mission, because it's most likely going to be a long one, especially for the team headed for Evakis to deal with my aunt." He shrugged. "Just little things, you know?"

She smiled kindly at him. "Sometimes, it's the little things that matter the most, if not to the mission itself, then to their morale."

Valis nodded. But her words stayed with him for the rest of his meal. He rolled them over in his head, because something about it felt precognitive, like a tug from Sovras that it was important. Was it immediately important, or would it be important in the future?

He sighed and sat back to enjoy his spiced milk now that it was cool enough to drink. He wondered if he could get away with some of that creamy spiced tea, but thought better. It sometimes made him sleepy, and he couldn't afford that right now. It was strange, though, because it usually helped wake everyone else up. Why was he so different in that regard?

"What has your forehead bunched this time?" Aenali asked. "You're thinking too hard. You should stop doing that. You'll injure yourself."

Valis almost choked on his spiced milk. When he could breathe again, he shrugged. "Seza's words felt precognitive."

"About morale?" Seza asked.

"Yes."

"Then you should see what you can do to help boost their morale even more." She shrugged. "Maybe we can all do something to help. It wouldn't hurt and may help in ways we can't foresee."

"Like what?"

She shrugged again and sipped her tea. "Don't know, but we'll figure something out. But, Aenali can draw them pictures if she wants. They'd find that adorable and cherish them."

"I can!" Aenali said. "I'd like that."

"Thank you." Valis's throat felt tight, but he smiled. "There are eighteen going after the anchors, if you're really interested in something like that."

"I'll write them letters on the backs of the drawings," she added. "I'll need all their names."

"You shall have them," Tavros said. "I'll write them down after we get back from breakfast."

With his friends all trying to think of things they could do or give to the anchor teams to boost morale, Valis glanced around the table. The conversation was lively, and it did much to erase the tension from the day before. And once again, he was left breathless that these wonderful people were his family.

CHAPTER SEVENTEEN

AFTER MORNING PHYSICAL TRAINING, Valis took a leisurely bath and dressed in his soft uniform, then led Tavros out of their suite and through the halls to Kerac's.

"You are a bit too glowy there," his husband remarked. "What has you floating around on your own little cloud?"

Valis snapped out of his reverie and grinned at his lover. "I had an idea, and I need your help."

Tavros's eyes widened, but he nodded. "Anything."

"I need you to go down and hitch Rasera and your horse to a rented wagon. I'll be down as soon as I can."

"What do you have planned?" Tavros asked, his eyes even wider.

"You'll see." Valis couldn't help his stupid grin. "I promise, though, it's nothing bad, and we're going to have a good time."

His lover smirked and pulled him in for a kiss that made Valis's toes curl. He panted into Tavros's mouth and clutched him close. It was only when a passing Aesriphos whistled at them suggestively that Valis pulled back enough to give the man a rude gesture that matched his husband's. The man laughed. Valis glanced at Tavros, and they both broke into laughing fits that made Valis feel so free in that moment that he wished it would never end.

"Go on," Tavros said, kissing him chastely this time. "I'll go get the horses ready and the wagon rented."

"Thank you."

Valis bounced on the balls of his feet for a moment, then headed into his father's suite with a grin stretching his face so wide that his cheeks ached.

"What has you so happy today?" Kerac asked. His eyes were brighter today than the day before. He looked more comfortable, and Valis's heart soared. "You're positively radiant with it. Tell me." He patted the bed beside him, and that was new. Before, he couldn't move his hands even a few inches without help.

"How strong do you feel?" Valis asked instead. He sat on the edge of the bed and took up Kerac's hand, his heart stuttering when Kerac's feeble squeeze felt so much stronger than it had just the day before.

"I won't be getting up and dancing anytime soon," Kerac teased, "but I am feeling much better." He frowned. "I still can't walk, or even sit up by myself, but I do feel... stronger.

Moving my hands and legs is still hard, but I'm getting better, especially with my hands and arms."

"Good," Valis said and leaned in to kiss Kerac's forehead. "Good. Because I have a surprise for you today, and I need to get you dressed in something warm."

Kerac's entire face brightened. "Really?"

Laughing, Valis went to his closet and pulled out his winter cloak, his warmer boots, and a clean uniform. "Yes. Really." He also pulled out a thick blanket from one of the cupboards inside and tossed it on the empty side of the bed. "Did you want a bath first?"

He shook his head. "Firil already came in and bathed me. I just need to get dressed."

Valis spent the next few minutes wrangling Kerac into clean clothes, tightening the drawstrings of his pants to make sure they wouldn't fall off, and punching a new hole into his belt so that it would actually cinch around his painfully small waist.

Though, Valis had to admit that his waist was fuller now that he'd been eating well. He no longer felt quite as light as he had when Valis had pulled him off his horse on the night of the Autumn Festival ten days ago. Hopefully when he came off the liquid diet and started eating solid foods again, he would start packing on more weight. He couldn't wait until Kerac was strong again.

As he dressed his father and laughed with him, Valis had a vision in his head of going through sword forms and physical training with Kerac in the mornings and evenings, making sure Kerac didn't hurt himself, but also keeping his spirits up while he struggled through the exercises. And the longer that vision stayed, the more Valis wanted to make it happen.

You can make it happen, my son, Roba murmured into his mind. *It may be after we deal with the Sovereign Priest of Qos, or at least after we rescue Darolen, but you can make it happen. I have faith in you.*

Valis smiled. *I have faith in* us, *Dad. You and I... we're a team. Forever.*

I only hope that is true, Roba whispered. *I keep feeling that I am a temporary guest in your mind.*

Let's not borrow trouble, Dad. Enjoy it while it lasts, and if it lasts forever, then so be it. If not, then we'll say goodbye and meet at Sovras's meadow.

Meadow?

Valis mentally shrugged. *When he pulled me to him, he was in the middle of a meadow. Lush green grass, a river nearby, trees in the distance. It was gorgeous and peaceful.*

And you think that is where we go when we die? Roba asked.

Probably not, but I have a feeling Sovras will make an exception for us. He's my friend, after all.

I hope so, my son. I do hope so.

Me, too, Dad.

"Where did you go off to?" Kerac asked. His lips twitched into a curious smile. "You were gazing out into middle distance."

Valis ducked his head. "I was having a conversation with

Dad. He's worried that he's only with me temporarily and was getting a little maudlin. Now that he's free of the darkness, he's become quite sensitive about some things."

"He really has changed so much?"

"So much, Papa. So, so much." Valis leaned in to hug Kerac gently and sit him up to get his cloak on. "Just remember, that he can't ever replace you or Father. I love you all, and always will."

"Your heart is so big." Kerac sighed and smiled up at him. "You've always been such a love."

"When I wasn't being a terror," Valis half-joked.

"It wasn't your fault that you were terrified."

"No, it wasn't. I was teasing, Papa." He settled the cloak around Kerac's shoulders more securely and adjusted the cloak pin, so the front closed better. Once he had Kerac's boots on him, Valis carefully picked Kerac up and headed for the door. "Can you get door knobs, do you think?"

"I can get them," Aenali said as she came in. "It was my turn to watch Kerac. You're going somewhere?"

"Yep," Valis said as he led the way to the door to the hall. "I'm taking Kerac for a surprise, but I have to go back to my suite to get winter cloaks for myself and Tavros."

"Okay!"

"Could you get the blanket for me, 'Nali? It's the one on the end of the bed."

"Sure!" She ran over and grabbed it, almost dwarfed by the thick material. "You gonna need me to take it wherever you're going?"

"Just until we reach the wagon," Valis said. "Thank you. It would be awkward as anything carrying Kerac *and* that heavy blanket."

Kerac stared at Aenali and muttered, "I can't believe how that little weed has grown." He playfully glared at the little girl and pointed a shaky finger at her. "You were so tiny when I last saw you, Aenali."

She grinned back at him and shrugged. "Can't help it. You'll get over it."

Kerac laughed so hard he ended up in a coughing fit. "Oh, Aenali," he chuckled again and struggled to catch his breath. "How I have missed you."

"I missed you, too! But not as much as Valis. It took him *forever* to get over you and Darolen leaving."

"Let's not talk about that," Valis said. "We want Papa to have fun today, not worry about the past. Right?"

"Right," she chirped.

When they entered Valis's suite, Kerac gasped and when Valis looked, he had wet eyes as he looked around. "What's wrong, Papa?"

He sniffled but shook his head. "Nothing. It's just..."

"You forgot I'm married?"

Kerac sighed. "Yes. And I missed it all over again. But your suite is stunning, Valis. I'm so glad you've taken the time to make it your own."

Valis sat him on the bed and kissed his temple. "It's okay, Papa. I missed you, too."

Kerac smiled up at him and sighed. "Don't worry about

me, my son. Let us make today a fun day."

"That's what I had planned."

He quickly grabbed his winter cloak, pinned it on, grabbed the one for Tavros and wrapped it around Aenali. She let out a belly laugh and glanced behind her. "It's training behind me like I'm a princess!"

"You *are* a princess," Valis said. "Our princess." He grinned and nodded toward the door. "Let's go, your highness. We have things to do! Places to go!"

He almost tripped on Tavros's cloak, but they made it down to the monastery's front steps and once Tavros relieved Aenali of his cloak, she made Valis kneel down so she could kiss Kerac's cheek and then his. "Have fun!" Then she raced back inside, chased in by the chill of the morning.

"We ready to go?" Tavros patted his horse and came back to Valis and Kerac. "How are we going to do this?"

"Get in the back of the wagon, and I'll hand him up to you. Then I'll ride in the back with him while you drive."

Tavros grunted as he hauled himself into the back of the wagon and reached down. "Where are we going?"

"The closest tree line," Valis said as he handed Kerac up. "Other than that, we'll see when we get there."

Kerac gasped, and when Valis looked into his eyes, he knew he had at least somewhat of an idea as to what Valis was doing, but he said nothing as he changed hands from Valis to Tavros, and then back into Valis's when he pulled Kerac back against his chest and wrapped him in the thick blanket.

The ride across the lake was soothing, as was the slow ride through the dangling fronds of the weeping whiptails. Valis had himself and Kerac situated so that they could see where they were going instead of back where they had been. And as soon as the forest's rich colors filled their view, Valis leaned his head down and whispered to Kerac, "You once told me that you wished we had arrived at the monastery in autumn, because you wanted to show me the colors."

Kerac's breath hitched, and he nodded.

"Well, it took a while, but let's do that now."

He cast his gaze forward and let the colors wash over him. The grass was still mostly green, not dead yet. But the trees… their leaves nearly blinded him with the array of red, gold, sunny orange, rust, and even a variety of pink and purple. And the crisp, cold air brought with it the scents of hearth fires, baked goods and so much life from the forest that Valis didn't know how to contain it all. It wasn't over-whelming, but it was close, like he wanted to capture this moment in time and have it painted, saved for the rest of his life, but devastated because he was no artist, didn't know any, and he had no idea when he would see such colors again. Even if or when he did, it would never be the same. It would never be *this moment* again.

"Thank you, my Valis," Kerac said, his voice tight. "Oh, my son…"

"I love you, Papa. Did you think I would forget something so important? It made you so emotional when you made that wish. I couldn't forget even if I wanted to."

"I love you, too," he whispered. "So much."

"You two okay back there?" Tavros called from the driver's seat.

"Yes," Valis called back. "Take us a little closer to the trees, then park and join us. We can all cuddle under the blanket, and our body heat will help keep Papa warmer."

"Sounds good."

Once they parked and Tavros came to cuddle, Valis sighed and they all sat quietly while taking in the beauty of the forest as it prepared to sleep for the winter. A gust of wind blew through the canopy, sending a rainbow swirl of leaves to the forest floor. Valis squeezed Kerac as tight as he dared.

"What troubles you?" Kerac asked. "You suddenly grew tense."

Valis sighed and told Kerac about his failed attempts at getting a mission to save Darolen sanctioned. "Brother Bachris keeps calling it a foolish mission and upset several Aesriphos when he confronted me about it. I'm pretty sure most of them were as pissed as I was, but better at keeping their emotions in check."

Kerac made a sympathetic noise. "I do not blame them, nor do I blame you. It is against our code to leave known captives in captivity if a rescue is even close to possible. He is asking every Aesriphos who was present during that confrontation to ignore the very code they have given their lives to uphold."

"Yeah. They mentioned that." Valis sighed and adjusted

the blanket when a breeze made Kerac shiver. "I'd go without a sanction, but I have a precognitive feeling that it needs to be sanctioned. And, most of the reliquary guards who are in support of the mission have made getting the mission sanctioned a requirement if they are to step in and accompany me."

"Then you go over Brother Bachris's head."

"I would do that in a heartbeat, but I also have a precognitive feeling that getting Brother Bachris's approval is also necessary. And *that* pisses me off to no end."

"You always were an impatient young man," Kerac teased. "I see little has changed except your body."

Valis snorted and kissed the side of Kerac's head. "Ass."

"I kn—"

Kerac's voice disappeared, as did the trees and the wagon. Valis gasped as he fell into the vision. Darkness started lightening. Whoever he inhabited opened their eyes, and they immediately began to burn, but he felt like the person was used to it. Then he noticed the stench and Valis's stomach rolled.

He was in Darolen's body. His father glanced at the door where lamplight shone, getting stronger as footsteps grew louder. Darolen tensed, but tried to keep his face straight, his eyes defiant.

It didn't work.

As soon as the door opened with the jangle of heavy keys, Darolen's eyes went to the floor like a kicked dog. Valis had the distinct feeling that Darolen didn't want to see his jailer's face.

Rough, gloved hands hauled Darolen up. They removed his shackles, but Darolen was too weak and emaciated to move, let alone fight.

Another man entered and gagged. He dumped a bucket of ice-cold water over Darolen's head. When he left, another man came in and did the same thing. After five buckets, the man who held him tucked Darolen's slight body under his arm and carried him like a sack of grain out of the room.

"Clean the filth, Carn." The man's grating voice made Darolen shiver. "The flies are getting into the rest of the holding, and the master wants to cut down on them."

"Yes, sir." That man gagged again, but Darolen didn't even twitch as the man with the grating voice carried him through endless halls and strapped him to a cross against a wall.

"Are you ready to talk?" He wrenched Darolen's mouth open and poured tepid, stagnant water down his throat. Darolen choked down as much as he could, the rest trickling down the sides of his face. "We might feed you more if you give us the information we require."

When Darolen was silent for too long, that hand left his face. Only a moment later, a crack sounded, and searing pain erupted in a line across Darolen's back. He cried out, his voice hoarse and weak. Wetness trickled down his back. Another crack, and Darolen's head fell forward. When it touched the wood of the cross, Valis's vision went dark again.

"He's shaking!"

"It's okay, Kerac. He's only in a vision. He's coming out of it. Are you hurt?"

"No. I am fine. But he's bleeding!"

"He sometimes gets nosebleeds from visions. It's normal. I promise."

Valis groaned and struggled to open his eyes. "Hear that? He's waking. He can probably hear us now."

"Yes," Valis wheezed.

"His nose isn't leaking anymore. Cuddle him while I drive. He'll rouse more on his own now."

Tavros kissed Valis's forehead. "I'll get us home, love. Just hang on."

Valis felt Tavros manipulate his body so that he was still laying down, but Kerac's head rested on his outstretched arm and he cuddled against Valis's chest. Once Tavros tucked the blanket around them, Valis felt the wagon shift as Tavros got into the driver's seat, and the rocking ensued as he drove them back toward Cadoras's shore.

"Valis?"

Valis cleared his throat. "I can't see yet, but I can hear you, and I'm coming around."

"Gods, I was so scared," Kerac whispered.

"I know, Papa. I'm safe, but I need to rest a moment."

"Of course."

While Kerac smoothed his bony fingers through Valis's hair, Valis concentrated as hard as he could on Thyran and tried to break into his mind. He knew he succeeded when he started hearing the man's thoughts.

Thyran, I had another vision.

Good Gods, boy. You nearly made me set myself on fire! Do not scare me like that!

Valis chuckled in his mind and shivered, earning another pass of fingers through his hair from Kerac. *I had a vision, Thyran. Tav and I took Kerac out to see the autumn leaves, so we're on our way back to Cadoras. But I wanted to tell you before I forget.*

Go ahead, Thyran said. *I am ready.*

Valis relayed the entire vision, speaking aloud for Kerac's benefit while sending the thoughts to Thyran at the same time. When he finished, Thyran sighed. *There is little we can do, but I have made note of it. Thank you, Valis.*

"Gods," Kerac whispered thickly. "I should—"

"Don't you dare, Papa," Valis said softly. "Darolen was so happy to hear that you're safe. Your safety is giving him the strength to wait for help."

Kerac shivered. "I know." He nuzzled into Valis's arm as if trying to console him as best he could in his weakened state. "Do what is in your heart, Valis, and shine your heart onto those who oppose you. Just... remember. Sometimes those in power *do* know what is best. Not always, but... it is something to consider."

"Yeah," Valis said on a sigh. "Not this time, though. Brother Bachris is wrong. And I will find a way to make him see soon. Very soon."

CHAPTER EIGHTEEN

THE STENCH of refuse nearly choked him. No matter what he did, he couldn't get it out of his nose. It rose up in a miasma so thick he tasted it with every breath, even when his mouth was closed.

The cell door creaked open. Fear gripped him. He hadn't heard the footsteps. Nor had he seen the light. Had he slept? Was he dreaming? A shudder of revulsion and fear swept through him, and all he could do was whisper prayers in his mind, begging Phaerith to make his suffering end, but also begging to be reunited with his husband and son again soon. It lapsed into the familiar mantra that had kept him going for these last months, kept his mind and heart strong, even as his body grew weak and frail, as his muscles disappeared, wasting away as his body repossessed the protein to fuel the rest of his body because he wasn't getting anywhere near enough to eat.

"Get him up," said a man with a permanent snarl in his voice. "For fuck's sake, you're supposed to rinse him once a day. His shit is everywhere. Clean it up. Get the water and get him rinsed off so we can get him to the Master without dragging or dripping shit through the fucking halls."

"Yes, sir."

Then the torture began. Water so cold it felt like needles poured over his head and body. Then they bundled him in a rough cloth. It abraded his already bruised and bleeding skin, but at least it offered him a bit of warmth.

The largest man tucked him under an arm as if he were a child. He resolved himself, as he always did, not to cry out when the whip fell. They would not see more of his weakness. But, deep in his heart, he knew that was a lie he told himself just to get through his nerves.

Only this time, they didn't take him to the whipping room, as he'd come to call it. They kept walking, winding through halls until the cadence of their feet rocked him to sleep.

A rough, hard hand smacked him so hard that he feared he'd broken his neck. "Wake up!"

He blinked and shrank back from the blinding daylight. When was the last time he'd seen the sky? He couldn't remember, and the harder he tried to figure it out, the more he wanted to fall to his knees and weep. But he was still held in an iron grasp. Only this time, it was shackles that held him to a pole, his arms over his head, and his ankles chained to the base instead of rough hands and burlap.

He only now heard the calls and jeers from an amassed crowd. "Kill him! Beat him raw! Kill the Aesriphos!"

It was a game to them, an amusement. Ending a life was *fun* for these people. The thought should have sickened him more than it did, but he felt so very far away from it all. The light was so blinding, and he tilted his head up to let the weak morning sun shine on his face, basking in its glow.

"End him." That voice... he didn't know whose it was, but it sounded vaguely familiar. "Send him to Qos."

He didn't register the pain at first. But then it flared, white hot across his throat. Sticky wetness coated his naked body as his life's blood cascaded down in weak spurts.

And the crowd cheered.

VALIS WOKE UP SCREAMING SO HARD THAT HE TASTED BLOOD, and for a moment, he thought it was from a slit throat. His body shook. Tavros clutched him to his naked chest and petted his hair. "It's okay, Valis. It's okay. I've got you. You're safe. You're *safe*, love."

Hearing his lover's voice settled something deep inside Valis and he sagged against Tavros until his husband settled them back down into bed. "Another nightmare." It wasn't a question. Valis had been having the same nightmare, or variations of it, since the night they'd found Kerac. "I'm so sorry, love."

"Me, too." Valis cleared his throat and winced. "At least it means he's still alive. I wouldn't be dreaming of him dying if he's already dead."

"These dreams may not even be precognitive," Tavros murmured against his head. "They may just be your fears coming to the fore when you're sleeping. It's normal, especially when you're stressed and scared. So, it may mean absolutely nothing except that your subconscious is being an asshole."

Valis groaned and rolled over, pushing Tavros onto his back so he could curl up on his husband's chest. "That could be it. I'm not sure if it's precognitive or not, because I'm so raw after waking that I can't tell one way or the other." He lowered his voice and cringed at how small he sounded. "I just want them to go away."

"I know, love. I wish I could make them go away for you." His sigh ruffled Valis's hair, and he kissed the crown of his head. "Need something to take your mind off it?"

Tavros wrapped his arms tight about Valis's back, rubbing warmth into his skin. He pulled the covers up around him, tucking them about his neck to cocoon Valis in warm bliss. "I know you haven't been keen on sex in the morning after these nightmares, but perhaps going to the arena early and getting some exercise might help calm and soothe your mind enough that you're not as tense during your classes as you have been this last week."

Valis groaned again and snuggled in closer. "That's probably a good idea, but you just got me warm..."

The bed shook with Tavros's quiet laugh and he hugged Valis tighter. "We'll go in half an hour. It's still obscenely early."

"Then what are we going to do until we leave?"

"I thought I just got you warm. I assumed you wanted to doze until we had to go."

Valis grunted and rubbed his eyes, trying to decide if he was ready to wake up or if he wanted to go back to sleep. "Ugh. Damn it. I don't think I can nod off again."

"Then don't," Tavros said softly. "Just relax and rest with me. We don't have to be moving at all times during our waking hours. Just let yourself *be* for a while."

"But that's when the frustration starts getting to me," Valis whispered. "I hate it."

"I know you do." Tavros's fingers trailed up and down Valis's spine in a hypnotic rhythm. "But, try it. And if your frustration gets the better of you, we'll go get you sweaty early."

After twenty minutes of resting, Valis's frustrations got the better of him, and he found himself standing in the quiet arena. It was so early that no one was around except them, and Valis stretched his arms over his head, trying to wake himself up a bit more. He wore only his uniform. They'd go back and bathe before donning their armor for the two classes. For now, though, Valis started his morning routine, easing into a gentle warm-up first so he didn't injure himself during his stretches.

"What do you have planned for me, oh wondrous mentor?"

Tavros chuckled as he did his own warm-up. "Our normal routine first, and we'll go from there."

By the time they were done with their normal routine, Valis's muscles burned pleasantly. The frustration still simmered, but Valis's mind was clearer than it had been after first waking.

"Take a jog," Tavros called. "Sixteen laps around the arena floor."

Valis hated running. Not because he wasn't good at it, but because it was boring. But, as he fell into the familiar rhythm of feet hitting stone, his mind blanked out again, and he started to feel the weight slowly lift off his shoulders. It wasn't an immediate thing, but by the time Tavros called him over, he did feel slightly better.

Tavros put his fingers to Valis's throat, checking his pulse. "You did twenty-five laps. Did you get lost?"

Laughing, Valis ducked his head. "I wasn't counting."

"Figures." Tavros didn't sound or look upset, having a small smile lighting his face. But it grew to an almost sinister grin when he motioned to the dreaded drag blocks. "Time for the dead drag. I'm starting you off with two blocks."

"Fuck."

"I did say I was going to get you sweaty and exhausted."

"You said nothing about the exhausted part."

"That's my secret to destroying your frustration. You should know this by now."

"Fuck."

"You said that already. Get over there, get that bull rope in hand, and get dragging."

Valis might have hated it, but he had to admit it was a genius plan. As the bull rope bit into his palms and his leg muscles started to burn, Valis had no room for frustration. The only thing he had room for was the movement of his arms and legs.

He pushed out for five steps, his arms shaking under the strain of dragging the blocks. His legs quivered. Five steps at full extension. Sweat dripped from his brow. Five steps, each step bringing the rope closer to his chest. Five steps with the rope biting into his breastbone. Over and over again.

Then the block got heavier, and Valis glanced back to see Tavros had added a third block. He groaned but kept up the rhythm. As much as he hated it, he needed it.

When Valis almost fell on his face, Tavros called for him to stop. Then Valis did fall, but he managed to do it on his ass instead of his face.

"You okay?"

"No," Valis groaned. "I'm dying. Send help."

His husband chuckled and went about returning the blocks to their base. "Get off that floor and take a jog. It will help your legs feel better."

Valis doubted that wholeheartedly but did as he was told. And when they made it back to their room, Valis tired and dripping with sweat, Valis's found his frustration had evolved. He wasn't frustrated anymore. He was *determined*.

Yes, he knew he'd been determined from the start. But now, he felt that determination on a whole new level.

"You seem… different," Tavros said as he drew the water for their bath. "What's up?"

"Just figured something out," Valis said. He chanced sitting on the vanity stool to give his wobbly legs a break.

"Care to share?"

Valis went to shrug but cringed when his muscles screamed at him. "I just feel determined. Nothing earth-shattering. But the frustration isn't as bad. So, the workout worked, even if my entire body *does* feel like jelly."

"Get in the bath and relax. We'll grab something to eat from the kitchens before we head out for you to teach your classes. We still have plenty of time."

Valis almost fell into the sunken tub, but for a well-timed catch of both arms from Tavros. He helped Valis in and climbed down beside him with a contented sigh that disturbed the steam rising from the water. Tavros drew it hotter than they usually made it, but it felt so good to Valis's overworked muscles that he didn't dare complain.

TRAINING WITH THE TRANSLOCATION STUDENTS WENT ON AS normal. But when the reliquary guards started filing in, Valis stomach pitted. No one looked happy, and Valis didn't like the downcast eyes as they all milled about.

"What's going on?" Valis asked the room at large. "Why does everyone look like someone kicked your favorite puppies?"

"Brother Bachris is still making a stink," Shyvus said, his voice a low growl. "Some of us went to the Grand Master Aesriphos, but Brother Bachris had gotten to them first, and... well, our meeting did not go well, Valis. Our Grand Master has denied us the sanction until we can convince Brother Bachris that it is a 'worthy' mission."

"Needless to say, none of us are happy," Netai said with clenched teeth. "Our Grand Masters aren't happy, either. They're rather angry at Brother Bachris and won't tell any of us what the Patron Priest has over them that their hands are so tied when they're essentially Brother Bachris's superiors."

Murmurs arose from the others, and Valis's gut felt so tight he wondered if it would shatter. "No..."

"I am sorry, lad," Shyvus said. "Truly, I am. We won't give up, and neither should you, but at this moment, the answer is still 'no.'"

Valis firmed his mouth into a thin line and nodded. "Right. I'll see what happens when I go see him after lunch. For now, line up. We have work to do. I want you all ready for this mission, because one way or another, I *will* get it sanctioned, or, as I've said before, I'll go alone with the mercenaries and Kalutakeni at my side."

"Never alone, my heart," Tavros promised. "I'll always be by your side."

Valis spared him a tense smile and nodded. "I consider you a part of me, so always assume when I say alone, it always includes you, Tav."

Tavros nodded and stepped closer to show his support.

"The rest of you, thank you for taking this matter further. I'll deal with it from now on. I don't think these men know quite how driven I am, or how stubborn."

Quiet chuckles arose from the men and women as if they were afraid to be any louder for fear of upsetting Valis or breaking some sort of spell. But, when Valis looked, each man and woman had hope in their eyes, when they had all entered with despair and defeat.

"I promise you." Valis looked around the room, meeting one pair of eyes after another. "I promise you I will rescue him. And any captured Aesriphos I find along the way. If I find bodies, they *will* have pyres. If I find them alive, they *will* receive as much healing as we can afford, and they *will* be returned home alive."

He straightened his back even more, raising to his full height. "And I promise you all... I *will* take out every Qos nest I find, and I won't rest until this war is at an end."

The raucous cheers nearly deafened Valis. They sounded almost exactly like those from his dream, only these were happy calls instead of zealous jubilance. Still, the similarities made Valis tremble and his skin erupt with sick sweat. Tavros noticed almost immediately and his face hove into view. He removed his gauntlets and threw them down with a loud clatter of metal hitting stone. Then his hands cupped Valis's face.

Everyone seemed to sense something was wrong at the same time whether they could see Valis or not. Kaltani came up to their side. "What is wrong?"

"I don't know," Tavros said.

Valis tried to still his trembling, but that made him shake more. His teeth chattered when he tried to speak. "Ch-cheer-cheering... l-l-like m-my dream. J-just—"

"Anxiety attack?" Kaltani asked.

Valis didn't trust his mouth again, so he just nodded.

"Get him on the bench," she told Tavros gently. "I'll go get a damp cloth to help cool him down."

She pressed the backs of her fingers to Valis's forehead in a comforting gesture. "Regulate your internal temperature, Valis. Just like we taught you. It will be over soon."

Tavros guided Valis to the side wall and helped him onto a bench while Valis fought to control his internal temperature. He wasn't hot or cold, but somehow, he was *both*. His skin felt like insects were crawling all over him, while his chest felt too tight, and his lungs struggled to pull in each breath. The sense of impending doom was so strong that Valis didn't know how to deal with it because he'd never had an attack quite this strong before. Nor did he ever have one that made him feel anything like *this*. They had all made him shy away from things, mainly crowds or going into different places. But this? He didn't know how to deal with *this*. This was more than an aversion to something, it felt like he was dying.

And suddenly, it was like living that nightmare all over again. He could see and hear the reliquary guards nearby, close but keeping their distance to give him breathing room. But in his mind, he was shackled to that pole, bleeding out, wishing he could see his husband one last time before he choked on his own blood and succumbed to death as whatever didn't go into his belly or lungs spurted down his torso and soaked the ground at his feet.

"Love, what can I do?" Tavros asked softly. "What do you need?"

Valis shivered and shook his head. He couldn't talk yet. Instead, he shifted closer, and Tavros caught his meaning and started removing his own armor. "Someone help Valis out of his armor. He needs body contact."

"Will he be okay?"

Shyvus and Phalin worked quickly but with great care to get Valis out of his armor. Shyvus looked at Tavros, waiting for an answer as his hands worked.

"I worked him really, really hard before his translocation class started because he was frustrated from the nightmare he has nightly. Your cheers might have sounded like those in his dream and caught him off guard. It's just stress from everything bearing down on him. I think it's finally reaching its peak."

"Poor bastard," Phalin said on a sigh.

They kept working until Valis sat shivering on the bench,

devoid of his armor and padding, his uniform sticking to his skin. Then Tavros was there, holding him and rubbing his back. Valis tucked his face into Tavros's shoulder, and as if a dam broke, he sucked in a breath and sobbed it out.

"Let it out, love. It's okay."

And Valis did. He cried hard—for his father, for his papa, for all the Aesriphos who were taken from that dank cell but never returned. He cried for the injustice of Brother Bachris's denial, and for the Grand Master Aesriphos' decision to defer to the Patron Priest's wishes.

But most of all, he cried for himself, because he missed his father, and it *hurt* to see his papa so frail and sick.

When the tears finally stopped, Valis leaned back and someone pressed a handkerchief into his hand. Tavros took it away and started mopping up Valis's face for him. "Are you okay now?"

"No," Valis said, his voice stronger now that he'd cried out all his panic. "No. I won't be okay until I get this mission sanctioned. I won't be okay until my father is home where he belongs."

CHAPTER NINETEEN

BREAKFAST WAS fraught with the remnants of Valis's anxiety attack. He picked at his food as he struggled to get it down. But as he calmed more, he found himself able to stomach more of his meal.

It didn't help that his friends all kept giving him worried looks. He smiled at them and swallowed his mouthful. "I'm okay. Honest. Or, at least, I'm getting better as we eat."

Everyone seemed to relax except for Seza. She stared at Valis for a long time before finally nodding and going back to her food. Then she looked up again and pointed her fork at him. "You *will* rest today. Do you understand?"

Valis ducked his head. Suddenly his food was *very interesting*, and he started making patterns with the last of his scrambled eggs. "Yes, ma'am."

She lowered her fork and muttered, "I swear, you boys

turn into toddlers when you're scolded. Not sure if it's hilarious, or endearing."

"Both?" Maphias asked hopefully.

Seza snorted but didn't grace him with an answer. Valis wondered if she did it on purpose to annoy her brother. He stared at her with a wilting smile and huffed before going back to his breakfast.

"So what are we doing this morning?" Jedai looked pointedly at Valis as if he had all the answers. "Anything interesting?"

Valis rubbed the back of his neck and stared at his now-empty plate, pondering a trip back to the serving line. "I had thought to make a trip to Cadoras proper and get more supplies to take to the Kalutakeni caravan. I'm deadly serious that I'm going whether this mission gets sanctioned or not. And I want those with me to be as ready and supplied as possible."

"I'm in," Jedai and Maphias said in unison. The two men looked at each other and laughed.

Seza rolled her eyes at them and nodded to Zhasina. "I think we'd better go to make sure they don't hurt themselves."

Her wife almost choked on her tea. "Of course."

Tavros shrugged and smiled at Valis. "I go where he goes."

"You two are disgustingly cute," Seza said and sighed. "Not even Zhasina and I are that cute."

"We rather are." Zhasina winked and nudged her wife. "We're just cute in private most times."

Seza grinned and ducked her head, a blush spreading over her face as it climbed up from her neck. "Shush, you."

Aenali bounced in her seat. "I want to come, too!" Then she stopped and frowned. "But then no one would be left to watch Kerac. I'll stay."

"You don't have to stay, Aenali." Valis gave her a small smile. "I can get another guard to replace the one who's with him now. It won't be a problem. Most of the guards stationed with him are his friends, anyway. So, it's not a hardship for them."

"Oh." She immediately brightened and sat up straighter. "Okay! If they're his friends, then I won't feel bad!"

"Can you handle a horse?"

She looked at Valis with huge green eyes, sparkling with hope. "Kind of!"

"Rasera should be good for you. We'll need a horse to pull the rented wagon." Valis chuckled as she did a little dance in her chair. "He's so pretty! I wish I could spend more time with him. You've only taken me out to play with you two a few times!"

"I'll try to take you out again before we leave," Valis promised. "But, when we're done shopping, I'm sure the Kalutakeni will let you play with the herd. They're all well behaved animals."

He didn't think it was possible, but her eyes got even bigger as she clasped her hands before her. "Really? You mean it?"

Valis laughed, and the last of the awful feelings from earlier drained away. "Yes. Really."

"YAY!"

Snorting, Valis gave up his fight and went back to the serving line for another plate of food. When everyone had finished their breakfast, Valis led the way to pick up more gold from his caches, giving his husband and each of his friends a heavy purse, but giving a much smaller, lighter one to Aenali.

"What all are we going to get?" the little girl asked as she peered into the purse. "There's enough gold in here to buy the entire market!"

Valis chuckled and ruffled her auburn curls. "Not quite, dollface. Today, we're going to focus on things Tavros and I will need, such as heavy winter clothes and boots, heavier cloaks, thicker bedrolls, scarves, gloves, and that kind of thing. We'll be journeying through snow and below freezing temperatures for part of our trip. And we'll be getting some things for the army at large."

"Like food and stuff?"

"No." Valis paused as he held the door to the courtyard open for everyone to head outside. "The mercenaries and Kalutakeni are getting all that, themselves. I'm thinking blankets for the horses so they're not freezing in the winter, wraps for their legs and necks, and just things to make sure our horses and army are warm and as safe as possible through the entire journey. We'll also need more tethers for each of our horses to carry the additional supplies, because each man will have to carry their own winter gear and that for their horses."

"That's so much!" She took his hand and held on as they walked toward the market. "Maybe we don't have enough money after all."

Valis smiled down at her. "If we don't, I can always run back for more."

"Good."

She remained quiet through the rest of the walk, but the moment she saw the stalls, she released Valis's hand and darted off. Jedai broke away from the group to follow her, always the doting and protective older brother. Valis's heart warmed as he watched them go.

"Where will we start?" Tavros asked.

Valis adjusted his winter cloak and kissed his warm lips as the autumn breeze swept through the square carrying scents of baked goods, warm fires, apples and spices, and a cooler scent that promised an early snow. "Probably best to rent the wagon and hitch up Rasera before we get any shopping done."

"I'll tend to that. You start putting in orders while I'm gone?"

"Done." Valis kissed him again and adjusted his own cloak. "I'll meet you back here." Then he added, "See if Aenali wants to go with you. She's in love with Rasera."

"Will do." Tavros grinned at him, waved, and headed off to find Aenali before heading to the stables.

Twenty or so minutes later, a cold hand touched the back

of Valis's neck and he squawked as he whipped around, ready to hit someone only to find Tavros cackling like a madman. "I almost decked you!"

Tavros couldn't quit laughing enough to reply, only pointed at him and wheezed between cackles, "Your face... Oh, Gods... I'm dying..."

Valis rolled his eyes and grinned. "Ass."

He couldn't help but chuckle and playfully shoved Tavros's shoulder as he went to greet Rasera. "Hey, Ras. Miss me?"

The tall black stallion nudged him with his entire face, making Valis laugh and hug it. "Yeah. I missed you, too. Be nice to Aenali, okay?"

"He's been super nice!" Aenali bounced and ran around under Rasera's neck to scratch under his jaw. "He remembered me!"

"Of course, he did. No one could forget you." He ruffled her curls and rested his forehead against the side of Rasera's neck. "And he's a big kid, so he's got about as much energy as you."

"A big kid?"

Valis smirked. "When we were waiting for the ground to dry during our journey to retrieve the Kalutakeni caravan, Tavros died and the mercenary leader, Jintas brought him back. Well, I was distraught and carried Tavros into our tent, and Seza and Zhasina came in with us. I had been training with Rasera, and... I'm part of his herd. He knows herd is supposed to stay together. And I think he knew that Tavros is part of *my* herd and knew he was hurt. So... Rasera laid on his side and stuck his head and neck into the tent, laying on Tavros's legs to check on him."

Aenali giggled and looked up at the beast with so much adoration, Valis thought she might spontaneously combust from the amount of warmth she radiated. "Aww!"

"Indeed. He's a sweet boy." Valis patted Rasera's face and stepped away. "And he's got some work to do, which, strangely enough, he seems to love as much as playing."

"Is everything ready?" Tavros asked as he came around from the back of the cart. "The back is down and it's ready for loading."

Valis nodded and took a deep breath, glancing around at the different shops and stalls. "Everything is ordered. They might be finished packing it all up now."

"I want to go get a few things," Aenali said, still giving Rasera love. "Can I?"

"If you can leave Rasera alone long enough, then sure," Valis teased.

She laughed and skipped off, again followed closely by her brother who seemed to materialize out of thin air from one of the shops to hustle after her. Rasera went to follow, but then must have realized he was attached to a cart. He snorted his displeasure and stamped his hoof.

"She'll be back you big baby." Valis ran a hand down his horse's face and smiled when Rasera lipped at his fingers, almost as if in forgiveness. "You'll get to play with her once we get back. Will that appease you?"

Rasera nickered and butted his head against Valis's chest, and Valis swore that horse understood every word he said.

Sighing, Valis left his horse and started gathering parcels from all the vendors, getting their word that the rest would be delivered to the caravan throughout the day and the next because more of everything had to be made due to space and stock limitations of their stalls and shops. And in a short time, Valis and the others rode the ferry across the lake toward the caravan parked along the shore.

"There's so many!" Aenali squeaked and started her excited bouncing again. "They're so pretty!"

She, of course, was talking about the herd of black horses grazing along the line of weeping whiptails. And the moment they docked, she didn't know where to go first—the herd, her brother for permission, or the Kalutakeni camp to ask *their* permission. She seemed to vibrate in place until Zhasina whistled and her horse, Zorar, came galloping toward them.

"I'll take Aenali to play with the horses," she said. "You all can deal with the parcels."

"Sounds fair," Valis said, waving them off. "Have fun, Aenali!"

"I will!" she cried.

Now that Aenali was occupied, Valis led Rasera toward the camp's center where most of the tribe sat around the fire as usual. They all seemed to look at the group at once, and Valis waved. "We've brought more supplies."

"More?" Venabi stared at him like he'd grown another

head. "What more do we need? You already gave us enough money to buy anything we need."

Valis motioned to the wagon. "You'll need a load of winter clothes. Things that will keep you warm through sub-freezing temperatures, through snow, possible blizzards. That means thicker bedrolls, blankets for you and your horses, and other things. I bought as much as I could. I saved out a few parcels for me and my group here, but the rest is for you and the mercenaries. More will be on the way as they're made throughout the day and tomorrow. But you may need to put in more orders. Just go through everything to see what I bought and buy similar for yourselves if you need it or nothing fits."

"Wise," Vodis said. He sighed. "We have never been through snow. I remembered we can't use our wagons but forgot our need for winter clothing."

Valis smiled. "Good thing I didn't." He looked from one person to another and nodded. "I want each person to have at least two winter cloaks, three if you can manage and fit it on your horse with everything else you'll be carrying. I also want each one of you to have at least five of each item in these parcels. When the temperature dips, you can add more layers. It might be annoying, but you'll be warm."

Venabi motioned to the wagon, and people filed by her to start unloading. Then she motioned for Valis and his friends to come have a seat around the fire. "You're thinking we will be out for most of the winter?"

"I'm making sure we're prepared for it, just in case," Valis said with a nod. "And I have a feeling that, if all goes well, we will be leaving soon. I asked the shopkeepers to bring in their apprentices for mass production, because I want everything ready to go within two days, again, just in case."

Venabi nodded and rubbed the scar on her cheek. "We can do this." She nodded and dropped her hand to her lap as she looked back up at Valis. "We will start gathering food stores for our journey. But we will need at least two carts for the heavy things."

"Buy four carts, just in case. If one breaks, we can shift the loads, save parts for spare, and ditch it along the way."

"Smart." Venabi glanced around and watched her men and women unloading the cart for a moment. "I also want two horses unburdened other than their riders in case we need couriers."

Valis nodded. "I appreciate that. I'll be doing most of our correspondence via two-way scry with Thyran during our journey, but if something happens to me, or we need something or someone not from the monastery, that will help greatly."

"My thoughts exactly."

"I know you have Kaliz as your courier. Do you have another?" Valis asked. "The mercenaries also have a trained courier, Sirvi."

Venabi tilted her head, staring off into middle distance for a moment. Then she focused on Valis again. "We will have our second-best on standby just in case we need a third. It is better to be over-prepared than under."

"Agreed."

After a few more moments of Venabi seeming *off*, she finally leaned forward, resting her elbows on her knees and stared at him intently. "Valis, I must tell you… I was not going to, but I believe you should know."

Valis's stomach pitted, and he frowned. "What is it?"

"A messenger came with a note from one of your Patron Priests, a Brother Bachris."

Valis groaned. "Fuck. Let me guess, he told you something along the lines that you're not to accompany me for an unsanctioned mission."

"More or less," she said, irritation lacing every word. "He said that, as allies of Avristin, we are under obligation to follow the monastery's rules. And that, should we find ourselves propositioned for a mission, we must refuse. And if we have already accepted this mission, we are to back out of our agreement immediately."

Snorting, Valis shook his head in disbelief. "I'll almost bet he sent a matching missive to the mercenaries."

Venabi shrugged. "I sent him a reply saying that yes, we were allies of the monastery, but that your actions and help are what solidified our relations, and our loyalty is to you and Seza first, as brother and wife to our Zhasina, and Avristin after." She gave him a feral grin that pinched her scar and made her seem sinister as anything. "I have yet to receive a return reply. Perhaps he forgets that he cannot command people who are not his and cannot expect loyalty when he shows disloyalty to one of his own. …I may have put those words in my reply as well. Just a fore-warning."

"I'm not sure if I've said this before, but if I did, I'll say it again," Seza said, "I really like you. You're my kind of girl."

That feral grin grew, and Valis lost it, laughing and leaning against Tavros. "Venabi… you're lovely and terrifying. Never change."

Zhasina came over with Zorar following along behind her, an excited Aenali on his naked back and Jedai walking along beside them to keep her from falling off. Zhasina winked at her countrywoman. "She *is* terrifying, isn't she?"

"In the best of ways," Valis said fondly. "The very best of ways."

He glanced behind him since he hadn't seen any of the Kalutakeni moving the packages in a while, and seeing the cart empty, he stood and adjusted his cloak. "Now that they're done unloading, we should be heading back. If you run into any trouble from Brother Bachris, let me know and I'll take care of it."

"You sound as if you are about to go into war," Venabi mused.

Valis grimaced. "That's more accurate than you might think. I'm about to go pay the Patron Priest a visit, and I'm not leaving until this mission is sanctioned and scheduled."

"I wish you luck, my friend." She stood and touched the center of his chest in solidarity. "We are with you."

Valis returned the gesture, avoiding her tightly bound

breasts. "Thank you. I couldn't do this without your help and that of the mercenaries."

"And you will not have to," Venabi said with a smirk, "regardless of what Brother Bachris wants."

As Valis and his friends rode the ferry back to Cadoras Island, Valis's glanced back at the caravan with a full heart and a renewed sense of hope. Now, it was time to plan. It was time to confront Brother Bachris for the final time, and he had to have a solid plan going into the meeting if he wanted even the slimmest chance of success.

"I'm not sure I like that face," Tavros muttered. He glanced over at Valis again and sighed. "That's your 'I'm going to ruin everyone's day' face that you usually get when going into battle."

Valis stared at the nearing city wall. "We've got everything in place and the only thing left is Brother Bachris."

He smiled at his husband and took his hand. "It's time."

CHAPTER TWENTY

VALIS TOOK A FEW DEEP, cleansing breaths before knocking on Brother Bachris's office door. He didn't want to go in there angry and ready to fight. If possible, he wanted to reason with the man, and prove to him somehow that he was doing the right thing.

"Everything will be fine," Tavros said at his side. "And if he still refuses, we'll take the matter up with the Grand Master Aesriphos ourselves. Keep calm, Valis. We can do this. Just remember that Brother Bachris is our friend, not an enemy to vanquish."

"Yeah." Valis sighed and shook the tension from his body. As he knocked a second time, though, and still received no answer, Valis opened the door and stuck his head in to find it empty.

"Brother Bachris is up in the Hall of Communion if you

are looking for him, boys," a passing priest said. "He should still be there. He only ascended about twenty minutes past."

"Thank you," Valis said with a kind smile for her. "We'll go up immediately."

She smiled back and nodded, then continued on her way through the hall. Valis turned the other way with Tavros close behind and headed for the stairs that would lead them up to the temple. Having Brother Bachris not be where Valis had planned threw him a bit, and as he ascended the stairs, he tried to regain his composure. He needed to shake this sense of being so wrong-footed and reroute his thoughts. His damned anxiety was getting the better of him and he didn't want to botch this meeting.

Once they reached the temple doors, Valis raised a hand to stall the Aesriphos from opening them. "Give me a moment, please. I need to get my head on straight so I don't make an ass of myself, or an enemy from my friend."

Kaltani grinned at him. "Good idea."

"Yeah, I thought so, too," Valis said as he leaned against the wall perpendicular to the doors. "And my anxiety's spiking again."

"Still from that nightmare?" Netai asked. "It must have been something."

Valis shuddered. "I dream, every night, of my father's death in horrid, gruesome detail. And I feel everything he feels so *vividly* and hear his thoughts."

He shook himself and rubbed his face. "I don't think this is from the nightmare, though. It's just... He's been like another father figure to me, you know? And having him deny something like this feels like such a betrayal. But... because he is another father figure, I want to make him proud, and I know that, no matter what I do in this situation, I'm disappointing him."

"Oh, Valis." Tavros squeezed his hand. "You and your giant heart."

Kaltani abandoned her post and cupped Valis's face, tipping it up so he looked at her instead of the floor. The warmth of her fingers bled out through the metal of her gauntlets, lending Valis a bit of comfort from her touch.

"You never had to worry about upsetting your father before, because until he died, your birth father wasn't a real father at all." She smiled and patted his cheek. "Your adopted fathers, Kerac and Darolen, never had anything to correct you on, at least nothing major. So you've never had to fight for your rights or beliefs against them."

When Valis frowned, she patted his face again. "Children always have, and always will come to odds with their parents at one point in time, Valis. Just because you do not agree on something doesn't mean they will stop loving you, just as you won't stop loving him for being an overbearing ass."

Valis huffed a laugh and wiped his eyes. "Thanks."

"Just remember that love is stronger than arguments, disputes, or even physical fights. It is how you men are *made*. You are prone to aggression sometimes, and in many cases, naturally assertive. He has been a leader for many years, and you have been a leader for a few months. You are both trying to lead and are butting heads. But, Valis... he will never stop loving you for fighting for what you believe in. Keep that in your heart, all right?"

Sighing, Valis leaned in and kissed her cheek. "Thank you, Kaltani."

She smiled gently at him and went back to her post. "You are welcome. Do you feel better?"

"Much."

"Good. Now go in there and fight for what you believe in." With that, she and her wife grabbed the ornate handles to the temple doors and pulled them open, revealing the Light of Phaerith shining down on the two people talking in hushed tones inside.

Valis studiously kept his eyes level. He didn't dare even glance up, or he'd be lost to Phaerith's Light until someone shaded his eyes to break his trance. He needed to be present and get this done. But as he entered and walked the sapphire runner toward the two near the reliquary doors, Valis wished he could get lost in the comfort that Light brought.

Brother Bachris turned to look who came and frowned. With him, the large woman wearing heavily ornate ceremonial armor glanced his way, too, and Valis gasped.

"Warmaster Isophel! I'm sorry to interrupt."

"That's Grand Master Aesriphos to you turds," she sneered, but Valis saw a hint of playfulness in her one good gray eye. "I am only the Warmaster when I'm training young pukes like you two," she said, her voice raspy and broken from shouting orders in battle. "But, you did well, lads. You made me proud."

Just like before, she had the top half of her fiery red hair pulled into a tight, high ponytail. The long tail trailed down her chest in an ornate braid that brushed past her waist. The lower half of her head seemed as if it was just recently shaved, only a hint of copper stubble showing. And when she smiled, the scar that trailed from her right temple, over her cloudy eye and down to the corner of her mouth pinched in a way that made her look completely evil.

Before, when she was in her regular armor, her shoulders had been almost as broad as Valis's own. But in that ornate armor, she dwarfed him and seemed so imposing that Valis almost shrank away. When she beckoned him forward, though, he went without hesitation. Duty always went before his own anxiety or aversion.

"What brings you?" she asked. Though, the way she asked, Valis doubted she didn't know, and the way she looked at him, with a hint of exasperation, Valis was almost certain she asked only out of social niceties.

Valis swallowed down his first reply and turned his attention to Brother Bachris. "I came to see the Patron Priest about a matter we discussed before. I wish to launch a rescue mission to save my father, Darolen Jaund, and I have come to petition for the sanction again."

"You are not going on that foolish mission!" Brother Bachris said with such ire that his face reddened. "I forbid it!" He sliced the air with his hand in a gesture of finality, and

Valis had to bite back the disappointed sigh that threatened to escape him. He had hoped, but somehow, he knew Brother Bachris would still be adamantly against him.

"If you call his request foolish one more time, Brother, I will have you removed from your station," Isophel warned. "Watch yourself. Rescuing an Aesriphos is *never* a foolish endeavor. And it never will be."

"I beg your pardon, Grand Master, but he is too young! Too inexperienced! He will die before he reaches his target, and then what? We not only lose the mercenaries who have vowed loyalty to him, and the Kalutakeni who also allied with him above the monastery, but four bright young Aesriphos and a few of our young laymen warriors. And for what? For an attempt at rescuing a man who will most assuredly be dead before they get a quarter of the way to their destination, *if* they can even learn the destination at all!"

Isophel shrugged, looking decidedly unimpressed. "But, if the mission is sanctioned, he would have reliquary guards and Aesriphos at his disposal and to help him become a better leader. This could be a great learning opportunity for him if we were to give him the assistance and men he needs."

"You do realize he will be going on a long mission during the full brunt of the winter months, even if he leaves tonight. It is a suicide mission, Isophel. All our sanctioned missions begin at first thaw if winter is close at hand. But I highly doubt Valis would wait even that long."

The Grand Master studied Valis for a moment, collecting

her thoughts before turning back to Brother Bachris. "How many rescue missions have you known? How many have you sanctioned?"

The Patron Priest paled and cleared his throat, clearly uncomfortable as he fidgeted with the sleeve of his tunic. "Three."

"And were any of them successful?"

He frowned. "You know they were not! And that is why we should not send Aesriphos straight out of Valiant training!"

"Did you ever think those failed attempts might have been *your fault?*" Isophel asked, her calm seeming brittle now. "Did you ever think that if you had not made them wait until first thaw to begin their mission, they may have had a higher success rate?"

"But—"

"There are winter clothes for a reason, Brother," Isophel went on. "There are provisions for the horses. There are supplies and measures our men and women can take to be as safe as possible in sub-freezing temperatures on a mission. And if the mission is thought to be a long one, we send them with these provisions in case they get waylaid and cannot make it home before the weather gets frigid."

"And," Valis said, reminding them that he was still there, "I've used my own personal gold cache to fund these provisions for myself, my husband, Seza, Zhasina, the Kalutakeni warriors, and the mercenaries, because I am well versed in traveling in cold weather." He stared into Brother Bachris's eyes, trying to press his point. "We arrived during a brutal blizzard if you remember, and we didn't have half the gear necessary for that climate. But we made it anyway. With the proper gear, we shouldn't have any casualties due to the climate."

The Patron Priest blew a long breath out through his nose and turned back to the Grand Master Aesriphos. "You are entertaining these *children* and it is giving them the wrong idea!"

Isophel rolled her eyes. "These two bested two of my best reliquary guards, Bachris. They've also seen battle. Valis, himself, has personally killed four men before his twenty-first birth anniversary. No one returns from killing another human being with their childhood intact. You should know this by now."

"That is—"

"I refuse to back down," Valis said as calmly as he could. "I *will* go after my father whether this mission is sanctioned or not. I would just prefer a sanction so that I have more Aesriphos on my team, because while I am strong, I know quite well that with only four Aesriphos, we are not strong enough to go against some of the larger Qos nests we may come across."

The Grand Master Aesriphos perked a cherry brow at him and smirked, the action tugging her scar in a way that looked painful. "I like you."

"Grand Master!"

"Hush, Brother." Isophel cast him another warning look

and turned back to Valis. "I have a proposition for you, if you will hear me."

Valis gave her a wary nod. "I'm listening."

She gave him an intent stare that made Valis feel small. He straightened his spine to stand taller under her regard to try to shake that feeling. It didn't work.

"If you can win in a battle against my wife and I," she paused to give him a menacing grin, "I will gladly sanction your mission and grant you fifty reliquary guards, one-hundred Aesriphos, and three-hundred laymen warriors to aid you."

"Isophel, you cannot be serious!" Brother Bachris rounded on her, getting into her personal space. "This is ludicrous!"

"Stand down before I have you arrested, Bachris." She rose to her full height, towering over the Patron Priest by several inches until the reed-thin priest looked like a toy in comparison. "This matter is officially no longer in your hands. As Aesriphos, these two men are under *my* purview, and I will deal with them accordingly."

"But if they win—"

Isophel laughed, the sound jarring but joyful, as if this was the most fun she'd had in ages. Her eyes twinkled with mischief when she finally calmed. "Exactly. Thrilling, isn't it?" She shrugged and stared hard at Valis. "I would, of course, stay on as his adviser."

"What do you mean?" Valis asked. He looked from the Patron Priest to the Grand Master Aesriphos and back again, trying to find an answer to his confusion. "What's going on?"

Brother Bachris grimaced and looked distinctly like he might be sick. "If you win against the Grand Master Aesriphos, you unseat them from power, and thus become the next Grand Master Aesriphos. Thus, you gain command of the entire monastery and are under no one but the Sovereign Priest, herself. But, if you fail, you might well die, my boy. Choose *very* wisely. This is not something you want to go into just to prove your worth or the worth of a mission." He frowned deeper. "This is *serious* boys. You have no idea how serious this is."

The Grand Master nodded, agreeing. "Quite serious. Especially for me. Think of all the jeers I would have to endure if I am bested by a team fresh out of Valiant training. But..." She smirked at Valis and turned it onto Tavros next. "But... if they *did* win this challenge, think of their future. The youngest Grand Master Aesriphos in history, and one wields black magic alongside his gold. It would be historic."

She shook her head as if she couldn't believe she was doing this, huffing a soft, amused laugh. "The things I do..." Then she waved at Phalin who stood guarding the reliquary doors with his husband, Shyvus. "I will guard your post. Please go fetch my wife."

"At once, Grand Master."

As he hurried out of the temple, Isophel narrowed her eyes on Valis. "So, lad. What will it be? Abandon your quest for a proper sanction and face expulsion from the Aesriphos

Order should you fail in your attempt to rescue your father, or fight me for my title?"

"Valis," Brother Bachris hissed, "you do realize what this means, yes? She has not been defeated since she has risen to the rank of Grand Master Aesriphos, and she beat the Grand Master before her!"

"I'm aware," Valis said. He took a deep breath and stared into Isophel's good eye. "I'd like to take a moment and discuss this with my husband."

Isophel gave him a curt nod. "You have until my wife arrives."

"Thank you." He led Tavros to the other side of the room and took a deep lungful of air because it had felt like there *was none to be had* while he stood so close to her.

"What do you think?" Tavros asked, he raked both hands through his shaggy black hair and sighed. "Do you think we can beat her?"

Valis glanced back at Isophel with a critical eye. She was large, and she hadn't come upon her title by accident. Nor had she come upon that scar by accident, either. She was battle hardened, but when was the last time she had actually seen a good fight? When was the last she had seen battle?

Another critical look, and Valis knew she still trained, and trained hard. She couldn't keep muscles that size by letting her title make her lazy.

But had she been training with the reliquary guards? Had they taught her and her wife the lessons he had taught them?

There was really no way of knowing, so he sighed. "I'm not sure."

Tavros stepped closer. "Then I have a better question. Do you really want to be the Grand Master Aesriphos? We will keep that position until we are bested, just like her and her wife. And we will constantly have hopefuls throwing down their gauntlets at the chance for our title. Especially due to our age. They will think we got lucky because we're young."

Valis pressed his mouth into a tight line and hung his head. "It's the only way to get this sanctioned. We'll have to, Tav."

His husband let out a quiet groan and looked toward the ceiling as if searching for answers. "At least it isn't a death match. She won't actively be trying to kill us, just knock us unconscious or put us in stasis."

Valis's shoulders drooped so fast he thought he might lose them. "Thank the Gods for that. That worried me the most. I don't want to kill her, and I thought to best her, we'd have to kill her."

"No, no, no," Tavros said. He took both Valis's hands in his and stepped closer. "No, love. I wouldn't allow the fight if that was the case. I'd have called it off the moment she posed the question to you, no matter if you hated me or not for it. I *won't* lose you. Especially not for something like this."

"I'd never hate you," Valis whispered. "I'd be angry, hurt, but I'd never hate you."

"I know." He took a deep breath and squeezed Valis's hands. "Regardless, it is still a very serious fight, and we've never fought anyone at her level of battle before. Do you think we can win?"

Valis stared into his husband's eyes and squared his shoulders. "We can win. We'll just have to use everything in our arsenal, everything we've been training with the reliquary guards every morning."

Tavros frowned. "It may not be enough…"

"It may not, but it's worth a shot," Valis said, putting his determination in his voice. "What have we got to lose? I was prepared to go without a sanction, and I still am. If we beat her that's definitely a great bonus. But if we don't?"

"We can do it," Tavros said. "I'm with you. Forever and always."

CHAPTER TWENTY-ONE

THE DOORS to the temple opened. Valis and Tavros turned to see who entered at the same time, and Valis couldn't hold back his gasp.

Phalin entered, and the woman who followed was nothing like Valis expected. Where Isophel was a beast of a woman, broad and tall, her wife was a petite thing, a head shorter than her wife, and while still strong looking, half as broad. She had her blond hair pulled up into a severe bun at the crown of her head, and her blue eyes seemed so kind that Valis could imagine easily becoming her friend.

She didn't wear the heavily ornate armor, but a normal set with dents and scratches all across the steel, proving it was her training set. The woman seemed so unassuming that Valis almost couldn't see her as Isophel's wife.

"Ephala," Isophel purred. "We may have a fight to attend."

Ephala brightened and went to her wife with a long, confident stride. "Fantastic. Anyone good? It has been so long since we have battled anyone worthy."

Valis gawped at her. She no longer seemed so unassuming.

"The little fish over there," Isophel said with a wave of her hand toward Valis. "He's actually quite good. Bested two of my best reliquary guards. If he can keep from having a vision during the battle, he may actually provide us some fun."

"Excellent!" She got on her toes and Isophel leaned down to meet her for a sweet kiss. "Hopefully this provides some good entertainment. We've been sorely lacking."

"You ladies are horrendous," Brother Bachris muttered. "I cannot believe you are going through with this."

Isophel turned her attention to Valis, ignoring Brother Bachris completely. "Have you made a decision, Valis?"

Valis pulled in a breath and nodded. "We'll fight."

"Then let's head to the arena."

She led the way, and they soon stood in the center of the arena. Valis spared a thought to shield the entryway once everyone was inside and broke it off from himself after adding impermeability from magic and physical force to it. He didn't want any passersby to get hurt during their battle.

"Oh, he's full of surprises," Ephala said as she adjusted her gauntlets. "Interesting."

"Indeed," Isophel said.

Then she rolled her neck, cracking it several times. "Okay. This is a magical battle, not a physical one. And there are two rules." She lifted her finger. "First, is you do not cast the stasis spell until one of the opponents is downed. If they are down for more than a moment, you may attempt the stasis spell.

"Second rule." She held up a second finger. "No one leaves this arena until both partners of one of the teams is disabled."

Nodding, Valis rolled his shoulders and shook the tension from his limbs. "Both are reasonable."

"Then let us begin."

Valis snapped up his shield, encompassing both himself and Tavros. Isophel did the same for herself and her mate. And in the next breath, she and her mate started launching volleys of gold magic to test Valis's shield.

Valis winced at the onslaught but added permanence and impermeability to physical and magical attacks from just one side, just like he had with the fish pen shields. Then he added another thought to siphon all attacks into his own magic reserves. When he broke it off from himself, he let out a sigh of relief and cast his first volley.

"Keep them busy," Valis murmured soft enough that only Tavros would be able to hear. "I have an idea."

"Hurry," Tavros whispered.

Tavros sped up his attacks, launching several attacks at once, his magical missiles arcing through the air followed by golden lightning. Valis could *feel* his lover trying to break their shield. He spared his lover a stream of his magic while he worked on his plan.

Inside himself, Valis started gathering magic in his hand, keeping it invisible with just a thought. The ball gathered in size until it nearly dwarfed Valis and Tavros. With the stunning amount of magic hitting his shield and absorbing into Valis's own magical reserves, Valis could almost imagine his magic would be able to encompass the entire monastery.

When it finally reached its peak, Valis aimed it like a spear. He launched it at Isophel's shield with the thought to shatter it and shock those inside with the residual blast.

The moment it hit, both women shrieked. Tavros's blasts made four direct hits to each woman, knocking them back and bowling them over. Valis was just about to cast the stasis spell when Isophel quickly erected another shield while still in obvious pain.

"What the fuck was that?" Ephala cried. "You little shits!"

Valis didn't answer. Instead, he released a series of concussive blasts that knocked both women off their feet, making them fly across the arena into the far back wall with a loud crash of metal against stone. Valis's stomach rolled. Had he killed them?

But no, their shield was somehow still up. Even as both women seemed to be too stunned to move, or unconscious.

Releasing another volley with the intent to shatter their shield, Valis started gathering his black magic into his left hand, keeping it invisible. The more he could surprise them, the better chance they had at winning. So far, it was looking to be in their favor. They had never seen Valis in a magical battle before. Isophel had only seen him really cast one or two spells during a physical battle against Shyvus and Phalin.

Their shield shattered, and Valis was a breath away from casting the stasis spell when they yet again cast another shield. It seemed somehow stronger this time, as if they hadn't been putting the full force of their magic into the ones before.

Ephala staggered to her feet, wiped at the blood on the back of her neck that must have trickled down from the back of her head and *growled* at them.

"You will pay for that, you little fucks!"

Isophel rolled around on the ground, still stunned. But Valis felt her sending her mate her magic, fueling Ephala in waves that he could almost see.

The woman screamed as she sent a wave of volleys, but all she did was fuel Valis, strengthening his reserves. And in turn, he sent a good portion of that magic into his mate, fueling Tavros as he renewed his attacks.

"Concussive blasts," Valis whispered, barely moving his lips. "Keep them off their feet. Try to knock them out."

Valis did the same, sending out waves of concussive blasts, but somehow, this time, they didn't work. The women didn't move an inch. They seemed completely unaffected.

Isophel finally found her feet. She staggered a step, leaned on Ephala to regain her balance, and glared at Valis with her one good eye. Blood trickled down her face, making her even more terrifying than the scar that went from her temple to her mouth, bisecting her bad eye.

"I think they're toying with us," Tavros whispered. "They're testing our magic, testing what we can do."

"I'm thinking the same," Valis whispered back. He studied the women as Tavros fought on. He could feel his husband's strain, smell the sweat that slicked his skin. His grunts of effort made Valis's heart hurt.

"Take them down," Isophel ordered, her voice ringing like a battle cry.

The ladies renewed their attacks. Their magic stronger. They tried concussive blasts, but because of the restrictions Valis put on his shield, they didn't work. It almost seemed they were at a stalemate. If they couldn't affect him, and Tavros could no longer affect them, then there was no reason to keep on except to exhaust the Grand Master Aesriphos. And who knew how much magic reserve she had.

But Valis's was greater and growing with every attack they launched. And it seemed neither woman realized that fact.

The fight went on for several minutes. Valis absorbing, Tavros attacking. The women were drenched in sweat, but so were Valis and Tavros. Nothing seemed to work now for either side.

And Valis was starting to get physically tired. With the nightmares that plagued him every night, he wasn't getting enough sleep. At least he'd eaten enough at breakfast, but if they survived this, he may need to make another trip to the serving line to refuel. Hopefully this fight didn't last until the kitchens closed.

Only you would think of your stomach at a time like this, Roba griped. *Sometimes I cannot believe you.*

I really need to concentrate right now, Dad.

Roba huffed in his mind. *It seems all you are doing is beating your head against a stone wall.*

Yeah. That's my thoughts. I've got a plan, but I need them tired, first.

Yet, you are the one getting tired.

Yeah. Valis groaned. *Yeah...*

Use a stream of your magic to fuel your body, Roba suggested.

And Valis wanted to smack himself. If he could make Kerac's immune system stronger, could he remedy his own fatigue?

Try it, Roba urged. *No harm will come from trying.*

Taking a deep breath, Valis turned his magic inward, focusing on his tired muscles and exhausted mind. He worked until he felt his fatigue draining away, his body and mind perking up, and his eyes feeling less like they were weighted down by bricks.

Then he did the same to Tavros, and his lover's eyes widened. "You can *do* that?" he whispered hoarsely. "Fuck, Valis!"

"We'll do that later," Valis promised. "Right now, let's finish this fight."

Tavros's laugh bolstered Valis's heart. They could do this. He knew they could.

Valis felt a shift in the air and tensed. Isophel was gathering magic for some kind of giant spell the likes of which Valis had never dreamed. He could see it forming in his mind. That much magic could devastate him. Could he even absorb that much magic at once?

He braced for impact, widening his shield to the full width of the arena so her magic would disperse across it. It would, hopefully, absorb and filter the magic into his reserves gradually instead of exploding into him.

It didn't work out that way.

The ball of pure, uncontrolled magic hit his shields, and Valis's vision whited out. He fought to keep the stream to Tavros going. The only thing saving them was the permanence to Valis's shield and the fact that he'd broken it off in case he was knocked unconscious.

"Valis!"

"I'm okay," Valis croaked. "Keep fighting."

It took long, painful minutes for Valis to regain his sight. His entire body felt like he'd been struck by lightning. He felt *burned*, but his skin seemed whole. His mind slowly came back to him. His blurred vision slowly cleared.

He couldn't take another blast like that. If he did, he'd be a liability to Tavros.

"I have an idea," Valis whispered. His voice was so hoarse that he could barely even do that. "Keep them focused on you. And don't freak out."

He gritted his teeth but nodded. "Got it."

Tavros's trust humbled Valis. He would reward that trust by ending this soon.

Using a trick he had used before in training, Valis drew on his black magic and made it invisible. He spread it across the arena floor in front of him, under the Grand Master Aesriphos' boots. It shimmered to his own sight, letting him know it was in place, even though he could *feel* it.

With a breath, he lifted it up violently. The women both let out shrieks of surprise as they hit the ceiling. Then Valis jerked them forward as that mist of black magic curled around their shields and tossed them to the left-hand arena wall. Then did it again, smacking them against the right. Another violent thrust, and they bounced off the ceiling again, landing hard on the floor.

Then, with a thought, Valis disappeared. He formed another shield around just himself, keeping it invisible. But this time, he made *himself* invisible.

The moment he winked out of sight, Tavros let out a startled cry. Valis placed a hand on his arm and squeezed, letting him know that he hadn't gone anywhere. And then, he phased.

He ended up behind Isophel and used a concussive blast to knock both women against their shield. He pummeled them so hard and fast with concussive blasts and mage bolts that they couldn't tell where they were coming from and had no defense.

Their shield shattered when he knocked Ephala unconscious with a concussive blast directly to her head. Isophel screeched and tried to find him, her fists swinging, knowing that he had to be there somewhere. But every time she got close, Valis would phase away, always behind her.

He caught her in the back of the head with a concussive blast that sent her face-first into the back wall, and she crumpled to the floor in a bloody heap.

When Tavros cast the stasis spell, Valis fell to his knees and drew the shields back into himself, reappearing to Tavros.

"Valis?"

"Exhausted."

"Me, too. Use your magic to do what you did before, love." He came up behind him and squeezed Valis's shoulders. "You did well. I never... I never thought I would see this... or be *here*. Valis... We *bested* the fucking *Grand Master Aesriphos*!"

Valis lolled his head back and rested it against Tavros's abdomen. "We did. Now, let's get these ladies back to the temple."

Tavros constructed the magical litter and Valis carefully levitated the women onto it. Both dragged their feet as they headed through the halls and ascended the stairs, followed by several gawping Aesriphos who had happened by to stop and watch the battle. Brother Bachris was also there, and when they passed him, he was whiter than his uniform.

"Boys..."

"Not now, Brother," Valis mumbled. "Too tired for that shit."

Once they made it to the temple, Valis lowered the litter

and removed the stasis spell from both women, drawing the magic back into himself. He set about healing their wounds while he waited for them to wake on their own. Then sat back on his ass and closed his eyes.

Tavros collapsed next to him. At the same time, they leaned against each other, holding each other up as the Aesriphos who had followed them laughed.

It took a few minutes, but after Valis rested a bit, he poured magic into them both, reducing their fatigue until Valis no longer felt like passing out. Then he stood and helped his husband up, hauling him to his feet with a grunt.

"Boys..."

"I really don't want to hear it, Brother Bachris," Valis said. He turned to face off against the man, who gave him a frosty stare. "I have *earned* the right to go after my father. And you will no longer stop me."

"Valis, you must see reason! Please!"

Valis sighed. "I do see reason. I see every reason to rescue my father from sitting in his own filth. I see reason to rescue him from freezing and starvation and pain and fatigue. I see *every reason* to rescue him from impending death." He glared at Brother Bachris. "Now, it's time for *you* to *see reason.*"

"See here, young man!" Brother Bachris rose to his full height and stormed toward him, his forefinger wagging like he was scolding an unruly child. "You—"

"That is enough, Brother Bachris." Valis whirled around toward the reliquary doors as Thyran threw them open. The reliquary guards stationed to either side barely caught them in time to keep their faces safe. "That is *quite* enough."

"Stay out of this, historian," Brother Bachris hissed. "This does not concern you."

"On the contrary," Thyran said in a calm, authoritative tone. "Anything and everything in this monastery is my concern."

"I fail to see how."

"You will hold your tongue, Brother."

Brother Bachris gasped as Kyris Yavih swept out of the reliquary behind Thyran. "Sovereign Priest!"

"Thyran is *my* superior, Brother Bachris," Kyris said. She gave him a chilly smile. "You *will* stand down."

"But—"

Thyran folded his hands before him. "I am now, and have been since Sovras's ascent, the August Patriarch of this monastery and our faith. Kyris and all Sovereign Priests before her have been tasked with keeping my secret, to keep me safe so that the monastery would never fall."

He waved a hand to Isophel and Ephala. "The only others who knew are my reliquary guards and the Grand Master Aesriphos. I am the *reason* we *have* reliquary guards."

Brother Bachris blinked at him stupidly for a moment. Then his face flushed with embarrassment. "I am... I am so very sorry, Aug—August Patriarch."

Thyran ignored him for the moment and focused on Valis. "As you have bested my Grand Masters, Valis and Tavros, that means you have taken their ranks. As such, they will stand in your place while you go on your mission."

Valis gasped. "Truly? Thyran... Thank you."

The August Patriarch gave him his usual grin, dropping the formality. "My boy, you have truly surpassed all my expectations."

"Why didn't you tell Brother Bachris or even the Grand Master Aesriphos to allow the sanction when this began?" Tavros demanded. "You've made him suffer so—"

Thyran lifted a hand and gave him a sheepish smile. "Because I had a vision." He motioned to Isophel and Ephala. "This... needed to come to pass before Valis went on his mission, and if I had interfered in any way, it would not have. I am the one who told them to humor Brother Bachris's demands to reject your mission request due to that vision. They were under my orders."

He walked over, gripping Valis and Tavros's shoulders, looking from one man to the other. "I truly am sorry for the heartache, sorrow and confusion. But, in some cases, I must let matters play out as they will so that the greater good can be accomplished. The fact that I can do this, that I can set my heart aside to listen to Sovras's wishes through my visions, is precisely why Sovras made me his August Patriarch." He frowned. "It is, indeed, not an easy position to bear. Especially when I care for someone so much and must watch them hurt to ensure the proper outcome comes to pass."

Valis stepped forward and hugged him. "It was worth it," he whispered. "Now that I know... it was worth it."

Thyran squeezed him tight and patted the back of his head. "I hope so."

Isophel groaned from the floor and when Valis turned to look at her, he pulled away and went to her side to help her sit up. "How do you feel? I tried to heal all your injuries."

"Little rat bastard," she grumbled. "Just bruised pride. I'll get over it, you shit."

Chuckling, Valis took a moment to rouse Ephala and help her up as well.

"So, you managed to beat us," Ephala said. "Interesting." She looked over at Isophel and grinned. "We finally get a vacation."

"Not quite yet," Thyran mused. "You are acting Grand Master Aesriphos in Valis's stead. You did promise him that if he bested you two, he would have his mission sanctioned and be afforded the men and women he needs to succeed."

Isophel grunted and stood, helping her lover up. "Yeah. I did say that, didn't I? Well... vacation can wait, I suppose." She looked at Valis and gave him a nod. "You did well, lad. Underhanded and dirty as fuck, but you did well."

"But—"

Valis looked over at Brother Bachris and frowned when he saw tears in the priest's eyes.

"No..." He blinked the tears away as his chin shivered. "You can't go," he whispered. "No..."

Thyran stepped over and rested his hand on Brother Bachris's shoulder. "Have some faith in him. He is stronger than you know."

"I have never lost a child," Brother Bachris said, sounding lost. "I don't want to start now…"

Valis scooped him up into a crushing hug. "You won't lose me, Brother. I'll be back. I promise."

"You'd better," he said in a watery voice. "You'd damned well better."

CHAPTER TWENTY-TWO

AT DINNER, Valis couldn't get away from the surge of congratulations that poured in from seemingly everyone in the entire monastery. How his victory against the Grand Master Aesriphos had spread through the monastery so fast was beyond his imagination, but apparently it had. He groaned when another person left and tried to focus on his food. He was still recovering from that battle. His stomach definitely wasn't happy about all the attention he was getting. It didn't help that even his friends were in shock and could barely stop staring at him and Tavros.

Tavros seemed to be taking it all in stride, or at least, he was better at hiding his discomfort. He ate quietly, accepting congratulations with grace, and patiently kept rubbing the back of Valis's neck when his shoulders started climbing up toward his ears.

"Love, you need to calm down."

Valis glanced over. "How are *you* so calm?"

Tavros smiled and kissed his temple. "Because you need me to be."

And with that, Valis fell in love with his husband all over again. "Thank you."

"Always," Tavros said. "Forever and always."

Not long after they began eating, Thyran sat down with them with his own tray and nudged Valis's elbow. "We have a meeting after dinner. I wish you and Tavros to join me outside the city at the docks." He glanced at the others who sat with them and smiled. "You all may come as well, but none of you may participate or interfere. The same goes for you, Tavros. This is for Valis only."

"He won't get hurt?" Tavros asked.

"You should know me better than that," Thyran said. "I would never intentionally hurt him *or* you."

Tavros nodded. "Then I'll be fine. But I *will* interfere if Valis gets hurt."

Thyran smirked and gave Tavros a respectful nod. "Very well. I will give you all an hour to let your food settle after dinner, then I will meet you at the docks. And be prepared. It may take a while."

"Yes, sir," everyone said in unison.

"I can go, too?" Aenali asked.

Thyran turned a gentle smile on the little girl and nodded. "You may, but you must stay on your brother's shoulders. That way you can both see what transpires, and also not get trampled. I won't have you hurt if something goes wrong. Jedai can get you out of there faster than you can, yourself."

"Okay!"

As they went back to eating, Zhasina tilted her head. "Do you have a date set?"

Valis furrowed his brow. "We need to give the Aesriphos enough time to amass their own winter gear, pack, and say goodbye to their friends. Three or four days should be enough."

"I will send the order," Thyran said. "Three days is enough. You will leave an hour after sunrise so you aren't facing the worst of the morning's chill."

"I'll keep in contact through two-way scry if I can't reach you telepathically." Valis glanced over as he sipped his creamy spiced tea. He needed the calming effects today. "And if anything arises, we have four trained couriers with us."

"Good." Thyran heaved a sigh and went back to eating, so Valis did, too. Then the August Patriarch turned again and rested a hand on Valis's shoulder. "Do make sure you see Brother Bachris before you leave. He is… distraught."

Nodding, Valis swallowed what was in his mouth. "I'll be making my rounds to say goodbye. I won't leave him out. I know he was only doing it because he's scared."

Thyran relaxed and nodded. "Then let us finish our meals and rest before we head out. It may be a long night."

Two hours later, Valis stood on the docks with his friends. He glanced up at the sky, watching the stars as he waited for Thyran to show. He pulled his cloak tighter about him. The evening brought with it a deep chill that threatened to settle into Valis's bones.

"Ah, you are here," Thyran said from behind them. Valis turned, and Thyran smiled at him. "Let us head across the lake. Everyone else is waiting."

As a unit, they all filed onto the ferry and set off for the shore. "What's going on?" Valis asked.

"You need to be as ready as possible for the coming months," Thyran said cryptically. "I am going to ensure you are."

That did and did not instill confidence, but Valis settled and tried to enjoy the ride across the lake.

When they made it to the other side, everyone followed Thyran past the Kalutakeni camp, through the dense weeping whiptails, and out into a giant patch of grass that held what seemed like every priest and Aesriphos in the monastery, including faces of people Valis had never met. Tall torches lit the area, stuck into the ground at even intervals, making it almost seem festive.

"Head to the center," Thyran said. "Everyone else, stay back."

Hundreds of people stood in the giant circle, spaced so that they all had a direct line of sight to the very center with some sitting, others kneeling, some in chairs while others stood. At the back, yet more stood on risers to see above those in front. It was all so grand that Valis's breath caught in his throat and he gripped Tavros's hand tight.

"Tavros may come with you," Thyran said gently. "He just cannot participate."

"Understood," Tavros said, his voice subdued.

Now that they were out here, Valis had an idea of what Thyran meant to do. Every person present was a magic user, and Thyran was going to have him absorb their magical attacks to further expand his already obscenely large magic pool.

Thyran gave him a quirked smile over his shoulder with a small nod. "Exactly."

Thyran guided Valis into the center of the circle, and Valis blushed as he was met with Kyris Yavih, the Sovereign Priest of Phaerith, as well as Brother Bachris, his wife, Sister Qisryn, and many others. His Sovereign Priest cupped his cheek and murmured just for him, "I am so proud of you, Grand Master. You have exceeded my expectations."

His blush deepened, but Valis managed to swallow down his embarrassment and murmur back, "Thank you. I've been trying hard."

"It shows. You have been a great wonder for us all."

Valis nodded. "Thank you."

She patted his cheek and stepped away to take her place within the circle and Thyran rested a hand on the back of Valis's neck, breaking his thoughts on their conversation, and lifted his voice above the din, "Your attention, please." When the crowd quieted, he let go of Valis's neck and stepped away into the sea of people facing Valis. "I have called you all here for a very important purpose. We are about to embark on a task that has never been attempted before, let alone accomplished."

Murmurs arose, but Thyran held up a hand. "When I give the word, every mage is to attack Valis with the full strength of your magic. Do you understand?"

"What?" someone shrieked. "You can't be serious, Thyran! That will kill the boy!"

Thyran grinned. "I highly doubt that."

Kyris stepped away from her place and lifted her voice, "As Thyran wills it, so it is ordered. On Thyran's mark."

"Erect your shield, Valis," Thyran said. "And trust in yourself."

Thyran smiled and said into his mind, *You can do this. Absorb until I call off the attack. By draining all of them at once, you won't drain them until they are all useless, but* you *will become exponentially more powerful, and I have foreseen you will need such power. Do you understand?*

Yes, sir.

"On my mark."

Valis erected his shield with a thought, strengthening it with all that he had, setting it to have permanence and to siphon all attacks into his reserves before breaking it off from his direct will.

"Attack!"

Nothing could have prepared Valis for this attack. The sheer power behind it nearly sent him to the floor. It took him several heart-stopping moments to get his head right and get back on his feet with the help of Tavros. But once that drain began, it was like nothing Valis had ever felt, not even when he drained the Grand Master Aesriphos. Not even when he drained the entire army of Qos adherents who had escaped the prison.

Elation didn't even come close. It was the highest euphoria. Something that made him feel godlike and humbled at the same time. As their combined magic flowed into him, Valis felt such peace that he could have wept for the joy of it.

As hard as the Aesriphos and Priests—even Thyran and the Sovereign Priest—tried, they couldn't break his shield, and their power flowed into it, and then straight into Valis.

Where taking in the magic of Qos made Valis feel agitated, murderous, and made his vision go into shades of gray, the magic of his friends brought on a heightening to his consciousness so powerful he felt he could almost touch Sovras in his ascended state.

Valis let his head fall back, his eyes closed in his euphoria. When he opened them again, though, he gasped. An orb of light hovered over the group and shined bright enough to light up the night. Rays of golden light shone down onto him, touching his shield as if it, too, offered magic for Valis to absorb.

Was it real? Could it be real? The Light of Phaerith had moved outside?

It is real, Thyran said into his mind. *It is still the Light of Phaerith. I have never seen it outside of the temple's dome...*

Valis could only nod, smiling at the awe in Thyran's voice. His eyes watered as emotion overwhelmed him.

Sovras, his friend and God, was blessing him with magic, and Valis could do nothing but accept. It felt like the onslaught went on for hours, magic pouring into him like floodwaters through a broken dam. He nearly crumpled from the intensity, and just before he succumbed, Thyran called, "Stop the attack!"

The golden light winked out all throughout the area save for the glow from the torches. Valis dropped his shield, drawing the magic back into himself. Soon after, someone attacked his face with a soft cloth.

"I swear, Child, you and that Light must stop if you are going to leak like this," Thyran muttered, though Valis heard the fond teasing in his voice as Thyran mopped up Valis's face. If he had gotten used to anything, it was having his face dried by random priests, and maybe a friend or two. The fond thought made him lift his head, and he straightened his posture. He looked Thyran in the eyes, and the historian regarded him seriously. *You now are more powerful than Kyris. Use it wisely and tell no one.*

Not even Tavros? Valis asked.

You may tell Tavros. If he asks. Otherwise keep it to yourself. And if he does ask, make sure he is sworn to absolute secrecy.

Yes, sir.

Brother Bachris came up to him and without warning, pulled Valis into a hug so tight he feared the Patron Priest would break his own arms. He hesitantly returned the hug and sighed. "I love you, too, Bachris."

"I'm so sorry, my boy," he whispered. "I just don't want to see you hurt or dead."

"I know. But, have faith in me." He squeezed a little tighter. "I won't let you down."

"I will, Valis," Brother Bachris said. "I promise I will if you promise to come back to us."

Valis grinned and rested his forehead on his friend's shoulder. "I will always come home, Brother. I promise."

———

BACK INSIDE THE MONASTERY, THE FIRST PLACE VALIS WANTED to go was to see Kerac. So much power swirled through him, that Valis needed comfort, and he needed to rest. And with Tavros tagging along by his side, Valis rushed through the halls toward Kerac's suite.

"Are you sure you're okay?" Tavros asked.

"Just jittery," Valis said. "And it's like a wave keeps crashing over me. It's making me tense. I just need time to let it settle like I did back in Lyvea after siphoning Qeraden's magic. It's not making me fall into darkness. It's actually a weird feeling of elation. But I still need to rest and let my body absorb everything before I go mad."

"Are you sure it was a good idea to leave our friends behind? You always calm down when you hold Aenali."

Valis smiled fondly. "Yeah, I do." He sighed. "They know where we're going. I'm sure they won't be far behind. They're just not running like we are. I just... I need..."

"I know, love. It's okay."

Once Valis reached Kerac's door, he threw it open and rushed into his fathers' bedroom, careful not to make much noise in case he was sleeping. But when he entered, he found Kerac in bed, awake, reading a book. He set the book down with shaking hands and smiled brightly. "Valis." Then he must have seen Valis's harried look, because he reached out. "What is wrong? Come here."

Valis went, but instead of sitting on the edge of the bed, he kicked off his boots and laid next to him on the vacant side, rolling until he carefully snuggled to Kerac's side.

When his Papa's familiar scent was all he could smell, all the tension that had been thrumming through him finally started to ease away. And as Kerac's bony fingers threaded through his hair, his body relaxed further into the mattress.

"He just had his power augmented," Tavros explained. "He said he's jittery and needs comfort. He'll be okay in a couple hours."

Valis felt Kerac shrug. "Then kick off your shoes and join us. No sense in you standing all the way over there while we laze about."

A few moments later, boots hit the floor, and the bed dipped behind Valis. Tavros's arm wound about Valis's middle, and he pressed a kiss to the back of Valis's head.

"Do you need sleep, or…"

Valis glanced up at Kerac. "No. I just needed you, and to relax for a while."

Kerac nodded, and as he went back to reading, Valis

dozed for a while. He didn't know how long. Didn't care. But the peace it brought was *everything*. After a while, he got used to the power that swirled in him. Then he realized that he didn't need to absorb anything. He had already done that part. All he had to do was get *accustomed* to it.

When that realization settled in his mind, the rest of Valis's tension left him, and he cuddled deeper against Kerac's side with a sleepy purr. Kerac chuckled and patted his back. "Someone sounds content."

"I am." Valis cracked a yawn and grunted as he shifted. Tavros had fallen asleep behind him, and he was a heavy weight against Valis's back. But at least he was a warm weight, so Valis didn't care.

"So, what have you been up to today?"

Valis tried to sit up to tell him about it, but Tavros muttered something in his sleep and rolled more heavily on top of him. Since he couldn't sit up, he gave up and settled for mumbling the story into Kerac's side. "I became the new Grand Master Aesriphos with Tav."

"WHAT?"

That woke Tavros up and he sat straight up in bed. Now that his weight was gone, Valis sat up and stretched his back. "I said, Tav and I became the new Grand Master Aesriphos. We beat Isophel and Ephala in a magical duel."

Kerac paled. "Oh…"

"And in the process," Valis went on, "we got the mission sanctioned, because I'm now the one who sanctions missions. We will have reliquary guards and Aesriphos amongst our ranks, and we will be leaving in a few days once we get all our plans finalized."

He gripped Kerac's hand and squeezed. "We're bringing Father home. One way or another."

Kerac sucked in a sharp gasp. He reached for Valis, and Valis didn't deny him. He scooted over and wrapped his papa in a gentle hug and whispered against his ear. "We're bringing him home. I don't know how long I'll be gone, but we *will* bring him home."

"I wish I could go with you," Kerac murmured miserably. "I should be going with you."

"You should be staying here and getting stronger," Valis said. "Because Father is going to need you when we get back. He'll most likely be in a similar state as you are now, and he will need tons of care. Care that *you* will be able to provide by the time we return if you do what Firil says."

"Come to me before you leave."

"I'll make sure he does," Tavros said. "He's been groggy in the mornings of late because of his nightmares. But we'll be here before we leave. It should be in a few days. We have most of the supplies already ready to go. We just need the last bits and time for the Aesriphos assigned to our mission to get their own gear ready for departure."

After a few moments of silence, just breathing each other in and holding on tight, Kerac pulled back and looked into Valis's face, his golden eyes wet and searching. "I finally know what it meant."

"What what meant, Papa?"

Kerac's face brightened with a contented smile. "That dream. I am sitting in the grass, and you come cresting the hill. And you cry out, 'Papa! I'm home!' The dream I had for so long in my youth." He snapped out of his reverie and smirked. "It almost caused me to brush off Darolen's proposal. But he was strong, and I thought 'This is real. This is a guarantee. That boy may never happen.' But…" He stared at Valis again like a hungry man at a feast. "It will happen, Valis. *You* will make it happen by coming home to me. Do you understand me?"

Valis swallowed the lump in his throat and nodded. "I promise, Papa."

CHAPTER TWENTY-THREE

ON THE EVENING before Valis and his friends were due to leave, Valis started his rounds. He wanted to find as many of his friends who weren't leaving with him as possible before dinner so that he didn't miss anyone. He and his friends would be making last-minute adjustments to their saddle-bags and gear in Valis's sitting room and then taking every-thing down to the stables so it would be ready and waiting on their saddled horses when they were ready to leave.

Tavros had gone to do his own rounds, and as Valis made his way to his next destination, he wished Tavros had joined him. But not because he wanted his lover's support. More that he wanted him to hear everything that was said, too.

He knocked on Brother Bachris's door, and when the man called for him to enter, Valis opened the door a crack and peeked in. "You busy?"

The Patron Priest set his pen down and smiled. "Never too busy for you, my boy. Come to say goodbye to an old man?" He motioned Valis to enter and shooed him toward the fire once he stepped in. "Come. Sit with me."

As Valis made himself comfortable on the couch, he watched as Brother Bachris poured two cups of tea and brought over a plate of cookies, setting them on the low table between Valis and Brother Bachris's favorite chair. "Qisryn made these earlier today. They're still fresh."

Then he busied himself with something else, and Valis got the idea that he was actually stalling because he didn't want to have to say goodbye yet. That feeling solidified when he saw Brother Bachris tidying up his desk and muttering something about missing reports. The man had never fidgeted like this before in Valis's presence, so it had to mean he was either nervous or avoiding something.

"Brother Bachris," Valis said. When the Patron Priest finally lifted his head and met his eyes, Valis smirked. "Come sit down before you accidentally start a fire from all that fidgeting you're doing. Paper's flammable, you know."

"Insolent brat," he muttered, but it held no heat. He came over and sat in his usual chair with a sigh. "I am sorry, Valis."

"I'll miss you, too, Bachris."

The Patron Priest combed his fingers through the frost at his temples and smiled into the fire. "I will miss you. I wish there was some other way…"

"But there isn't." Valis reached for his tea and took a sip

before going on, "There is only one way, and I'm going to succeed. You'll see."

Bachris sighed. "I hope so, my boy." He smiled sadly at Valis, his blue eyes as soulful as Valis had ever seen them. "I truly am sorry. I should not have put you under so much stress, especially for something that, deep down, I knew was inevitable. All I did was make things worse, and I apologize."

"Apology accepted, Brother." Leaning forward, Valis set his cup down and took one of the cookies. He wasn't going to let Sister Qisryn's baking skills go to waste. Not that he thought Brother Bachris would let such a travesty happen, but he would pull his weight. "At the end I knew what your fears were."

"Still…"

"That's enough, my friend." Valis sighed and looked over the stately man across from him, watching the firelight play across half of his face, casting the other in shifting shadows in a comforting way. "I want you to promise me something."

"What is it?"

"Keep an eye on Kerac and Aryn for me. Visit them often and let them know they're both still loved. Especially Aryn. He's prone to depression in prison, and he needs someone who isn't his therapist to visit him."

"Now that is an easy promise to keep, my boy."

Valis spent another hour with him. After dinner, he and his friends made a trip down to the prison. The last person Valis needed to see was Aryn. None of them could leave without telling him goodbye. He wouldn't understand. Not in his current mental state. And it didn't take much energy.

They waited in the Duty Captain's office while the guards went to get Aryn from his cell and into the interrogation room. Then they all filed into the room with that tiny cell in the back corner. The dingy walls seemed to close in, and as everyone stood around, wondering how to say goodbye, Valis eased to the front and reached through the bars.

"You're leaving…"

Valis smiled as Aryn leaned into his touch. "We head out in the morning to rescue my father, yes. I got the mission sanctioned, and we're waiting for daylight before we leave."

"But…"

Taking his hands, Valis pulled Aryn closer to the bars and rubbed his arms. "Brother Bachris will come visit you often. I asked him to come apart from your therapy sessions and spend time with you since we won't be able to. I've asked the Duty Captain to always let Aenali come in, too, and to allow you to have any books she brings you."

He gripped Aryn's arms. "Just because we're leaving doesn't mean you'll be forgotten. Papa said that when he's able to move around, he'll even come see you. He's actually planning on convincing some of his Aesriphos friends who promised to sit with him on watches to carry him down here to spend time with you. So, please don't think you'll be forgotten, Aryn. Don't break my heart like that."

Aryn wiped at his damp eyes and nodded. "I'll miss you

guys. Just be careful, okay?" He stared hard at his brother. "And you make sure Valis comes home safe."

"Always, little brother. You've got my word on that."

Then Aryn turned wet eyes on Valis, his tears falling over his lashes. "And make sure Tav comes home safe. Please, Valis."

"I promise," Valis whispered thickly. "We'll both come home, and we'll have my father with us. You'll see."

"And we just don't matter," Seza remarked to Zhasina in a conversational tone. "Aryn only loves those two. So glad we're loved, Zhas."

"It *is* great, isn't it?" her wife replied. "We should be—"

"I haven't gotten to you two yet!" Aryn protested. "I'll miss all of you, damn it. I just can't see most of you because of Valis and Tavros's big heads."

"My head is not big!" Tavros cried.

And all Valis could do was laugh. He moved out of the way after giving Aryn an awkward hug and a kiss to his forehead, letting the others have their turn for love. By the time Aenali got done with him, they all said their final goodbyes, and it was time to head up to finalize their packing.

Aryn stopped them as they got to the open door to the interrogation room. "Valis…"

Valis turned around and frowned at the way Aryn clutched the bars. "What is it?"

The boy took a deep breath, his lower lip wobbling. "I'm sorry. I wish I could take back the last few months. I just… I'm so sorry. Neither you nor Tav deserved what I did."

Tavros stepped in and went to the bars, Valis close behind. They pulled Aryn as close as they could with the bars in the way as Tavros whispered, "That's all we needed to hear."

Aryn clutched at their shirts, his hands trembling. "I couldn't let you go... Not without saying it." He sobbed and rested his forehead against the bars. "I couldn't. Couldn't risk you never knowing how sorry I am."

"Aryn..." Valis reached in and stroked a hand down the boy's hair. "We will be back. I promise."

"You can't make that promise." Aryn stared at him with wide, wet eyes, his face turning red from trying to keep his emotions in check. "Anything can happen on a mission. And I just wanted you to know..."

"It means everything," Tavros said. "And we'll be careful. *That* is something we can promise."

———

KERAC CLUNG TO HIM WITH FRAIL, TREMBLING ARMS. IT wasn't even dawn yet, but his papa had been awake, waiting for him, tears already in his eyes and they hadn't even said goodbye yet. Valis kissed his forehead and leaned in, resting their heads together. "Be strong for me, Papa. Be strong and brave and do your best. I won't let you down."

Kerac shuddered and held on tighter. "And *you* do everything you must to stay alive. As much as it pains me to even think it, Darolen may be a lost cause, but *you* are *not*. Do you understand me, my son? You are not expendable. You *must* return." His voice cracked on his last words, and Valis rubbed his back while Kerac tried to regain his composure.

"I understand, Papa."

"Then go," he whispered. "And serve us well. We are counting on you."

Valis knew Kerac was talking about himself and Darolen rather than the monastery or even the city. That thought was what made Valis break down, but he reined it in, if barely.

"I'll see you as soon as I can."

And before either of them could get more emotional, Valis strode out of the room and went to collect his bags and his friends.

The morning dawned bright and clear and cold. Valis stared at the sky, his heart heavy but hopeful as hundreds of men and women checked their geared horses, making sure they had everything. Valis had already checked his and Tavros'. Twice. He'd already been to the Kalutakeni camp, and they were packed and ready to go, their caravan wagons locked up and moved into tight rows to make a smaller dent on the shore for when winter came, and space might be needed. The mercenaries had mounted up not long before and now waited outside the city along the banks with the Kalutakeni.

Everything was ready, and Valis wanted to remember this

moment forever. No matter the promises he had made to everyone, this might be the last time he saw Cadoras. It might be the last he saw of the only home he had ever known, the only place he had ever felt safe and loved.

When he glanced back at the monastery, hordes of people stood around hugging their friends and family, wishing them well, or waving to those already ahorse with tears in their eyes and shouting wishes for their swift return.

Valis had never seen the city so busy and full of people except for the night of the Autumn Festival, and it seemed the entire city had come to see them off, not just the monastery.

"Valis!"

Valis turned toward where he heard his name and his eyes widened. Aryn ran toward him, still in his prison uniform and with a prison blanket wrapped around his shoulders in place of a winter cloak. Two guards strode after him, though at a slower pace followed by Sister Qisryn. Aryn launched himself into Valis's arms and clung to his neck. "Come home safe."

"Since he's progressed so far, I asked the Duty Captain to remand him to my care for the day," Sister Qisryn explained when she caught up. "He has earned this."

"Thank you, Sister."

She leaned in and squeezed his shoulder. "Be safe. I expect your mission to be a success, young man."

"I promise."

He hugged Aryn tighter, and something inside himself, a

precognitive feeling that tugged at him made him press his hand to Aryn's back. Magic flooded through him, and he unlocked Aryn's magical reserve, allowing it to start regenerating. Aryn's gasp against his neck told Valis he was successful.

"Why did you do that?" Aryn asked in a strained voice. "Why?"

"Because Phaerith demanded it," Valis whispered. "And I will always obey."

The boy shook in his arms and he pulled back. "I won't let either of you down, Valis. Never again."

"I know you won't." Valis motioned back toward the guards. "Go on and say goodbye to the others so they can get you back inside. It's freezing out here." He bent down and picked up the blanket, wrapping it around Aryn's shoulders. "Be good and stick with your therapy."

Rising on his toes, Aryn kissed Valis's cheek with a soft, "Promise," and ran after his brother.

"I have something for you, Valis." Brother Bachris stepped forward into the space Aryn had just vacated and held out a small paper sack. "To remind you of home."

Valis opened the bag and looked in but saw tons of little paper-wrapped sachets. But the smell was wonderful, spicy and sweet.

"The spices the kitchen puts into the spiced milk you guzzle at every meal," the Patron Priest explained. "The instructions on how to mix them are inside with the spices."

He shrugged and sighed. "It may not last you the whole journey, but if you use it sparingly…"

"It's perfect, Brother Bachris," Valis said. He coughed, clearing his throat and turned to stuff the bag in his already overfull saddlebags. "Thank you. I was wondering how I was going to live without it."

The old man laughed and clapped him on the shoulder. "I figured. Now, I must get back inside. This frigid weather does mean things to an old man's bones. Be well, Valis."

"You, too."

The stream of people seemed never ending. Everyone he had ever known or met who wasn't part of the army leaving with him came to say their goodbyes and wish him luck. It had started off a welcome thing, with just his closest friends, but then it started to get overwhelming.

"Deep breaths, Valis," Thyran said.

Valis almost jumped out of his skin. Thyran had appeared from thin air, having apparently phased before him. Clutching at his heart, Valis gasped, "Don't *do* that!"

The August Patriarch laughed and pulled him into a tight hug. "My apologies. I could not get through the throng of people, and I saw my opportunity."

He pulled back and held Valis at arm's length. "Remember what I told you. Tell no one."

"Yes, sir."

"And contact me for anything, and with any news, whether via telepathy or scry."

"Yes, sir."

"And stay warm."

"Yes, sir."

"Do you have your pocket watch?"

Valis laughed. "Yes, sir."

Thyran sighed. "And come home safe, Grand Master. That is an order."

Valis stood straighter and grinned. "Yes, sir."

"Now..." Thyran looked distinctly uncomfortable as he stared at the ground. He sighed. "I have not had to say goodbye to anyone I truly cared for in so long, I forgot how heartbreaking it is."

Valis smiled and squeezed his biceps. "It isn't 'goodbye,' Thyran. It's 'until we meet again.' I'll be home. Have as much faith in me as I've had in you since we met."

He smiled a little at that and looked up from the ground. "I will endeavor to do so." Letting out another sigh, Thyran snatched Valis into a fierce hug and pulled away. "Safe journey. I expect a report soon."

"Of course."

When Thyran turned and left, Valis noticed that the crowd was hanging back, and that meant it was time for them to leave. He hauled himself into his saddle and adjusted his winter cloak, then his gauntlets before grabbing his reins from the handler. He took one last look at his home, saying a prayer to Sovras for their safe return, and guided his horse around, pointing them toward the gates.

As he led his army out of Cadoras and across the lake, he gazed back at the high walls that protected his home. If he committed the place to memory, he felt he might just make it back.

"You okay?"

He glanced to his side and smiled at Tavros. "Yeah. Just memorizing home."

Tavros looked over his shoulder at the wall and sighed. "I get it. But we'll be back."

"Yes. We will."

Once the last of their men had crossed the lake and everyone was in formation, Valis urged Rasera into a canter. He wanted to give his horse his head, let him gallop until nightfall, knowing that Rasera could and would. Most likely happily, too. But he needed to keep their numbers tight, keep everyone together, and keep their horses fresh.

Because in the journey ahead, he had no idea what they would run into. And he had no idea how long their journey would be. Endless miles separated him from his father. Snow would come all too soon. And Valis was new at commanding so many.

He had to be careful.

He had to stay safe.

But most of all, he had to come home.

"Yes," he whispered to himself again. "We will."

To Be Continued in *Anchors*...

Read it now!

WANT TO KNOW MORE ABOUT GOD JARS?

Visit the wiki to get more information about The God Jars Saga.

There you will find interesting things like an overview and map of the continent of Peralea, a glossary of terms, the ranking list of the Aesriphos order, the full book list, and more information on each character. The information there grows with every book written.

Come find out more about the intriguing and volatile world of The God Jars, and continue your immersive experience!

Head to the Wiki now!
www.devonvesper.com/wiki

ALSO BY DEVON VESPER

The God Jars Saga

Fated (Newsletter Freebie)

Saviors

Avristin

Possessed

Support

Mentor

Betrayal

Marshal

Anchors

Incursion

The God Jars Holiday Single

Solstice

Adradis Singles

Soulbond: The Omega's Assassin

ABOUT THE AUTHOR

I'm a mother, furbaby spoiler, and a girl who can't get enough of pretty, pretty boys. As a kid, I traveled the world, too young to appreciate the gift I was given, but now those adventures spur on stories that my brain just can't keep up with. Well, my brain tells me it keeps up just fine, but my fingers are the slow ones. I'll let you decide. But the boys, man. The boys I remember make my heart sizzle looking back on them. Being a kid at nude beaches, I never cared, but looking back on those memories of Sicily, WHEW! There are some really great childhood images that I wish I could have been an adult to savor.

Home is some place I call "rustic". I'm used to large cities, stores everywhere, gas stations on every corner. Here in rural Pennsylvania, it's rustic and beautiful. And quiet. Too quiet. With all this quiet, all there is to do is write stories, and let the hot men in my head out to play. We all benefit, yes? I like this development. The only thing I dislike about this rusticness is the fact I can't find a coffee shop that sells a proper chai latte. They make it from powder. Ew. This makes for a disgruntled Dev. Ugh. I miss my chai.

Most of all, I am a down-to-earth southern girl at heart from spending 16 years in Florida. If you chat with me, you'll hear endearments like darlin', sweetheart, and hon/hun/hunnie. It's who I am, and if we chat, you're almost instantly family, so get used to it.

Don't forget to join my newsletter!

And if you want to chat at me, find me on:
www.devonvesper.com

facebook.com/AuthorDevonVesper
twitter.com/DevonVesper
instagram.com/devonvesper
bookbub.com/authors/devon-vesper
amazon.com/author/devonvesper

Dear Reader,

Thank you so much for reading the God Jars Saga! I hope you enjoyed it. Valis has been one of my favorite characters since 2014, and I'm so stoked I get to share him and his adventures with you!

If you enjoyed the books, I would be honored if you would leave an honest review. It only takes a few minutes, and it can mean the world for your favorite authors.

Please, take a few minutes to review this book, give your honest thoughts, and help me continue writing stories so you can lose yourself in my next great book.

You are my hero.

Sincerely,

Devon Vesper